A CASE OF CONSUMPTION

CALEB LOTT

authorHOUSE®

AuthorHouse™
1663 Liberty Drive
Bloomington, IN 47403
www.authorhouse.com
Phone: 1-800-839-8640

The following is a work of fiction. Any similarities to any persons, living or dead, or any events, are purely coincidental and exist only in the mind of the reader.

Published by AuthorHouse 10/22/2014

ISBN: 978-1-4969-4786-4 (sc)
ISBN: 978-1-4969-4785-7 (e)

This book is printed on acid-free paper.

To Megan

Revenge is the poor delight of little minds.
JUVENAL, Satires, c. A.D. 100

CHAPTER 1

1977

Mama Ce Ce's Grocery usually closed at ten each night. When Mark Hatchett drove his Mercury Cyclone into the parking lot, it was ten of, and there were no other cars in the lot. Hatchett hoped that the clerk had not yet locked the front door.

He parked his car in the angled space farthermost from the front door and got out. Highway 80, which ran east and west in front of the business, seemed oddly deserted for a Friday evening, and he stopped for a couple of seconds to listen for the far off rush of cars and large trucks on the nearby interstate. It was an unusually warm spring night, and there was a steady breeze out of the west.

As he walked toward the entrance, through force of habit he slowed to look into the two large picture windows on the left side of the entrance. He saw no one, so he pulled on the handle of the glass door. It opened, and a small bell made a tinkling sound, thereby announcing his arrival.

A woman with a dumpy figure and long, stringy, dishwater blonde hair was standing behind the counter. She wore one of those smocks that identified her as an employee. Hatchett looked at her. She didn't smile.

"Hey," he said.

She nodded acknowledgement, but said nothing.

"Closing time, huh?"

She nodded again. The woman had a strange look on her face; by that it is meant that her brows were raised, her mouth was set in a line, and her eyes were opened wider than normal.

Hatchett couldn't tell if something was wrong or if the woman was just annoyed at getting a customer this near quitting time. He decided to ignore her and walk toward the back of the store to get a soft drink from the cooler.

He shook the ice water off the can, rubbed the top of it with the heel of his hand, and then started toward the front, picking up a pack of peanut butter crackers on the way. When he reached the register, he put the can and the snack down on the counter.

The woman, who had not moved, began to punch keys on the register. Then, Hatchett knew something was wrong. Her eyes sought him out, and he could see her cutting them to her right, to a location behind the wall that separated her compartment from another room, probably the office.

Hatchett was sure it was a robbery, and he began quickly to conceive a plan of action while reaching for the wallet in his left hip pocket. He opened the bill compartment and was extracting a single when a young boy jumped up from behind the counter with large revolver in his right hand.

"Be still, man!" the young boy shouted.

"Whoa, hey, what's this?" Hatchett said stepping back while raising his hands mockingly.

The clerk began to shake. Her mouth fell open in a silent scream, and she backed into the corner away from both young boy with the gun and the register, the drawer of which was standing open.

"Gimme that wallet, bitch," the robber said to Hatchett.

Hatchett stepped back from the counter and closed the wallet he held in his right hand.

"Now, come on. You don't think I'm just gonna give it to you, do you?"

"I'll kill yo' ass." His voice was loud, but not a yell.

"Easy, easy. I'm not sayin' I won't give it to you, just come over the counter and get it, and leave the clerk alone."

The boy looked around at the woman then back at Hatchett. He was no more than seventeen, with a smooth, chocolate face and a one inch Afro. Hatchett had two inches and thirty pounds on him.

Then, with seemingly no effort, the young boy bounded over the counter and was within four feet of Hatchett, his gun arm outstretched toward his victim's face.

Instead of backing up, as the boy would have expected, Hatchett took a step toward him with his arm extended, wallet in hand. Hatchett could see the boy's right index finger was in the trigger guard, but was not against the underside of the trigger. He waited for the boy to take his eyes off him and put them on the wallet, and then he struck.

"Okay, here it is."

Hatchett flipped the wallet over the boy's left shoulder. He watched as the boy's head turned that direction then he reached for and grabbed his right wrist.

As he bladed himself to the boy's chest, Hatchett held the gun arm steady. At the same time he gave him three quick elbow strikes to his nose. Blood spurted onto Hatchett's white shirt.

The young boy fought back. Hatchett could feel his left arm on his shoulder. When he did, he dropped to one knee and, grabbing the boy's belt with his right hand, threw him over his shoulder. The boy fell hard onto the floor, his head bouncing off the concrete. Hatchett wrenched the revolver from his hand, put his knee onto his throat, and pointed the muzzle of the weapon right into the boy's open mouth.

"Dumb ass," Hatchett grinned. "I only had six dollars in my billfold. There was a hundred times that in that open cash drawer. You jumped right past it."

Hatchett looked up at the clerk. Her mouth was open in fear as well as surprise as she watched the action.

"You want a piece of him?" he said to her.

She said nothing, but as she looked at the scene, and saw that the danger had subsided, her visage turned from fear to anger. Her brows narrowed, she set her jaw in a hard line, looked around, and picked up a beer bottle off of the shelf behind her. Then she walked around the counter and strode quickly to Hatchett, who was still holding the semi-comatose young boy at bay.

At first, she acted as if she didn't know how to do what she wanted to. Hatchett looked up at her.

"Go ahead. It's okay."

At that, she bent over and swung the brown, twelve ounce, Jax beer bottle as hard as she could, hitting the boy square on the forehead, sending him into complete unconsciousness.

Three hours later, inside the Investigative Offices of the Manipi County Sheriff's Office in nearby Mauvilla, Alabama, Hatchett was busy telling, for the fourth time, his side of the story of the robbery at Mama Ce Ce's.

He leaned his elbows on the metal table in the interrogation room and wiped his face with both hands. The room was painted light green and there was a drop light hanging over the table.

"Look, Sergeant. I told you, I grabbed a beer bottle off the shelf next to me and hit him. I didn't think I could hold him down, and I didn't have anything to tie him up with. I figured that if he was unconscious, he'd be easier to handle 'til you guys got there. So, I clocked him."

"That's not the way the lady tells it," said Andrews, a stout man with carrot red hair and freckles. "She says she's the one that hit him; and that you told her to do it."

"Well, who knows what she saw, or did. She was over in the corner, behind the counter, scared shitless. She probably don't remember anything. You know how things are at a time like that."

"Where'd you get the beer bottle from?"

"I told you three times. I got it from the shelf next to where he was layin'."

"But there were no other beer bottles there."

He shrugged. "I don't know how it got there; maybe some customer left it there; maybe they were gonna buy it and didn't have enough money to pay for it; maybe they were gonna steal it and decided at the last minute to put it back."

"Well, we know it was her that hit him."

Hatchett leaned back. "Well, what does it matter? He was robbin' the place. He stuck a gun in my face – in hers, too. I defended myself."

"What it matters is . . . the boy's dead."

Hatchett wasn't surprised. He didn't think the woman had hit the boy hard, hard enough for a skull fracture. But when Hatchett threw him and his head had bounced off the floor that was another matter. He could tell by the way the boy had grunted and moaned after he landed that he was really hurt.

Hatchett had decided to take the blame for hitting him after he saw the kid's eyes roll back in his head and his face slump to the right. The store clerk could no doubt ill afford the stress and anguish that the lick would cause her, and, after all, it was Hatchett's idea. Anyway, he was used to living and working through these kinds of situations.

"Well, hey, one less thug on the streets. What was on his rap sheet?"

"Three or four robberies and one ADW."

"See, I did the taxpayers a favor."

"Tell that to his mama."

Hatchett snorted "She knew it was coming. She just didn't know where or when."

Just then the door of the interrogation room opened and in walked Lieutenant Patrick McRae, the Major Crimes Bureau supervisor.

McRae was an average looking man, slightly under six feet, with a medium build, brown hair, and blue eyes. His face was completely unremarkable except for a long scar on his right mandible, a scar that stretched from the point of his chin to just below his ear. He looked hard at Hatchett.

"You gettin' the truth out of him, Sergeant?"

"We're still working on it, sir."

"Well, don't sweat it. Mr. Hatchett killed a felon who was attempting to perpetrate an armed assault and robbery. He's confessed to it. That's all we've got, and that's the way we're gonna write it up."

"That's just exactly what happened, Lieutenant." Hatchett folded his arms and leaned back with a satisfied look on his face.

McRae looked at Andrews. "Have you got what you need?"

"Yes, sir."

"Okay, you can go. I'll take care of Mr. Hatchett."

Andrews rose, gathered his notebook and some papers, and walked out of the room. McRae took a seat at the table.

"Are you still in business, Hatchett?"

"Business?"

"You know, that PI thing you had going. What did you call it?"

"Clandestine Solutions."

"Pretty swanky name for a gumshoe."

"Well, I do other things."

"Yeah, I know. You leave a red trail where ever you go; blood, you know."

Hatchett smiled. "A little melodramatic, don't you think?"

"Maybe. But true."

"Hey, things happen. I never killed anybody that didn't deserve it."

"Right. I know, I know."

McRae was familiar with Hatchett's work. The situations had been varied, but they had all ended the same way. He had delivered ransom demands on at least two cases, collected child support on a dozen others, and had even rescued a kidnapped woman, all the while using just enough force to get the job done - force that had led to the deaths of three people.

Hatchett didn't enjoy hurting people. It was just that he had a strong sense of right and wrong. When he saw injustice or lies, he felt compelled to act. He'd been that way since childhood. He was no angel himself. He was just someone who hated it when things were out of balance; when the bad people were winning. His Christian mother used to call him, 'Jesus in the Temple' - referring to the time that an angry and enraged Jesus Christ had cleared the moneychangers from the Temple in Jerusalem.

"How would you like to do some real detective work for a change?" McRae said.

"That's all I do, Lieutenant."

"No, I mean a case; a missing persons case."

"I'm listening."

"Her folks came in today to make a report. They said they hadn't heard from their daughter in a month. She lives here, but they're from Mississippi."

"Did you take the report?"

"We had to, but, frankly, I don't think she's missing." He paused. "The girl's a dancer, uh, a stripper, a prostitute. I told them we'd put out an APB on her, but they should probably just be patient; they'd hear from her if they'd just give her time."

"Let me guess. The mother wasn't satisfied."

He nodded. "Right. Her 'intuition' told her something was wrong."

"She may be right."

"She may be. But, well, you know, it's not what you feel, it's what I can prove. And right now, I can't prove there's anything wrong with this woman."

"So you want me to get'em off your back."

"Oh, no. She asked for some private help."

"And you thought of me."

"I thought of someone who was comfortable dealing with the people that run in this young woman's circles."

"Pimps and whores."

McRae nodded and chuckled. "And probably a few addicts as well. So, I gave them your number."

Hatchett looked down, took a deep breath, exhaled, and looked back up. "Have they gone back to Mississippi yet?"

"If they have, it doesn't matter. They live just across the state line and can be back in town pretty quick."

Hatchett shook his head. "I'm probably going to regret this." Then he paused and smiled. "Better yet, you're probably going to regret it."

CHAPTER 2

Hatchett was in his third floor office in the Albright building at the corner of 5th Street and Park Avenue in downtown Mauvilla at nine on Monday morning when the Boatmans arrived. It was the first Monday in April and it was warm. He could see the outlines of two people through the smoky pane of glass in the door, and he sat up straight in his leather chair behind a metal desk.

Hatchett wore a starched white shirt under a tan safari vest, khaki slacks, and leather desert boots. He was armed with a .45 calibre Colt, model 1911 pistol, in a holster, in the small of his back, and a switchblade knife in his right front pants pocket.

"Come in," he said in response to their knock.

A man and a woman, both in their fifties, walked through the door and toward the two wooden chairs across the desk from him. They sat down hard with only nods as a greeting.

"You, Mr. Hatchett?" the woman said.

"I am."

"We got your number from Mr. McRae at the Sheriff's Department. I called because we thought we might get more help outta you than him." Her accent was decidedly southern.

She had called the day before to set up the appointment. When they spoke, Hatchett thought that she had sounded at some times hopeless and at others combative.

"Well, Mr. McRae is a practical man with limited resources."

"We know that, but . . . well, it helps if you sound like you care. He didn't."

The man, Arnold Boatman, sat with his arms folded above his huge abdomen. He had a disinterested look on his face; the look of a man who had given up on his daughter long ago and was only there to please his wife. He wore jeans and a plaid shirt, and tan work boots. His hair was gray, and horn rimmed glasses sat astride his bulbous nose.

"Just exactly how can I help you?" Hatchett said.

Mary Boatman did the talking. She had a bouffant hairdo and a round face with fair skin and puffy, red cheeks. Her white blouse was thin but opaque, and her black skirt was a modest length.

"We want you to look for our baby girl, Mindy, uh, Melinda."

"Melinda Boatman?"

"Yes."

"Is she missing?"

"We think somethin' bad's happened to her."

"How so?"

"Well, she used to call ever two weeks. We hadn't heard from her in a month now."

Hatchett took out a pad and a pen. He looked the woman in the eye.

"Where does your daughter live?"

"She lives in Swanwood, right outside'a town, with her, her man friend, I guess you'd call him. They got a house out there."

"Have you been over there to look for her?"

"We stopped over there a week or so ago, but he told us that she was gone, and he hadn't seen nor heard from her in a couple'a weeks." She paused. "He wouldn't even let us in the door."

"I take it you all don't get along?"

She looked at her husband who as yet was silent. "He's a little colored man she drug up somewheres, and, well . . . we think she could do better."

Hatchett nodded. "So you talked to her a month ago. What was going on in her life?"

Again Mary Boatman looked at her husband. "She said she was doin' fine; said she was goin' outta town for a few days, to work; said she'd call when she could."

"What kind of work does she do?"

"She dances. At clubs, I mean." She paused. "We're not happy about it, but she makes a good livin', and it's what she does – and wants to do."

"How old is Mindy?"

"She's thirty; born on Valentine's Day."

Ironic, Hatchett thought.

"Do you know of anyone who has any reason to want to hurt her?" Hatchett paused. "Mr. Boatman, you haven't said much."

The heavyset man took a deep breath and cleared his throat. "There ain't much to say, really. She run with a tough crowd. I guess I always thought this day'd come."

"Hush," Mary Boatman said looking hard at him. "We don't know anything's happened to her." She looked back at Hatchett. "She's okay. She may be hurt, or sick, but she ain't . . ."

"Again, do you know of anyone who would want to hurt her?"

"No, not really; unless, well, Mindy has used drugs in the past. It could'a been one'a them folks."

"Know any of them?"

She shook her head. Hatchett could think of a couple of places near Swanwood where she could get dope.

"What kind of drugs does, did she take?"

"I think it was cocaine, mostly. 'Course she drinks, too, workin' in them clubs and all." She paused. "But you'd never know it to look at her. My baby's beautiful."

"What does she look like?"

"She's got honey colored hair; about five feet eight and a hundred and twenty pounds. She's got green eyes and a little mole right here." She pointed to a location under her lower lip, toward the left corner of her mouth.

Hatchett wrote down the description. "Any scars, marks tattoos, amputations or deformities?"

She shook her head. "If she's got any tattoos, she keeps'em hid. As for that other stuff, no."

"Has she ever been in jail?" He asked with an eye toward getting her mugshot.

Mary Boatman shook her head. "Not that she ever told us about; or that I remember, anyway. I'm sure she didn't tell us ever thang about her life."

"I didn't want to know about it," Arnold Boatman spoke up.

"That's your daughter you're talkin' about," Mary Boatman said sharply.

Hatchett wrote on his pad. "Anything else you can tell me about her? Where she hangs out? Who her friends are? Does she have any health problems?"

Mary Boatman looked down. "I, I can't really tell you about her friends and all. She just don't talk much about things like that." She paused. "I guess she don't want to cause us any hurt. But as far as her health, now, she never complained about nothing."

The unspoken question that Hatchett wanted to ask was: did she hook? He thought about it quickly and decided that he could assume the answer was yes, and there was no need to even bring it up.

He was thinking that Melinda Boatman - not a dancer's name, to be sure - was, in fact, either laid up stoned, or dead. And if she was dead, and it wasn't a drug overdose, the suspect list would be long and varied. It was a fact that her high risk lifestyle would lend itself to injury or death.

"What was her stage name?"

"She calls herself Lisa, Lisa Lemon." She shook her head. "I don't know where that come from."

"Does she dance around here?"

Mary Boatman shook her head. "Oh, no. I think she does all her work outta town. She comes back here when she ain't workin'."

"And she calls about every two weeks?"

"That's right."

"Who's her best friend?"

The couple looked at each other. After three seconds, Mary Boatman looked back at Hatchett and shrugged her shoulders.

"I guess we just don't know her very well anymore."

She spent the next hour talking about Melinda Boatman - Lisa Lemon - and her childhood; where she grew up, how she grew up, her first day at school, even the toys she played with. Hatchett listened but was uninterested. None of that had any meaning when trying to locate a prostitute who was most likely out on a spree.

Hatchett was able to maneuver her into giving him her daughter's address and phone number. Then she broke back into the subject of her dance lessons and the school plays in which she had performed. After taking all he could, he decided to get to the matter of his fee.

"I bill on an hourly basis for the work I do."

"That's fine. We'll pay whatever it takes."

Arnold Boatman had to be awakened out of a trance by a sharp elbow from his wife. "Oh, yeah, yeah, sure," he said.

The Boatmans handed over a five hundred dollar retainer, in cash, and Hatchett pocketed the money. They didn't ask for a receipt, and he didn't offer one.

"I'll get you something every week. Just let me know how much you need," she said.

"And, what do you want me to do if I find her?"

"Just tell her to come home."

Hatchett foresaw a situation where the girl was stoned out of her mind and so far gone that she didn't want to go home.

"And if she blows me off?"

"Just tell her we love her and miss her."

Touching.

CHAPTER 3

It took another thirty minutes for Hatchett to convince the Boatmans to leave and give him a chance to look for their daughter. It was almost as if they just wanted someone with whom to talk. Hatchett envisioned an exasperated and impatient McRae at the Sheriff's Office either running the two out of his office or handing them off to another detective as soon as he could.

After they'd left, before he did anything else, Hatchett telephoned the three hospitals in Mauvilla and made inquiries as to the existence of any Jane Does in the morgue. All three were negative, however they each took his number and promised to call if anyone materialized. He also called the jail with similar results.

With no real idea of where to start looking for Lisa Lemon, Hatchett decided to begin at the last place she was known to have been: her home.

The address her parents had given him was on 17th Court off County Road 52; a location not far from Mama CeCe's. Hatchett made the trip in his Mercury from downtown to the north side in twenty minutes.

The house, the last one on the right, turned out to be a small, wood structure, painted white, with green shutters and a red shingled roof. It had seen better days. There was a rusted and beat up, red pickup in the dirt driveway, under a spreading oak with new leaves. Hatchett parked, got out, and looked every direction. Then he strode up the brick sidewalk and onto the wooden porch. He rapped three times on the door facing and waited.

A short, thin, man with straightened hair opened the wooden door and stood behind the screen. He was still in his boxers and a t-shirt, even late in the morning. He wiped the three day old growth on his face and yawned.

"Yeah," he said.

"You Alphonso Watkins?"

"Who wants to know?"

"My name's Hatchett."

"What'chu want?"

"I'm looking for Lisa."

"She ain't here?"

"Can I come in?"

He thought for second. "No. I don't know you."

With that, Hatchett yanked open the screen door and stepped inside hard and fast, pushing Watkins back with a straight arm to the chest in the process.

"Wait! Now, what the - you can't do that."

"I just did."

"Who is you, man? What'chu you want?"

"Where's Mindy?"

"Who?"

"Lisa, Melinda, Mindy, your girlfriend; the woman that lives with you. You know who."

Hatchett stood over the man who had fallen back into a dirty and faded club chair, and watched as he lifted up his arms in defense. His face said that he didn't know what was coming next.

"Look, I don't know where she is. I ain't seen her in two'a three weeks." He talked fast and his voice rose an octave as he spoke.

"I don't believe you."

"Well, it's true. We had a argument, and she took off on a Sunday night, I thank it was. I ain't heard from her since."

"Argument? About what?"

"What'chu thank? Money."

"What about it?'

"She done spent up all the money she made, and I made too, doing coke."

"You work? Where?

"I fix lawn mowers over to the hardware store in Slocumb." He paused and looked at Hatchett with wide eyes. "Who is you, man?"

"I told you, I'm the man looking for Mindy Boatman."

"Who?"

"Lisa Lemon. Is that how you know her?"

"Well, yeah, das what she tol' me her name was."

Hatchett looked at Watkins with hard eyes and a clenched jaw. Thinking that he was about to be hit, Watkins recoiled noticeably.

"Look, mister, I don't who you are, or what she done, but I ain't seen her in three weeks. Now, dat's the truth. She lef' here on a Sunday night."

"How long ago?"

"'Bout three weeks ago."

"Where would she go?"

"I'on't know."

"Bullshit. Think again." Hatchett balled up his fist.

Watkins talked fast. "Look, maybe she went to the Plantation; maybe she went to Washington Park, I don't know."

"Who would she go see?"

"She buy her dope from T-Bird in the Plantation."

"What about women? She got any woman friends?"

Clearly rattled, Watkins was silent. He looked at the floor as if his mind was wandering. Hatchett reached and slapped him across the side of the head.

"Oww! Man!"

"Come, on. Every woman has somebody they talk to."

"Okay, okay. Look, try Jasmine up to the club."

"Which club?"

"Uh, uh, up to the, The Platter, over in Johnston."

"Who else?"

"Uh, ah, her mama and daddy, I guess. Dey come by here lookin' for her the other day."

"What did you tell'em?"

"Same thang I told you. I ain't seen her."

"Did you kill her?"

The shocked look on his face was indescribable. "No, no, no. Wait a minute. Who said dat?" He paused. "Is she dead?"

"You tell me."

"Man, I don't know. I don't know where she is."

"You got the best motive of all: money."

"Man, I ain't kilt that girl." He was almost whining now.

Hatchett, who was now bent over next to the flustered and afraid Alphonso Watkins, took a deep breath and exhaled. He wanted to ask Alphonso more questions, but he was of the impression that he had learned all that the man knew. Hatchett had found out the names of Melinda Boatman's drug connection and her best girlfriend, and that was about all he could expect to find out.

There was only one thing left to do. Hatchett reached and took Watkins by the upper arm and lifted the thin man to his feet.

"Come on."

Shaking, Watkins stood. "Where is we goin'?"

"Looking for blood."

Hatchett felt Watkins tense noticeably. They started walking - Hatchett walking, Watkins being drug - through the house. Hatchett looked at the floors, as well as the walls and ceilings of every room.

"Which is the bedroom?"

Watkins nodded toward a short hall off the dining room. Hatchett dragged him that direction. They both stood and surveyed the space.

"How long you two been together?"

"Two o' three years; a good lil' while."

"She got any stuff here?"

"Jus' a few clothes; nothin' else. She took 'bout ever thang else wid her."

It was unusual for a woman to leave and not take all her clothes, unless she planned on coming back. But Hatchett saw nothing to indicate that violence had occurred in the house. Any closer examination would have to be done by the Sheriff's Department. Hatchett turned Watkins back toward the living room and prepared to leave.

"If you hear from Melinda Boatman, or Lisa, or whatever it is you call her, I want you to call Lieutenant McRae down at the Sheriff's Office. If you don't and I find out about it, I'm gonna come back out here and smack you. You got it?" He pointed his finger at Watkins for emphasis.

Watkins, sensing that he was finally out of danger, took a deep breath and exhaled.

"Man, ain't you ever heard of catchin' flies wid honey?"

CHAPTER 4

It was late afternoon when Hatchett parked at the north end of the parking lot of The Silver Platter Lounge on the Merle Ray Highway in Johnston, north of town. He had been to the club once in the past, trying to catch a man who had stolen his boss's income tax check, and had found it to be typical of every other strip joint he had ever seen. The outside had a solid wood veneer and a large pink and green neon sign that advertised dancers 'on a silver platter.'

Inside, Hatchett paid the five dollar cover charge to the large man behind the podium in the vestibule while at the same time checking out the photos of the headliners on the wall next to the door. Lisa Lemon's photo was not present.

Hatchett took a seat on a vinyl couch, on a slightly raised level in the back. The lights were low and a busty blonde was strutting down the middle of the stage.

"What'll you have?" the thin, brown haired waitress said.

"A tall glass of orange juice."

"With vodka?"

"Without."

She raised her eyebrows. "Sure." She turned to walk toward the bar.

"By the way, is Jasmine working today?"

The young woman turned back. "Yeah. She just left the stage."

Hatchett reached in his pocket and handed her a five. "Ask her to step up here for a dance."

She woman took the money and nodded. "Okay."

It was fifteen minutes before a large, full figured, bleached blonde young woman walked up to the table where Hatchett was sucking up orange juice through a straw.

"You the guy that wants a dance?"

"You Jasmine?"

"Yeah."

"That's me."

"Okay, I'll wait 'til this song's over before I start."

She plopped down on the couch next to him and began adjusting her sequined brassiere to better cover her huge breasts. She was tall, tanned, and big boned, and Hatchett could spot no flaws in her complexion.

He reached in the front pocket of his slacks, took out a twenty, and extended it toward the young woman.

"Rest your feet. I just need some conversation."

She took the bill and put it inside the cup of her bra. She raised her eyebrows but said nothing.

"I'm looking for Mindy Boatman. You might know her as Lisa Lemon."

"Lisa? Hey, I haven't seen her in a week or so."

"Know where she is?"

She shook her head. "Nope. She come in one night to say hello. We had a drink, and she took off."

"Know where she went?"

She shook her head. "She said she had to meet a guy. Then she just took off."

"She say who this guy was?"

"No. Just said he was a guy."

Hatchett paused. "How'd you meet Lisa?"

"Look, 'fore I start talkin', who wants to know? You the cops?"

"My name's Hatchett. I'm working for her mother and father. They're worried about her."

She eyed him suspiciously, but decided that she could talk without hanging her friend out to dry.

"We met a coupl'a years ago in Nashville. I was dancin' up there before I come down her."

"How come Lisa didn't work here?"

"She worked here for a little while. But she mostly works outta town; in Atlanta and New Orleans, and the bigger cities. She always said she could make more money that way."

Hatchett took another pull from his glass. The DJ was introducing 'Destiny' who was striding down the catwalk.

"How bad was Lisa's habit?"

Jasmine looked down then toward the stage. She was obviously ambivalent about answering.

"Look, I don't know nothin' about that."

"Yeah, come on. Her old man told me she had a habit."

"Ha. Alphonso? I wouldn't believe him if he said it was dark at midnight."

"You know Alphonso?"

"Yeah, he come in once or twice, with Lisa. I thought he was dirty."

"You're sayin' she didn't carry a monkey around?"

Jasmine shrugged. "Maybe. She makes enough money for it, I think, but I never saw her strung out or anything like that. She works and makes enough to take four or five months off. I guess she's got to have something to occupy her time."

"What kinda' person is she?"

"She's okay, I mean, when she comes around here she kinda' acts like she's better than ever'body. But for the most part she gets along with most of the girls."

"Anyone in particular that she had a beef with?"

She looked up. Hatchett could tell that she didn't want to hang anything on anyone.

"Nobody in particular. You know, just girls gettin' together; sometimes they can get a little catty."

"Lisa ever do any time?"

"You mean, jail?"

"If you know."

"She never mentioned it if she did."

Hatchett stopped to think. "Did she have a manager, or did she use an agency?"

"Her man's name is, uh, Nick, I think. He's in Nashville. I know 'cause he tried to sign me, but I turned him down. He gets gigs for more than just dancing, if you know what I mean."

Hatchett nodded. "And Lisa didn't use dope?"

"Well, hey, what she did out of town, I don't know about."

Hatchett took another pull on the juice. Then he said: "You gotta number for Nick?"

"I think I got one of his cards back in the dressing room. I'll hunt it up and give you a call."

Hatchett reached in his shirt pocket and pulled out a business card. "If I'm not in, leave a message with my service."

Jasmine nodded. She put the card in her bra with the twenty and started to rise. Then she stopped.

"You think she's okay?"

He looked at her hard. "No. I think she's dead."

When Hatchett left the lounge, he was even more convinced of the opinion that he had shared with Jasmine. There were just too many aspects of Lisa Lemon's life out of which enemies could arise.

There was Alphonso the boyfriend with whom she was living but with whom she had apparently been unwilling to share expenses. There was her addiction, which, incidentally, was probably the rat hole down which most if not all of her money was flowing. And there was her manager/pimp in Nashville who had who knows what against her.

But, for now, Hatchett thought, she wasn't dead. He mentally went over the suspects again in his head. He was not yet ready for a trip to Nashville, and Alphonso was useless for now. That left only Lisa Lemon's connection to locate and lean on. Watkins had said his name was 'T-Bird,' from the Plantation. Well, in the morning, after a quick phone call to the Sheriff's Department, that was where he'd start.

CHAPTER 5

Hatchett was up and eating breakfast at Walt's Diner on 2nd Avenue by six the next morning. He chose the booth in the back by the picture window where he could watch the ducks swim and forage along the grassy banks of the muddy Raccoon River. Occasionally, an alligator would surface and send the birds scurrying for shore, honking and raising cain.

He was on his second cup of coffee when Wiley, the owner and cook, answered the phone on the wall on its fourth ring. He said, 'Yeah,' twice then held out the receiver toward Hatchett.

"It's the Sheriff's Office; some guy named McRae."

Hatchett rose from his table and wiped his mouth before picking up the receiver. "This is Hatchett."

"Hatchett? McRae."

"What a coincidence, I was just about to call you."

"Well, now you don't have to." He paused. "Did you hitch your wagon to the Boatman's star?"

"I did."

"Well, I've got something you'll want to see."

"You've got the body of Melinda Boatman."

"Flies don't land on you, do they."

In thirty minutes Hatchett was at a remote location at the end of Northeast 52nd Street, about ten miles north of downtown. It was a farm road, it was dirt, and it serviced several soybean fields in the area. The dead end butted up against the interstate and was separated from the busy four lane highway by a stand of trees and a chain link fence.

It was against that fence that a farmer, while in the process of turning his tractor around, had noticed what he thought was a mannequin lying in the weeds. He got down off the machine to investigate and finally decided that the arms, legs, and torso looked enough like a human being to call the Sheriff's Office.

Hatchett parked his Merc at the end of a long line of unmarked detective and marked patrol cars. He got out and walked toward the end of the road, his eyes scanning for McRae. He found him talking to the farmer. It took a minute to get his attention.

"Can I have a look?" Hatchett said.

McRae turned away from the farmer and toward Hatchett. "You didn't do this, did you?"

A smile crossed Hatchett's lips. "No."

"Yeah, you can look. Not much to see, though."

Hatchett stepped under the crime scene tape and walked up a slight incline to a location next to the departmental photographer, a bald man with glasses wearing a brown uniform, who had stopped to stare at the sight and was making a face. The ground was full of berry briars and jap grass, and a fair amount of stray soybean plants. Butterflies fluttered about and yellow wild flowers were in full bloom all around. Hatchett leaned in and scanned the corpse from toe to . . . .

It wasn't a shock, nor was it even startling to Hatchett, but it was a sight that he hadn't expected. The body of the nude female had been thoroughly and completely decapitated.

The woman was lying prone, with her right leg bent at the knee and both arms above her head. He leaned in closer and looked at her feet. There was something that looked like either brown paint chips or wood shavings between her toes. Other than that, she was clean, as if she'd been washed down. Her skin was pale and shiny, her nails painted crimson. He noticed a yellow butterfly tattoo on her leg. It was small, about one square inch, just above the outside of her right ankle.

She was of the height and weight of the young woman that Mary Boatman had described, but at that moment, Hatchett realized that without her hair and eye color, he had no way of making even a preliminary ID on scene. He turned and walked back under the tape toward McRae, who was making notes.

"How do you know it's my girl?"

"The tattoo of a butterfly on her right ankle was on her jail record; and, we've got her fingerprints downtown."

"She was arrested?"

"For robbery, about six or seven years ago."

"Convicted?"

He shook his head. "No record of a conviction, just that she was arrested."

Hatchett nodded. "Any idea where her head's at?"

McRae looked around. The wind blew a shock of brown hair into his eyes.

"Not right now. But we're gonna get the dogs out here and take a look off the road and in the fields. If it's not already somebody's souvenir, it shouldn't be too far away."

He was speaking of trained cadaver dogs that specialized in locating human beings - dead human beings. Hatchett had seen them work in Vietnam.

"As a matter of fact," McRae said, "here they come now." He gestured down the road at a marked county van.

The vehicle stopped and a brown shirted deputy exited the driver's compartment. He walked around to the back, opened the door, and removed four Beagle dogs, all restrained by leather leads.

Hatchett backed away as McRae walked that direction. He turned and watched as the evidence people and the photographer finished up with what was left of Melinda Boatman.

Technically, he was out of the picture. His job was to find her, and she had been found.

His eyes scanned up and down the girl's body. Like a bad wreck he couldn't look away. He went over it once, twice, three, four, five, six, eight, ten, twenty times. And, the more he did, the madder he got. No person, no female, not even a prostitute, he thought, should have to die a death like this. With each pass, the sight became more fixed in his mind.

Hatchett's concentration was broken by yelling, away from the body, about a hundred yards down the road to the east. He looked up and saw McRae walking toward the handler and the four hounds. A uniformed deputy was waving for the photographer to come to the same location. Hatchett knew that they had found what they were looking for.

As he stepped back and leaned against one of the patrol cars, he began to think about his suspect list. The pimp was not eliminated, but unlikely. This was too dirty and bloody a job. Unless there was a huge amount of money involved, a 'businessman' like him wouldn't even pay to have it done.

Alphonso didn't look the part, either. He acted too mousy, too much of a wimp for decapitation.

That just left her drug friends. The right amount of money or product could certainly drive them to all sorts of mayhem.

McRae walked up to where Hatchett was standing. He wasn't smiling.

"I'm gonna need everything you've gotten so far," the lieutenant said.

"It's only been one day."

"My guess is you've got a suspect list already."

"A couple."

"We'll meet in my office at noon for a debriefing."

"I'll want to talk to my client first."

McRae smirked and turned away.

CHAPTER 6

Hatchett pulled into the driveway of the Boatman residence at ten o'clock that same morning. It was a two story colonial on old Highway 45, two miles north of Waynesboro, Mississippi. A tricked out Ford pickup truck and a tan LTD sat in the gravel driveway surrounded by a manicured front lawn.

He was admitted after one verse of 'Dixie' from the door chimes. Mary Boatman was in jeans and a plaid shirt.

"Ms. Boatman."

"Come in." She ushered him into the living area.

Hatchett sat down on a brocade club chair. Mary Boatman took a seat on a couch. The room was cluttered, yet warm.

"Is Mr. Boatman home?"

"He's out with the cows. Did you find out anything?"

Hatchett paused. "I may have some bad news."

Mary Boatman put both hands to her mouth.

"The Sheriff's Department has located a young woman who they think, but have not confirmed, is Melinda." He paused again and swallowed. "She's deceased."

Mary Boatman began immediately to hyperventilate. Just as suddenly, she stopped and took her hands away from her face.

"But they're not sure, right? It might not be her."

Hatchett sat stone-like in the chair. "They're still waiting for a fingerprint comparison," he said.

"But until then, she's, I mean, she could still be alive?"

He wanted to tell her that if believing that made her feel better, she should just go with it. He said:

"Ms Boatman, I think you should go ahead and begin to prepare yourself for the worst."

Mary Boatman looked at the floor and stared. "What, what happened to her?"

"She was the victim of a homicide."

"How?"

"It was a sharp force injury."

"You mean she was stabbed?"

"Yes, ma'am." Not exactly the truth, but close enough.

"Where is she now?"

"I'm sure the police have taken her in for an autopsy."

Hatchett took a business card out of his pocket. He wrote McRae's number on the back.

"You should contact Mr. McRae. He can tell you more."

"Oh. McRae." She smirked. "He was that one that was so ugly to us when we come over to report Mindy missing. Is he working on her case?"

"Yes, ma'am."

She paused. "Well, can you still work on it, too?"

"If you want."

"I'd ruther have you workin' on it, if you still can. I don't have much confidence in that McRae fella."

Hatchett hated parallel investigations with the police. He didn't want them in his way, and he was sure they didn't want him in theirs.

"I'll do what I can."

They both looked around the room but said nothing. The sound of the tick-tocking clock on the wall was magnified by the silence.

"Is there anything I can do for you?" Hatchett said.

She shrugged and let her hands drop carelessly onto her lap. "Nothin', I guess."

"Well, I'd better go then." He rose. "By the way, do you know anything about Mindy being arrested? For robbery? About five or six years ago?"

"Arrested? No. She was with a old boy that robbed a gas station or a shop or something over there, downtown. She got picked up, but they dropped the charges on her."

"Why?"

"'Cause she testified in court. The boy that was with her got sent off, I think."

Suspect number four.

CHAPTER 7

It was shortly after one when Hatchett stopped his Merc in the parking lot of the county courthouse, a stone building at Fifth and Mulberry, downtown. He was a little late, but he didn't care.

He didn't like the idea of giving everything that he knew about Lisa Lemon's death away to the county detectives. In his mind, he would be hurting the case. He knew that law enforcement would be handcuffed in how they could approach the witnesses and suspects, and he knew that they wouldn't get the results that he could.

Hatchett walked down the tunnel and through a wooden door into the basement where the Sheriff's Office Detective Division was located. The receptionist ushered him to McRae's office, in the back.

"You're late," McRae said. He was sitting behind his desk chewing on a cigar.

"I got hung up."

"I know. She called us."

"Did you tell her?"

"Yeah. Tommy made the comparison over at the morgue."

"Well, Lieutenant, what are you gonna do?"

"I'm gonna solve this thing."

"Not if I solve it first."

"Yeah. She said she'd retained you to work with us."

"Not with you; instead of you."

McRae looked surprised.

"She said she doesn't have much confidence in your ability."

"Well, that's just her tough luck. We clean up our own messes over here." He paused. Then, softer, "She say why?"

"She didn't like your bedside manner."

"Is that all?"

"It's a woman thing."

McRae nodded. "I know." He paused. "So I can count on your help?"

"Sure, why not."

The lieutenant got out a pen and his pad and prepared to write. "What have you got so far?"

Hatchett shrugged. "I've only been working on it one day, but I talked to her boyfriend, housemate, whatever you want to call it, Alphonso Watkins. He's got motive, but he just didn't strike me as the type who'd saw off his old lady's head." Hatchett gave him Watkins' address.

"She's got, uh, or had a pimp in Nashville, 'Nick' somebody. I don't know anything about him, or how to find him."

McRae was writing quickly. When he finished, he looked up.

"That it?"

"For now."

"You'll let me know if you hear anything, right?"

"Hey, I'm a good citizen."

"Yeah."

"You just work on that human relations problem." Hatchett smiled.

"Get outta here," McRae said with a wave.

Hatchett hadn't told him about T-Bird, Lisa Lemon's connection in the projects, and the state's evidence case that she'd been involved in; what he considered his two most promising clues. In his mind, they were the two best suspects, and judging from the crime, they would have to be dealt with firmly; something the police couldn't do.

Hatchett knew that the best evidence in his case would be the dead girl's body, and since he had no access to anything that the police had gathered, he decided to pay a visit to the county coroner's office. He arrived at two.

The morgue was located in a now closed, World War II era, US Army base off 14th Street in Saylor, a north side suburb. The actual facility was in the old munitions magazine. Hatchett parked in the back.

The large woman in the lobby smiled as he walked through the front door. She handed him a visitor's badge and directed him to the office of Doctor Lucy Leopold. Leopold was a rarity for the times: a female coroner.

She was a transplanted northeasterner who did her pathology residency in Baltimore. Leopold was all business when she was at work and a free spirit when she was not. She was a thin, middle aged woman with sandy blonde hair and a large mouth.

The doctor was seated at her desk wearing a white surgical gown when Hatchett knocked on the door. The two knew each other, but not well. Leopold didn't like him.

"Mr. Hatchett. We meet again," she said.

"How do you do, ma'am."

"Just fine. I believe I saw a little of your handiwork last week."

He paused. "Oh, you mean the guy from the grocery store? Hey, he had it coming."

"Still, that was a pretty hard lick."

"Not as hard as the bullet that was about to come out of the barrel of his gun would have been."

"Still . . ."

"I wanted to ask you about Melinda Boatman," Hatchett said quickly changing the subject.

"How are you involved in that case?"

"I'm working for her mother."

"Oh, yes. I just talked to her. She seemed a quaint person, who, of course, is in some real pain just now."

At that moment, Hatchett wasn't interested in anyone's pain. "What can you tell me?"

"Not much, really. It appeared as if her head came off with one blow from a large single bladed instrument; an axe, or a machete. The wound was between the second and third vertebrae. She had apparently been washed down and drained of her blood prior to being left on the side of the road. There were no other significant injuries."

"Do you think she was awake when it happened?"

"I've got no way of knowing. There was nothing to indicate that she was struck about the head. There could have been some type of chemical sedation, but we won't know that for a while. I see no sign she was choked to unconsciousness."

"It looked like there was some foreign material on her foot. Did you notice it?"

"Yes, I did. I sent it to the laboratory for some analysis. It looked like wood, but I'll have to let you know for sure what kind."

Hatchett paused and thought. He wasn't getting much.

"Your conclusions?" he said.

"Well, first of all, you're looking for a crime scene with a tremendous amount of blood. She was drained almost completely dry. Second, one chop, and her head was gone. My guess is an axe, however, look for anything long and sharp."

"How about her head. Anything to work with there?"

"Nothing, really, well, except the fact that her tongue was missing."

Nothing? That was a huge fact. Lisa Lemon had talked about, or was planning to talk about, something that she shouldn't.

"Missing tongue, huh. Post or ante mortem?"

"Most likely, post. It's hard to cut out the tongue of someone who's alive, even if they're unconscious."

"Anything else?"

She took a deep breath and exhaled. "Not that I can think of right now. I can let you know about the wood a little later."

"Dr. Leopold, I sincerely thank you for your time and your expertise." Hatchett said in exaggerated politeness. He rose and extended his hand.

"Mr. Hatchett, you are quite welcome," she said in the same tone, while smiling slightly and shaking his hand.

Outside in his Merc, Hatchett reflected on what he had heard. The facts of Lisa Lemon's death had done nothing to shrink his suspect list. In fact, some things he had heard had opened up a couple of new doors.

The fact that her tongue had been excised shined a greater light on her drug friends, and took the spotlight off her manager. It also took a little more heat off her housemate, who Hatchett had begun to believe might be homosexual. Really, what was a woman like her doing living with a little mouse like Alphonso, he thought.

As he drove away from the morgue, he had one thing on his mind and that was to find out more about Lisa Lemon's criminal history; and without going through McRae.

Back at his office, Hatchett called Tammy Hobson at the Records Division of the Sheriff's Office. Hobson was a low level clerk that he kept on a small retainer to surreptitiously provide him confidential information, information that would not ordinarily be available to the general public, even to private investigators. She was young, she didn't make much money, and she enjoyed a drink.

"Call me back on the private line," Hatchett said when he got her on the phone.

She called back in two minutes. "What's up?"

Her voice was cheery, and if Hatchett hadn't known better, he would have said she was tight.

"I need what you have on a Melinda Boatman. I'm looking for information about an arrest about five or six years ago, on a Robbery charge." He supplied her with a birthdate and other particulars.

"She that murder victim from today?"

"Right."

She spoke in low tones. "What do you need?"

"Anything you can get. Who was she arrested with; when; where; who made the pinch; what happened; just a good run down."

"How soon you gotta have it?"

"Tonight, if possible."

There was silence on the other end. "I'll try. The usual place?"

"Yeah. At eight."

That night, Hatchett slid into back corner booth at Willard and Mike's, a greasy spoon at the corner of Dean Avenue and 30th, across from the entrance to the Fairgrounds. He ordered coffee and sat back to wait. It was five of eight.

At fifteen after, Tammy Hobson walked slowly through the front door. The choice of meeting site wasn't her idea, and she had always felt a little uncomfortable, especially late at night, coming to that part of the city. But it was far from downtown, and no one from the Sheriff's Office was likely to see her. Spotting Hatchett's face calmed her, and she walked confidently to the booth. She was a chubby girl with black hair worn in a flip.

"Hey," she said sliding in across from Hatchett.

"You got it?"

"Well, I have something. I don't know if it's what you're looking for, but I've got something."

She slid a manila envelope across the table to him as the counter man came to take her order.

"Just coffee, please."

When he brought the cup, Hobson reached in her oversized purse and pulled out a pint bottle of Old Forrester and poured a small shot into the mug. Hatchett ignored her, spending his time on the papers from inside the envelope.

What he read was that Melinda Boatman had been arrested six years ago by the city police for Robbery with a firearm. The victim business was the Style and Curl Beauty Parlor on Grand Avenue. Her co-defendant had been a man named Louis Hart.

"So," Hobson said as she sipped her brew, "what do you think?"

"We'll see. There may be something here I can use."

She looked at him with raised brows. "So?"

Hatchett knew what she wanted. He reached in his inside vest pocket, took out a folded envelope, and laid it on the table. Hobson picked it up and looked inside. She thumbed through the bills, then looked up and smiled.

"You need anything else?" she said.

"Not right now." He paused and looked at her. "What have you got planned for that?" He nodded at the envelope.

She looked hopefully at the money. "I'm saving up to do some things; you know, like to change my appearance." She placed the envelope into her purse.

"Like how?"

"I'm gonna get a nose job; maybe take off some of this weight; get my boobs done."

Hatchett didn't know what to say. He had a good enough grasp of human nature to know that the young girl was lonely and wanted a man. She thought she had to change herself to get someone to want her.

All he did was nod then look back at the papers. There was a county jail arrest report, a copy of a fingerprint card, a mugshot, and a criminal history card detailing all of her other arrests. Lisa Lemon had in the past been picked up for shoplifting, a couple of counts of prostitution, and once for Public Intoxication.

He looked hard at the photo. Lisa Lemon was smiling broadly - probably drunk, he thought - and her head was tilted slightly to the right. She had an earthy quality to her; by that it is meant that she was large boned, olive complexioned, and she had a thick nose and full lips. There was a gap in between her two front teeth on top. In spite of her smile, she looked tired, and her hair was askew.

Tammy Hobson slowly sipped her Irish coffee. Her face was deadpan.

"You know, drinking that stuff won't help you get a man any quicker."

"But, it'll keep me from getting too depressed until I do."

"I'm just sayin', sometimes that monkey is hard to get off your back."

"I can handle it."

"That's what they all say."

"I can. Besides, it's just until my surgery. Then I'll look like what I want, and . . . you know."

Hatchett nodded again. "Well, I hope it works out for you." He paused and looked at the papers. "Can you get home alright?"

She nodded. "Yeah." She patted her purse and prepared to leave. "I'll be okay. I just want to finish my drink."

Hatchett rose, gave her a fatherly pat on the head, and walked out into the warm evening.

CHAPTER 8

The next day, Hatchett set about trying to locate and contact the men that he had in mind were the best suspects in the death of Lisa Lemon. He was in his office early.

His first call was to the City Police Vice and Narcotics Bureau, known colloquially as the 'Mod Squad.' Vincent O'Leary was an acquaintance who owed him a couple of favors. O'Leary was a fat man with a full black beard and a bald head. He'd spent a lot of time undercover and there was no way he'd be mistaken for a policeman.

"I need a name for an alias."

"Who is it?"

"A dealer at The Plantation; name's 'T-Bird.'"

The Plantation was a black settlement off 14th Avenue in the southeast side of town. It was low income, rundown, and crime ridden. Officers in every division were familiar with it.

"'T-Bird'? Sure. That's Theodore Roosevelt Adams. But you'll never find him askin' for him by that name."

"How can I locate him?"

"Just look for his car."

"Don't tell me, let me guess."

"That's right. It's black and gray with mag wheels and suicide doors."

"Is that where he gets his name?"

"Nope. He gets it from the wine. He luuuvs the juice of the grape."

"Anywhere he's most likely to be?"

"Just cruisin'." He paused. "You goin' huntin' for him?"

"I thought I would, yeah."

"Well, be careful. We got word he carries a sawed off shotgun under the front seat."

Hatchett felt his abdomen tighten. "I'll be careful."

Next, he checked with the national book and found a private investigator in Nashville. He called the Towson Detective Agency. A female answered. She identified herself as Linda Towson.

"I'm trying to get a line on the clubs that headlined a particular dancer up there. Can you help me?"

Her voice was high and soft, but clear. "I'll try. You got a name?"

"Yeah. Lisa Lemon. See if you can find out where she dances. She's usually up that way in the fall and winter."

"Just the names of the clubs?"

"Yeah, to start. I'm really tryin' to locate her manager; or pimp, or whatever he is."

"You know anything about him?"

"Not a thing. I just know this Lemon girl works around the southeast and there's a guy in Nashville that books her. His name is thought to be 'Nick.'" He paused. "If you've got the contacts, it's maybe a two phone call job."

There was silence on the other end. "Okay, I'll give it a try. I get fifty an hour, but I'll do this one for a hundred flat."

"Got it."

Hatchett gave her the address of where to send the bill. He didn't haggle because he knew that the Boatmans could afford, and would gladly pay, any price to find out what happened to their daughter.

At nine thirty that morning Hatchett was driving slowly through The Plantation. The area was so-called by both races because of its exclusively black population and because it was said to have once been part of a large cotton farmstead. It was about a twenty square block area of numbered streets running east and west, and lettered avenues running north and south. Hatchett drove his Merc slowly down first one road, then up another that was pitted and potted and just barely paved. He was looking for the distinctive automobile hoping it would be parked in front of one of the ramshackle wood houses.

The neighborhood was deserted and eerily quiet. Not an overwhelming number of people in the Plantation worked, so most slept late. It was a bright sunny day, and the only movement he saw was out of a couple of dogs who raised their heads to watch as he drove past, and one or two squirrels tempting death by scurrying along the power lines overhead. It was as if the entire population was still sleeping off a drunk from the night before.

Hatchett found the car on 6th Street at Avenue K. It was behind a weathered house that appeared to be vacant and looked as if it was about to implode. The vehicle was parked in the back, between spreading oaks, next to what was once a chicken coup. There were no other vehicles around. Hatchett pulled the Merc around behind it, turned off the engine, and exited as quietly as possible. He walked soundlessly on sand toward the T-Bird and peered inside.

The situation was turning out better than he had hoped, for there, asleep on the back seat, his head on the driver's side, was a fat man with a large Afro lying supine under what looked like a short windbreaker jacket. Hatchett couldn't see the man's hands, but he could tell he was asleep by the rhythmic motion of his chest.

It would be tricky, but Hatchett had to get into the car and put T-Bird in an untenable situation before he had a chance to go for a weapon. It would all depend on whether or not the vehicle's back door was unlocked.

Hatchett reached around and got his .45 out of the holster in the small of his back. He flipped the thumb safety and then reached for the driver's side rear door handle.

As he engaged the handle with his left hand, it clicked once, then again, and then it opened. Luckily it didn't squeak. T-Bird, who smelled strongly of wine, was dead to the world.

Keeping an eye on where his hands would normally be, Hatchett leaned in and took his left hand and pinched the man's wide, flat nose. Within two seconds, T-Bird's mouth opened. When it did, Hatchett shoved the muzzle of the forty five in it and quickly yanked the windbreaker off him. The sawed off shotgun was lying across his chest.

T-Bird's eyes opened widely, and he started to rise.

"Unh, unh. Not yet, Theodore."

Hatchett liked calling thugs by their real names. He thought it took them by surprise; got them off their game.

Grabbing the short double barreled weapon, Hatchett tossed it out of the car about ten feet. Then he took his left hand and put it around the surprised man's throat while resting his left knee on his chest.

"Now, listen here, Theodore. I know who and what you are. I can put that pea shooter over there in your possession, and I bet the police would sure be happy to hear about that. But that's not what I'm interested in. All I want is some information. Understand?"

"Mmm, hmm," he said with wide eyes and a full mouth.

"Now, if you give me any trouble, all I got to do is step back, shoot your balls off, and then put the pop gun over there back in your hands. You're dead, and I'm the town hero. Sound like a plan?"

He shook his head vociferously.

"I kinda thought you'd feel that way. So, I know you're gonna give me what I want to know. Right?"

He nodded.

"Good. Now, I know that you and Lisa Lemon were on terms."

His brows knitted in confusion.

"Yes, you do. She's that white whore with the honey colored hair; the dancer. She bought dope from you."

His brows went back up in recognition.

"That's right. I need to know when you saw her last."

Hatchett pulled the barrel out past his teeth slightly.

"I 'on't know, man."

Hatchett took the barrel of the pistol and whacked him across his capillary-rich forehead. Blood trickled out of the wound. He quickly pointed it back at the shaking man's mouth.

"Bullshit. Listen, it's not too late for Plan B."

"Owwww! Come on, man! Ah'ite, look, I seen her two weeks ago."

"Bullshit. Now you're just making things up." He reared back his hand.

"No, no, man. Look here, I don't 'member when it was. Look, she come over here to get some powder, oh, a week or so ago, I 'on't know. I ain't had none, so I sent her ta Peahead. What happened ta her after that, now, I 'on't know."

Hatchett halfway believed what he was saying. It was detailed and, though it took him out of a bad light, it gave the girl's actions some continuity.

"Where does Peahead stay?"

"Over to the Highway, off Avenue A."

"What's his real name?"

"Uh, uh, Demetrius."

"Last name?"

"Come on, man." He paused. "'Likely,' I thank. Yeah, his name be 'Likely.'"

Hatchett guessed that knowing the man's last name would have been too much to hope for.

"How do I know all this is the truth?"

"Hunt up Peahead. He know. He saw her after me." He paused. "What up wid dat girl, anyway?"

"She's dead, Theodore. So you," he emphasized each word with a smack to the forehead with the muzzle of his pistol, "get your alibi ready, 'cause the police is comin'."

Hatchett reached and patted T-Bird's pockets.

"You got a knife on you?"

"No."

Hatchett patted both front pockets. He felt something moist on his fingers, and it was then that he realized the T-Bird had wet himself. He stepped out of the car and backed up to the location of the shotgun. He picked it up, and after holstering his own weapon, removed two shells from the breech of the gun. Then he flung them as far as he could into the wooded area behind the house.

T-Bird had rolled over and was watching as Hatchett worked.

"I got mo' shells," he said.

Hatchett nodded. Then he took the shotgun and slammed it against one of the spreading oaks four or five times until the stock had broken off and the trigger guard was hanging. He looked at the shocked T-Bird.

"You got mo' guns?"

In ten minutes Hatchett was near Avenue A and the Highway looking for a mailbox that said 'Likely.' There were two houses, one each on the northeast and west corners; neither had any identifying information on or near them.

As he drove slowly and looked from side to side, Hatchett decided that this Peahead lead was one best handled by McRae and his deputies. The more he thought of it, Lisa Lemon's death at the hands of the dopeheads from The Plantation was not a viable likelihood.

First, he thought, if she dies, they lose money. Apparently, she was a regular and a well-known customer. Second, even if she snitches on them, who cares. Everyone knows they sell dope up here, anyway. There was no evidence that she had turned or was intending to turn on them and start putting these guys away. If the police wanted to bust them, the undercovers could buy dope from them any time they wanted.

Finally, chopping the head off a victim just didn't seem to be T-Bird's style. This was a man who had wet himself when he had awakened and found a gun in his mouth. He would not want to get as bloody as he would have to in order mutilate a person. As hard as they tried to be tough, he and his friends were just good ole boys trying to make a living selling drugs rather than doing honest work. In Hatchett's mind, Lisa Lemon's killer was most likely white, and very, very angry.

CHAPTER 9

The next morning, Hatchett put in a call to McRae. He informed him of the Peahead lead. It would better suit Hatchett's purposes if law enforcement was working this particular angle and was out of his way.

"Yeah, I heard about your handiwork with that T-Bird character."

"How do you know it was me?"

"I know. He called me today and described you to a tea."

"We all look alike, Lieutenant."

"Nope. I recognized his description of your forty five and your smart assed mouth."

"Hey, I'm glib, and I'm well-armed. Soon everyone will be."

"I get the message." He paused. "So who is this Peahead character?"

"Demetrius Likely, I think. He was supposed to be the last person to see the Boatman broad alive, that we know about right now."

"Have you talked to him?"

"Negative. He lives up near Avenue A and the highway."

There was silence on the other end. "Don't hold out on me, Hatchett. The list of things I could run you in for is growing longer."

"What? You mean, T-Bird? What would it do to his street reputation if everybody found out a skinny white boy like me made him suck on the end of a bean shooter?"

"Just watch your step. I got better things to do than to be running down everybody that's got a complaint against you."

It was noon when Hatchett heard from Linda Towson in Nashville. He had expected it to have taken her much longer to get his information.

"I have the name of an entertainment agent up here. He handles a lot of the out of town strippers that come in and out. If he doesn't run your girl, he'll probably know who does."

"I'm listening.

"His name is Arthur Nicholas 'Nick' Peters. He's got an office on Broadway. Nothin' fancy, a second story walk up, not far from the Opry." She supplied him with the address.

"Peters, hunh. Is that his real name?"

"That's what's on his business card, and that's what's on the business license."

"Have you been to see him?" Hatchett said.

"No. I thought I'd save that for you."

"Okay, thanks. The check'll be in the mail."

It was the unwritten code among private investigators that they all pay their debts. If they didn't, word got around and they could expect no help in the future.

Hatchett sat at his desk and thought about what to do next. The idea that some talent agent in Nashville came to south Alabama and killed one of his clients, for any reason, did seem to be a bit implausible, unless the motive involved enough money. If so, then somebody in Mr. Arthur Nicholas 'Nick' Peters industry would surely have enough shady contacts and could hire someone to come and take care of Lisa Lemon.

But what bothered Hatchett the most was the tongue. What could she have known, or told, or was going to tell, that would do anyone enough harm as to warrant a murder of such violence?

He decided that the only way to find out was to take a trip to Nashville and see this Peters character and find out what he knew about Lisa Lemon. Getting a feel for him and his answers would go a long way in confirming or eliminating him as a suspect.

Hatchett was on the road by one, and he was in Nashville at eleven where he checked in to a motel close to the highway. Then he took a ride downtown to get a look at Nicholas Peters' office. He found it in the 300 block of Broadway near 4th Avenue. It was just as Towson had described it; a second floor walkup over a guitar store, with an exterior staircase.

Hatchett drove slowly down the extraordinarily deserted street. He looked closely up at the second floor window and saw a light burning, after which he brought the Merc to a stop in a space across the street.

He watched for ten minutes, but saw no movement around the doorway or the window. If anyone was in the office at eleven thirty, it was either Peters, who was used to nightlife, and or it was a cleaning crew. Hatchett was banking on it being Peters.

At the top of the stairs, Hatchett found a wooden door with the words, *Nicholas Peters,*

Theatrical Agent, painted in cursive lettering. He knocked twice and waited. In ten seconds, the sound of heavy feet answered.

"Who are you?" the man asked.

He was short with a pale complexion and dark hair that was long and flowed down his neck. He wore a polyester shirt, coordinated trousers, and patent leather loafers.

"I'm a friend of Melinda Boatman. I was wondering if I could talk to you."

"Who? I don't know any Boatman." His voice indicated that he was not from the south.

"You know her as Lisa Lemon."

A look of recognition overtook his face. Peters looked Hatchett up and down and apparently decided that he wasn't a threat. He stepped aside, and Hatchett walked in.

Peters took a seat behind his cluttered desk. Hatchett parked in a vinyl chair almost directly in front of him, with his back to the door, and with a view of the window. The light that he had seen from the street was a standing lamp close to the window, behind and to the right of Peters.

"I'm afraid I didn't catch your name, sir?"

"My name is Hatchett. I'm looking for Melinda; or, Lisa."

Peters smiled and shook his head. "Lisa Lemon, the best little dancer in my stable. She could be a millionaire – make me a millionaire, too – but she won't work more than six months out of the year."

"What makes her so good?"

He thought for a minute. "I don't know. She's just got a way. She can make every man in the place think she's goin' home with him."

"When's the last time you saw her?"

He steepled his hands and looked at the ceiling. "Oh, I guess it was probably in February. She made the circuit and her last stop was here, at Conway's Lounge."

"How was she, when you saw her?"

"She looked fine. She was clean and sober; and she was working at everything I sent her on. She told me she was heading home for the summer."

"She have a pretty big habit?"

"I don't know. It's just an expression."

"Have you heard from her since?"

Peters shook his head. "We don't usually talk when she's off. I mean, I used to try to get her to come back to work early, but she always said, 'no.' She wanted to go home and take a vacation. If she'd work the year round, man . . ." He shook his head and clucked his tongue.

"Was she having any trouble with anyone?"

Peters paused before answering. "You some kinda cop?"

"I'm an Inquiry Agent. I'm helping her mother find her. She hasn't called in a while."

"Missing?" He leaned forward. "That's not good; I mean, you think something's happened to her? Surely she'll turn up before next fall."

"Well, that all depends. Was she having trouble with anyone?"

"Hey, she never said anything to me. Lisa and I are, well, pretty close friends. She depends on me a lot. I think she would have told me if somebody was after her."

Hatchett measured Peters' words. He was convinced now that Peters and Lisa Lemon were lovers, or at least sex partners. It shed a little different light on things.

"Did Lisa do private parties, conventions, bachelor get-togethers, things like that?"

"Sure. She probably does two or three a month."

"Here?"

"Sometimes here; sometimes out of town. You see, Nashville is kind of her home base. She comes here, oh, say, right after Labor Day. I usually have her set up for a regular run at one of the clubs here, and then she works her way out of town. When I get a private thing for her, I give her a call, and she goes wherever the party is. She works steadily through Christmas, until right at the end of February, sometimes a little later."

"Where does she stay when she comes to town?"

"We have contracts with hotels in each of the cities that she plays in, including here in Nashville."

"These private parties; industrial, political, what?"

"All of the above. They're very high end gigs."

Hatchett noticed that Peters was relaxed and confident. He never talked about Lisa Lemon in the past tense and the fact that they were lovers would have made it harder for him to cut her head off; but not to have someone else do it for him. At that moment Hatchett couldn't think of any possible motive for Peters to kill his star.

"Do you do strictly dancers, or do you handle anyone outside of the sex trade? Actors, animal acts, that sort of thing."

"I don't know if I like the sound of that. I'm no pimp."

"I never said you were. But, you can't deny that Lisa was probably turning tricks at all of these shows."

"If she did, I had no knowledge of it."

"Look, I don't need the police answer. Tell me if she was doing the clientele. It's very important that I know."

Peters looked away. When he looked back at Hatchett, there was reservation on his face.

"Why is it so important to know?"

Hatchett didn't want to, though it did seem like the right time to break the news to him that Lisa Lemon was dead. Peters hadn't said anything to implicate himself, but Hatchett still had things he wanted to know first.

"How did you meet Lisa?"

"I found her. I saw her at a club in Memphis and told her when she came to town to stop by and see me. She knocked on my door a couple'a months later."

"Have you ever been down south where she's from?"

"You mean Mississippi? No. I wanted to come down one year to talk her into coming back to work, but she wouldn't hear of it; said that was a part of her life that her family didn't know about, and she wanted to keep it that way."

"How about her home in Alabama?"

"She lived in Alabama? I didn't know that. I thought her family was in Mississippi."

Peters began to get an impatient look on his face. It was clear he wasn't going to be forthcoming with information for much longer.

"Now," Peters said, "what's this all about?"

Hatchett took a deep breath and exhaled. "Brace yourself. Lisa Lemon's dead."

He leaned forward. "What? You're not serious."

"I couldn't be more."

"When? How?"

"She was murdered. About two or three days ago."

"Oh, no." He looked away. His face was white. "Who?"

"I don't know."

Peters dropped his head to his chin and his shoulders slumped noticeably.

"By the way, where were you last weekend?"

His brows went up. "Surely you don't think . . ."

"Hey, it's not what I think."

He snorted. "I was here all weekend. I spent Saturday and Sunday with a woman."

"Well, keep her name handy. The police'll be wanting to get in touch with you very soon."

"Look, I didn't kill Lisa. She and I were in love."

"Touching."

"No, really."

"Sure."

He smirked. "I know, I know, but, when she's gone . . ."

Hatchett was silent. He waited to see if Peters would say something else.

"Well, I'm not a pimp."

"Okay, okay, look. Think hard. Who did Lisa dance for last winter that might have had a reason to shut her up?"

Peters exhaled loudly and looked at his desk. He reached and picked up a date book and thumbed through the pages. He found one and ran a finger down one side.

"Okay, here. She had a gig in Atlanta, a party for some bankers," he flipped a couple of more pages, "and in New Orleans, a group of union people." He flipped another page, then back to the first. "That's about it. I just don't see anyone who might have a reason to kill her."

A bunch of drunk, up tight bankers, and some mobbed up union people, Hatchett thought. Both groups were too smart to let a coked-out prostitute see or hear something that could be used against them.

Hatchett thought quickly. Was there anything else that needed to be asked before he left? As of yet, he hadn't felt the need to lean on the small man with the long hair. But Peters needed to know that things were serious.

Hatchett rose from his seat. "Mr. Peters, I certainly hope you've been truthful with me." His tone was stern.

Peters sat up straight. He had an indignant look on his face. Hatchett watched as his hands slid under the desk.

Before anyone could say or do anything else, Hatchett's hand flashed to the small of his back and in a millisecond his arm was extended and the .45 was pointed at the pimp's head.

"Don't even think about it."

Peters put his hands back on top of the desk, and Hatchett lowered his weapon not really understanding how things had broken so badly so quickly.

"Now, is there anything that you neglected to tell me that might help me find out who killed Lisa Lemon?"

Peters paused. "No," he said. "And I'm not a pimp."

CHAPTER 10

Hatchett left Nashville at nine the next morning, right after calling and giving Peters' name and address to McRae. Let the police work him over a while, he thought. If they came up with something - maybe with the union thing - at least he would have given them the lead.

He arrived back in Mauvilla exhausted and no closer to a solution than when he had left. He went home immediately and took a pill that enabled him to sleep from seven that evening to five the next morning.

The next morning, at this office, Hatchett started thinking about all the people who might have the know-how and the ability to cut the head off of a human body. Butcher came to mind quickly; surgeon, chiropractor. Of course anyone who had ever hefted an axe or swung a machete, or had butchered some type of animal could also be suspect.

There was only one major lead left to check out. That was the robbery case about which Lisa Lemon had testified seven years ago.

An hour later at the County Courthouse, Hatchett was pouring over a case file in one of the reading rooms off the Circuit Clerk's office.

It was a dull case. According to the record, Melinda Boatman aka Lisa Lemon, and a man named Louis Hart were riding around one afternoon when, according to Lemon, apparently on a whim, Hart had decided that the two should rob a local beauty salon. It was Lemon's testimony that they parked in front of the Cut and Curl Style Shop on Grand Avenue where Hart entered, displayed a weapon, and robbed the three lady stylists, one of whom was a recent immigrant from Liberia, and six frightened customers of about two hundred dollars total.

According to the file, the police located the two about an hour later after an intoxicated Hart, who was driving Lemon's Chevy Impala, ran it into the lake at the city's municipal park, some three miles from the scene. Hart and Lemon were rescued, and, fortunately for them, evidence of the crime was lost in the lake. They would have gotten off scot free, except for an inebriated Lemon's willingness to tell police where they had been and what they had been doing prior to the accident.

Both were arrested, but Lisa's lawyer cut a deal with prosecutors, and she was given immunity in return for supplementing the hairdressers' testimony at trial. Hart was convicted and sentenced to a ten year term, split to serve five in custody and three on probation.

It was a sordid story of a stupid crime perpetrated by base people, Hatchett thought. He hated robbery, just like he hated murder. As he read, he wished that he had the two of them in front of him right then so he could beat them both to a bloody pulp. The very thought of threatening people who were only trying to make an honest living, and then taking their money, was, to Hatchett, despicable. The longer he read, the higher his blood pressure went. If he could have shot them both at that moment, he would have.

When he finished, he sat back in the wooden chair and took a deep breath. Hatchett had seen a lot of crime in his life, and the older he got, the worse it affected him. He despised it with every ounce of whatever was in him, and whenever he read of it, thought of it, or reflected on it he always had to spend some time afterwards coming down from the anger that arose in him; anger that made him want to hurt someone.

Hatchett looked back at the file and then copied down the last known address of Louis Hart. It turned out to be an apartment on University Avenue, not far from Glendale Cemetery. He left the courthouse and drove there without stopping.

The complex was old. Seven wood buildings were arranged in a semi-circle facing the road. He parked in a space on the street, a half a block away, and walked up. Hatchett knocked on D-6, Hart's address, upstairs in the third building from the right.

"Who is it?" said a female voice through the door.

"Louis Hart?"

"Who?"

"I'm lookin' for Louis Hart."

The door cracked. Hatchett could see that the occupant was a fat woman wearing a blue print moo-moo that had a stain on the front. Her coarse hair was cut short, almost lower than a man.

"Who you lookin' fo?"

"Louis Hart. He live here?"

She chuckled. "He ain't lived her in fo'a five years." She paused and looked him up and down. "Who is you?"

Two small children tugged at the woman's dress as she stood. Both wore diapers that just barely hung on their hips, and nothing more.

"I need to talk to him. It's about some money I owe him."

"I'm his wife. You can give it to me." She held out her hand.

He smiled. "I better give it to him. Where's he living?"

"I 'on't know where he stays, but he got a business down on Ingersoll Avenue."

"Whereabouts?"

"Down by the river."

"You know what it's called?"

"It's jus' a junk shop; secon' han' furniture and thangs. I thank it's called Louis' Junk Shop."

Hatchett nodded. "Those Louis's children?'

"Mmm, hmm."

He nodded again. The thought of Hart leaving his wife and children to spend time with a woman like Lisa Lemon was a little galling to him.

"Well, listen." He reached in his pocket. "Here's the money I owe him." Hatchett handed her a twenty dollar bill.

She reached and took it. "Okay, I'll see he gets it."

"You know what? Keep it. I'll let him know."

"Thank you, suh."

It was getting close to noon when Hatchett drove by Louis's Junk Shop in the 2200 block of Ingersoll. The building sat on the opposite side of the road from the Raccoon River. It was a brick structure inside a six foot chain link fence with razor wire on top. Hatchett made the block and slowed down when he was right in front of the place.

There was a double gate in front of the driveway to the right and another smaller gate in the middle. Both were open. Hatchett parked his Merc and walked through the smaller gate. When he was within five feet of the front door, it opened and a man walked out. His hands were empty.

"Hey," he said cheerily, with a smile on his face.

Louis Hart was a very light-skinned black man with white features; or maybe he was a very dark skinned white man, Hatchett couldn't tell. He was of less than average height, thin, but with big forearms, and his black hair looked as if it had been chemically straightened and combed over. He had a pencil thin mustache over thin lips and gleaming white teeth, and he had an imitation diamond stud in his left ear.

"Can I help you find something?"

"Yeah. You Louis?"

"Just like the sign says."

"I need to talk for a minute. My name's Hatchett."

"Yes, sir. What can I do for you?"

"When's the last time you saw Lisa Lemon?"

His face froze, and he was clearly struck. He recovered quickly, but there was a noticeable change in his disposition.

"And your interest is what?"

"I'm an Inquiry Agent. I'm doing some work for her parents."

"I see." He shook his head. "Lisa? Wow, I haven't thought about her in years."

Hatchett noticed that he hadn't 'thought' about her, but he didn't mention when he had seen her.

"When did you talk to her last?"

"Oh, I suppose it was the night we got pinched. About five or six years ago, I guess."

"How'd that happen?"

He paused and looked at the ground. "I don't really want to talk about it, if you don't mind."

"Hey, ancient history, right?"

"Well, yeah. It's not exactly something I'm proud of. You understand."

"I heard she hung you out to dry."

He cocked his head to the side. "The bitch did me wrong, now."

"How so?"

"Well, you know, hittin' that place was her idea, but I swung for it." He paused and shook his arm from side to side. "But, hey, I got over it."

Hatchett nodded. It didn't sound much like he'd gotten over it, he thought.

"Besides, like you said, ancient history, right?" Hart said.

"You haven't heard from her since?"

"We haven't run into each other. And, I'm pretty sure it'd be a violation of my probation if we did."

"Okay." Hatchett paused and looked around. "What kind of place you got here?"

His countenance brightened a bit. "Oh, you name it. I've got one of everything, but not two of anything."

Hatchett saw some mounds of sod over against the fence. "You got plant and gardening things, too?"

"Some. I mostly deal in nick naks, bric a brac, junk, throwaways. You know what they say about one man's trash."

"Right. You work it alone?"

"No, well, my hired guy just quit. I'm looking for somebody else."

Hatchett didn't want to get completely away from why he was there. "If you don't mind my asking, how would you characterize your relationship with Lisa? Back then, I mean."

His eyes dropped to the ground. "We was, you know, friends with favors, I'd guess you'd say. When we was together, we got on pretty good."

"How'd you meet her?"

"Is that important?"

"Well, yeah. It might give me somewhere to start looking."

Hart looked around, obviously thinking about whether he should answer or not. In Hatchett's mind, this guy was guilty of something, maybe not murder, but something. Hart had answered most of the questions and still hadn't asked about the purpose of the interview.

He smacked his lips. "Hey, I bet'chu that old boy she lives with knows where she's at. That's the first place I'd go."

Hatchett noticed two things: that he had neglected to answer the question and had just assumed that Hatchett was 'looking' for Lisa Lemon; and he knew that Lisa Lemon was living with Alphonso, though they'd only been together two years or so.

"You ever met him?"

"Once." He stopped short as if he couldn't remember what he'd already said and didn't want to get caught in a lie.

"When was that?"

"Uh, I don't remember, really. I think it was back before I went off."

Hatchett nodded again. He looked around the property. There was a small metal outbuilding behind and immediately to the right of the brick one. Next to the metal building was a rusting, vintage tractor. Weeds grew up around the two large tires in the rear.

"Well, I guess that's all I can think of Mr. Hart. One day I'll come back here and take a look around inside your store; see if you got any bargains." He looked toward the outbuilding. "What's that over there, some kind of African art?"

Hart looked that way. "Oh, them figurines? Yeah, I import those from Liberia. Then, I knock'em off. You got an eye for antiques, do ya?"

"I got an eye for money."

"Well, I'll make sure you get the good stuff."

"Well, okay."

They shook hands. Hatchett recovered and wiped his palm on his pant leg. He had a feeling about Hart, and it bothered him greatly that he hadn't found a reason to slap him hard across the mouth.

CHAPTER 11

Back at his office, Hatchett put his feet up on his desk and leaned back in his chair to think. The killer of Lisa Lemon was not going to walk in and bite him on the ass, he thought. He would have to be rooted out. Hatchett decided to go back to the beginning and go over what he knew and what he didn't.

Lisa Lemon, or Melinda Boatman, obviously a whore - but a whore with a family that loved her and missed her - was dead. She was last seen at her summer home, which she shared with her common law old man, two weeks ago on a Sunday night. It was her summer home because she spent the six cold months of the year stripping in the major metropolitan centers of the south, and the six warm months in south Alabama resting and smoking dope. She was found at the dead end of a farm road in the north part of the county, decapitated, her head being removed to a field about a hundred yards away. She was naked, drained of blood, and her head was minus her tongue. Hatchett took his hands and wiped his face hard.

Each of the players with whom he had spoken, players in some way related to Lisa Lemon, all had motives. Yet, in Hatchett's mind, none of them really fit the part.

Alphonso Watkins, had a motive: money. As long as Lisa Lemon was smoking up the money she made during the year, Watkins had to pay the bills and feed the two of them himself. Of course, getting rid of her by changing the locks on the door would be a whole lot easier than killing her, but if, by some stretch of the imagination, he cared for her, it wouldn't be out of the question for him to lose his own head and do something violent. But, chop off her head? That was way over the line, he thought. Besides, now that she's dead, he gets nothing; no money, no sex, no dope, nothing.

Nicholas Peters' motive was harder to identify. If he was in love with Lisa Lemon, then it was probably hard for him to know that she was moving about the southeast undressing for lots of men and having sex with many of them. If he wasn't, and he probably wasn't, then it didn't matter. He was trying to get her to dance full time, which would mean more money in his pocket. But, if he killed her, or had her killed, which was a more likely occurrence, then she was of no monetary value at all.

That left T-Bird, Peahead, and their crowd. The dopers seemingly had no motive for killing Lisa Lemon. If she was dead, they lost a customer. Unless she was somehow about to turn them all in, they would most certainly be happy with the status quo. There would have to be a personal reason for killing her, and killing her in the manner that she was.

Louis Hart was another matter. He had the strongest motive of all: revenge. He gave up five years of his life because she informed on him to the police. But, he also had the strongest incentive to forget her treachery. He had been to prison and knew what it was like. Inasmuch as the correctional system was working, he should have been discouraged from harming her in order to avoid another stint of incarceration - or even the death penalty.

Actually, there was another possible suspect. The injuries that Lisa Lemon had sustained more logically lent themselves to some thrill murderer; someone who killed completely at random; a serial killer, the FBI called them. One of those guys who roamed the country killing for the fun of it. He'd read about them in a Bureau journal. They were even starting up some new unit to deal with crimes perpetrated by these people. A serial killer, of course, could have come from anywhere and could be anywhere. Like an ill wind he entered from the west, swirled around, and then left as suddenly as he came.

A professional killer acted in almost the same way. He came onto the scene with little or no connection to the victim, did his deed, and left quickly. But killers for hire usually didn't take the time and effort to kill the way that Lisa Lemon was. They normally killed quickly, disposed of the weapon and the body as unobtrusively as possible, and if they had to send a message at all, sent it subtly, not with a lot of fanfare.

Hatchett was asleep fifteen minutes after he sat down. Asleep with visions stamped on his brain; visions of headless naked women lying in the weeds, with wildflowers, and blackberry and kudzu vines over, under, and around their arms and legs, and butterflies fluttering about where their heads would've been.

He was awakened by the telephone. McRae was on the line.

"What are doing?" the lieutenant said.

"I was sleeping."

"Nice. We've got a whodunit on our hands – that is half yours, by the way – and you're sleeping."

"Hey, murder is your business. I'm just making a couple of discreet inquiries."

"Speaking of discreet inquiries, we talked to Demetrius out in the Plantation."

"Demetrius?"

"Peahead."

"Oh, yeah, right."

"We ran into to T-Bird, too. He told us again how badly you treated him."

"I just took some pre-emptive action that's all. T-Bird tell you about the shotgun in his lap?"

"No."

"I didn't think so. He's the kinda guy who might forget how to be forthcoming with information. I just reminded him. I'm surprised he mentioned our little encounter."

"Well, he did. And, by the way there was a witness: a little ole lady watching from her window." He chuckled. "She was proud of what you did."

Hatchett was silent. "So, what did Peahead tell you?"

"He said that Lisa Lemon was a regular visitor to the Plantation; he said that she had about a thousand dollar a week habit, and he said that she'd do anything for a hit."

"Anything?"

"Yep; up to and including sex."

Hatchett suddenly got a mental picture of Lisa Lemon on her knees in front of her dealer while next to her sat a mirrored table with lines of coke and little bitty spoons.

Hatchett wiped his eyes. "I could've gone all day without that image."

"Well, here's another. Peahead said that when she got high, they'd take her into one of the old houses, and she'd put on a show for them."

"This woman just gets gets better and better." He paused. "Don't spread that to her family, okay? I don't know if it's true or not, but they don't need to hear it."

"Sure. But don't you think they deserve to know the truth?"

"If it's the truth. Besides, I think they already do, especially her father."

There was silence on the other end of the phone. Then Hatchett spoke.

"How about Nicholas Peters? You done anything with him, yet?"

"Just some preliminary background stuff. He's got a sheet."

"What for?"

"Pandering and Simple Assault."

"Was he ever in Alabama?"

"Not that we've been able to tell as yet. But we're still looking."

"Let me know what you find out."

"If you do the same."

"You know I will."

Hatchett wasn't purposely withholding the information about Louis Hart. In fact, McRae already had it, and would have learned it if only he had done his due diligence with regards to Lisa Lemon's victimology. It wasn't Hatchett's fault if he didn't recognize the significance of her criminal record.

"What else have you heard?" McRae said. His tone was polite and hopeful.

"I was just sitting here dreaming that a serial killer was afoot in the county."

"Don't even joke like that."

"Oh, don't worry. I was just dreaming."

The object of Hatchett's game was to feed McRae a little useless information in exchange for some information that was valuable. Today he had put the thought in McRae's head that there might be a serial killer operating, and in return he had learned that the crew at the Plantation had all but eliminated themselves as being involved.

"By the way, did Peahead and T-Bird say exactly when was the last time that they saw her alive?"

"Exactly twelve days before her body was found, on a Saturday night."

Hatchett made a mental note of the date and then cleared his throat.

"Okay," he said, "it's time for me to make a few more discreet inquiries."

"Fine. But try not to be so rough. I had to talk T-Bird out of a complaint."

"Next time, tell him I'll give him something to complain about."

"Just be careful. Okay?"

"Tell that to the skels."

The next day, Hatchett came to the conclusion that what he needed was a larger suspect list. At his office, in the morning, he picked up the phone and called a contact at the Southeast Violent Crimes Information Center in Tampa. Tom Jensen was an Army buddy who had served with Hatchett in Intelligence at Fort Huachuca, Arizona. He was a bookish man with a precise way of speaking and no sense of humor at all.

"Tom Thumb, the man with his finger on the pulse of what's happening. How are you doing?" Hatchett said.

"Hatchett. What are you up to?"

"I need some information."

"And what might that be?"

"I've got a prostitute with her head chopped off. Does that MO ring any kind of bells for you?"

"Hmmm. Let me think." There was silence on the Florida end of the phone. "As a matter of fact it does. Let me see."

Hatchett could hear papers shuffling on the other end of the line. Then he heard a file cabinet rattling.

"Here it is. The New Orleans Police Department is working just such a crime as you described. Looks like a prostitute, beheaded, and found in a garbage dump."

"Naked?"

"Doesn't say. Just says she strolled on Bourbon Street."

Hatchett jotted down the contact information, a Sergeant Justin Thibodaux with a 504 area code, and cleared his throat.

"Anybody under arrest?"

"Doesn't say. However, after cases are submitted, agencies are often tardy or even remiss in supplying additional information regarding arrests."

"Let me ask you this. Would you have a list of physicians that have gone bad? You know 'docs on the rocks'?"

"You mean doctors who have been incarcerated or otherwise arrested for murder or assault?"

"Yeah, something like that. Somebody who'd be familiar with how to cut off a head."

"I wouldn't, but the AMA might. But, it's going to take some time. I'll have to get back to you."

"Sure. You know how to find me."

"I'll let you know just as soon as I hear of anything."

Hatchett enquired after Jensen's family and then hung up. He dreaded the thought of a trip to New Orleans to compare notes with their detectives, but he saw no way around it.

There were suspects with good motives for killing Lisa Lemon. But making a case against them, if they were indeed guilty, was not in the cards just yet.

CHAPTER 12

The next morning at nine, Hatchett was in New Orleans. He parked his Merc on the east side of the Police building, right off Tulane Avenue, and stepped out of the car and into an obnoxious stench of creosote, fish, and raw sewage. The humidity was high, even for the morning, and it made the odors hang in the air.

The Homicide Division was on the third floor. A dumpy white female with blonde streaks and a big smile greeted Hatchett at the front desk. The top three buttons of her blouse were unfastened, and she leaned forward in her chair.

"Yes, sir. Can I help you?"

"My name is Hatchett, ma'am. I'd like to talk to someone about a case you guys are working on; a beheaded prostitute."

"You have some information about a case, do ya?" She was no longer smiling.

"I may have. I'm working on one like it over in Alabama."

"So you're with an agency?"

"I'm an Inquiry Agent."

"A what?"

"A private investigator."

She cleared her throat, and Hatchett noticed that her face had changed to a full blown frown. She picked up her phone.

"I'll see if I can get someone." Her friendly tone was gone.

Hatchett took a seat on the wooden bench along the hallway. The receptionist's demeanor was not lost upon him. She must have had a bad experience with PI's, he thought. He guessed it probably had something to do with a wayward husband.

The woman replaced the phone and looked up. "Sergeant Thibodaux will see you. He's the second office on the right."

Hatchett rose, gave her a half smile, and walked past her, down the hall. He found the second office on the right and knocked on the door.

Inside, a fat man with thick, salt and pepper hair wearing a light blue dress shirt pulled tightly across his belly leaned forward and nodded toward a chair.

"Sit down there, son," he said in the expected south Louisiana brogue.

"Thank you, sir."

"I hope the receptionist wasn't too hard on you." He was grinning.

"I kinda got a bad vibe from her; she doesn't like private dicks."

"You got that right. She got stung once. One of'em took her money, but he couldn't catch her old man running around on her. I think she ended up blowing about two thousand dollars on the deal."

"Was he really cheating?"

"Nope. I think that's what made her so mad. She wanted to get shed of him but couldn't find a reason."

"What finally happened?"

"Nothin', really. She stayed with him; still hates him and still hates PI's." He paused and then leaned back. "Now, what's this information about a whore without her head?"

Hatchett had decided to measure his words carefully. All he really wanted to know was if the PD had made an arrest, and if that person could be placed in Alabama at the time of Lisa Lemon's death. He also wanted to run a couple of his suspects by Thibodaux to see if any of them rang a bell. If nothing clicked, he wanted to find a thread and then hit the street and do a little snooping of his own.

"I'm working for the parents of a woman killed over in Manipi County, Alabama. She was a dancer and prostitute who was found dead outside of Mauvilla. She was beheaded also."

He nodded but said nothing.

"I just wondered whether or not you guys have made an arrest in your case and whether or not we could put that person back in Alabama at the time of my girl's killing."

"You got any suspects?"

"A couple."

"Mind sharing them with me?"

Hatchett could see it was going to be harder than he thought. "Well, she had a manager up in Nashville that doubled as her lover. And she did a lot of dope on the southeast part of town. The police are chasing those leads."

"So, you just thought you'd come over here and pick our bones and beat'em to the punch."

"I'm just trying to do right by her mama and daddy."

He nodded again. "Well, the answer is 'no,' we haven't made an arrest, yet." He picked up his pen. "So, what about this manager guy?"

"Was your girl a dancer?"

He shook his head. "Used to be, but she got a pretty bad habit, so they put her on the street."

"What was her name?"

"Darla Hedrick."

"Where'd she dance?"

"At a place called Leo's, over on D'Iberville, right off Bourbon."

Hatchett took a deep breath. At least he had somewhere to start. "My victim's manager was Nicholas Peters. He's got an office in Nashville, on Broadway; calls himself a 'Theatrical Agent.'" He paused while Thibodaux wrote. "The doper she used was Theodore Adams; they call him T-Bird. But, as far as I know, he's never left the city."

Thibodaux jotted the names down. Hatchett could tell that the detective was hoping for something a little more substantial. I'd give it to him if I had it, he thought.

"By the way, did you guys find her head?" Thibodaux said.

"Yeah, about a hundred yards from the body. You?"

"Nope. Never did." He paused. "Who's working your case for the PD, over there in, what is it? Manipi County?"

"His name is McRae. He's a lieutenant at the Sheriff's Office. And, yeah, it's Manipi."

"Sounds kinda queer."

"It's Cherokee. It means, 'amazing.'"

In thirty minutes Hatchett was in the Vieux Carre walking down an almost deserted D'Iberville Street. He found Leo's about fifty feet off Bourbon. The front door was shuttered tightly, but the sign in the window said that a lunch buffet was served everyday starting at eleven thirty. Hatchett made a note of it and walked on, content to wait until they opened.

The dirty streets of the entertainment district stank of beer and urine and were littered with cups and hot dog wrappers, and an occasional newspaper. It appeared as if the street sweepers had come through earlier in the day and had succeeded only in turning the papers and sand into a thick muddy paste.

Hatchett made the block twice. When he got back, a thin man with a receding hair line and wire rimmed glasses was hooking back the front doors at Leo's. Hatchett waited until he'd finished and then followed him inside.

When the thin man went behind the bar, Hatchett spoke.

"Are you Leo?"

"Nope. Leo's dead." His attitude was dismissive.

"Well, maybe you can help me. I'm looking for Darla Hedrick. I heard she danced here."

He froze for just a second then reached for a towel to wipe the bar. "I guess you hadn't heard. She don't dance here no more."

"You know where I can find her?"

"Nope. I had to let her go about three months ago. Where she went after that is not my problem." He went on about his work as if unconcerned.

His lying was obvious. The startled look, the evasion on where Darla Hedrick actually was, both betrayed him. Hatchett was incensed. He looked to his left and right, then over his shoulder. The only other person in the building was, apparently, the fat, Creole, female cook wearing all white and walking back and forth from the kitchen to the barroom with pans of food for the steam tables.

When the cook was back in the kitchen, Hatchett reached across the bar and grabbed the man by the collar of his plaid, oxford shirt. He walked him toward the end of the bar and toward a door marked 'Office.' The man went through it face first, and went hard up against a wall just inside and to the left. Hatchett took his left hand and bent the man's right arm back and pushed it up as far as it would go. With his right, he grabbed a hank of the man's hair.

"Okay, Leo, or whatever your name is. You're holding out on me. Now, where is Darla Hedrick?"

"Ahhhh! That hurts! She's dead, all right?"

"Who killed her?"

"I don't know."

Hatchett pushed his right arm up higher. "Bullshit."

"I don't know, really. Ahhh! The police have been out here four or five times. I don't know, I tell ya."

"So why not say so."

"Some guy who used to be her manager told me to play dumb."

"Who?"

"Some guy named Peters. I don't know. He's out of town."

"Why'd he want you to clam up?"

"He called and said not to talk; said he'd pay."

"What did he want you not to talk about?"

"Her connection."

"Her dope connection?"

"Yeah."

"Who's that?"

"I don't know."

Hatchett pounded his head into the wall.

"Ahhh! I don't know, some guy in Alabama."

"Where?"

"I don't know; somewhere down south. Mauvilla, I think."

Hatchett thought he had gotten all he could out of the man. He let go of his hair and with his right fist gave him one good kidney punch. The man crumpled to the floor. Hatchett stepped out of the room quickly and was on the street in seconds. In two minutes he was in the Merc and in less than ten he was on the interstate. In twenty, he was across the Mississippi River, out of state, and on his way home.

CHAPTER 13

The revelation that there was a connection between the dead prostitute in New Orleans and Nicholas Peters was unexpected.

The knowledge also that a drug dealer from south Alabama was involved meant little. There were hundreds of drug connections with hundreds of fish on their lines and the fact that this Darla Hedrick was one of them meant little except that it was unusual for an addict to get her medicine that far from home. But the question of the day was what connection did Peters have to the death of Hedrick?

Hatchett was back in town, and back at his office by five. After he put his feet up on his desk, he dialed his answering service. The husky voice of Marilyn, one of the operators, answered.

"Hey, Peaches. Anything for me?" Hatchett said.

"Hi, sweetie. Oh, I don't know. Let me see."

"Busy?"

"Oh, no. I've just been filing my nails and reading a magazine."

"Cosmo? 'How to Please Your Man,' maybe?"

"Oh, no, honey. I already know how to do that."

There was a smile in her voice. Hatchett had never seen Marilyn but had often wondered what she looked like.

"Looks like you've got one call."

Hatchett fumbled for a pen. "Shoot."

"It's from a girl named Jasmine. She says that she found out that Lisa was seeing a guy named Mike out in the county. She said she didn't know what his last name was, but he worked at a Christmas tree farm out in Pleasant Hill. She said she thought it was Abner's, Abner's Tree Farm." She paused. "Oh, she also said she couldn't find the number for the man in Nashville."

"That's alright. I found him."

Hatchett wrote quickly. He didn't ask if there was anything else. Marilyn always gave him everything she had in one swoop. She didn't question the callers for additional information, and he didn't expect her to.

"Okay. I'll run it down." He paused. "Hey, Marilyn, you maybe want to get dinner some time?"

There was silence on the other end. "On, no, I don't think so. I'm kinda' involved . . . for right now."

"Okay. Well, good luck with that." He hung up, disappointed, but not unhopeful.

Hatchett was familiar with Abner's, located off Vandalia Road in Pleasant Hill. It was about two hundred acres of small and large seedlings that the owner sold to landscapers, builders, and, at Christmas time, to the general public. They marketed several species of pines and other evergreens, and a fair number of oaks. Hatchett had only seen the place from the outside, but locating an employee didn't seem as if it would be a problem, with the right story, that is.

The next morning, at nine, Hatchett parked the Merc in front of the small clapboard building that was the office of Abner's Tree Farm. He pulled open the front door and heard a not so loud buzzer.

An elderly woman with gray hair coiffed in a late sixties style sat behind a desk in the front room. She removed her glasses and smiled sweetly when Hatchett stopped in front of her desk.

"Yes, sir. How may I help you?"

"My name is Hatchett, ma'am, and I'm an investigator for lawyer J. Edgar Haggerty. He handles estate disposition and tax law with a large firm over in Biloxi. He sent me to find the last known relative of a client who just died out in Denver. All we know is his name is Mike."

"Well, we've only got one Mike that works here – Mike Allenwood."

"Would it be possible for me to steal him away from his duties for about ten minutes?"

"Oh, sure," she said smiling. "You can probably find him in the barn. It's down that path about a hundred yards." She stood and pointed out the window at the back of the room.

"I think I can find it, ma'am. Thank you. You've been most helpful."

Hatchett walked out the door of the office, around the side of the building, and began making his way down between the rows of pine seedlings toward the wooden barn some three hundred feet ahead.

When he got to the large door in the front of the weather beaten structure, he stopped. The place seemed deserted until he heard a banging in the rear near the door on that side. He walked toward the sound.

As he neared the back, a short, fat man wearing a plaid shirt and jeans stepped out from behind a small tractor about fifteen feet away. He had a wrench in his right hand, and he wore work boots. He looked up as he was dusting off his jeans.

"You Mike Allenwood?"

"Who wants to know?"

"Name's Hatchett. I want to talk to you."

"What about?"

Hatchett took two steps his direction and stopped. "About Lisa Lemon."

Allenwood froze for just a second, but then he drew back and threw the wrench at Hatchett. He bolted out the back door of the barn and took off into the maze of trees. Hatchett ducked to his right and the crescent wrench missed him by a foot. He hit the back door ten yards behind Allenwood.

Hatchett's legs were longer, and he was obviously in better condition, so he was easily able to keep him in his sight. After fifty yards, he had made up the space between the two. He reached and grabbed Allenwood's right shoulder.

The fat man stopped suddenly and swung about. Hatchett pulled up short and was startled to see a hooked bill knife in Allenwood's right hand. He displayed the blade threateningly.

"Okay, buddy. Now, wait a minute," Hatchett said holding out has arms in a calming motion.

Allenwood was breathing hard. He dropped into a half crouch and tossed the knife from hand to hand menacingly.

Hatchett thought for a second of pulling his forty five from the holster at the small of his back and ending it all right there; but Allenwood obviously had information, and Hatchett wanted to know what it was.

Standing straight, he spoke. "Look, buddy, I just want to ask you about Lisa. No need for any of this."

Allenwood took a step forward and swung the knife through the air in a roundhouse effort to put a smile in Hatchett's abdomen. Hatchett jumped back. Allenwood made the move again. This time Hatchett waited until he fanned, then he pirouetted to his left and leveled a side kick into the fat man's torso that sent him sprawling backwards, and the knife into the air.

After he landed, Hatchett could hear him trying to pull air into his temporarily collapsed lungs. Hatchett walked leisurely to the location of the knife, picked it up, then walked to Allenwood. He knelt down, putting his right knee on the fat man's chest and his left foot on his right wrist. Then he grabbed a hank of Allenwood's hair and pulled his head up.

Allenwood was still gasping, but was beginning to recover. His rapid, shallow breaths were becoming deeper and slower. When Hatchett thought he could talk, he looked around and, seeing no one, he put the blade to the fat man's throat.

"Now," Hatchett said matter of factly, "you're going to tell me all I want to know."

Allenwood's eyes were wide with fear, but he managed a nod. Beads of sweat rolled from his forehead down the sides of his face.

"When was the last time you saw Lisa Lemon?"

"About a month ago," he grunted.

"Where?"

"At the Platter."

"Keep talking."

"She was supposed to pick up a load and take it north."

"A load. A load of what?"

"Coke, man."

That was it. Lisa Lemon was a mule. Then it made sense, Hatchett thought. It also widened his suspect list immensely.

"So?"

"She wouldn't take it."

"Why not?"

"Said she was gettin' out. She didn't want the hassles; she said she was through."

"So, what did you do?"

"I said, okay. I'd just tell the boss."

"Who is?"

He paused. Hatchett saw his hesitancy. He took the knife and quickly cut a short gash under Allenwood's right eye. Blood appeared immediately.

"Don't stop now."

"Owwwww," the fat man said, squinting his eyes tightly. "Look, I don't know his name. He calls me. I think he's out of town."

"Where do you get the stuff?"

"Come on, man," he whined. "I need the money."

Hatchett paused. He now knew more about Lisa Lemon than he did before. Did he really need to know the name of her drug connection? Whoever it was formed another link in the drug chain that might have led to her death. He decided he needed the information.

Hatchett put the knife to Allenwood's right eye. "Who is it?"

The fat man's eyes opened wide. "Okay, okay. His name is Whitey Sansome. He drives a truck. I meet him out at the stop off the interstate."

Hatchett relaxed, and so did Allenwood. "Tell me all you know about Lisa."

He shook his head hard and fast. "That's it. I met her at the Platter about three or four years ago, and that's when she got on board. Six months out of the year, she met me about every couple'a weeks and picked up a load. Then she took it to wherever she was goin' next. It was no big deal."

"I thought she danced out of town?"

"She did, but she'd make a pass through here and pick up merchandise. The out of town people, they set up her schedule."

"Did you kill her?"

"No!" He shook his head hard once again. "Why would I do that? All I had to do was walk in that club and get some other bitch to pick up right where she left off."

"What else?"

Allenwood looked away. He took two short breaths and shook his head. "That's it. I don't know, she gave good head, I guess."

At that, Hatchett took the knife and cut a slice out of the skin under the other eye. This laceration was deeper and longer and bled much more.

"That's for bein' funny."

CHAPTER 14

Hatchett was confident that his confrontation with Allenwood would not become a police matter, so he thought no more of it. If the fat man tried to report Hatchett's handiwork, it might throw attention onto his own illegal dealings and that would be fatal to his narcotic enterprise. So, Hatchett went back to his office and chewed on a sandwich while rolling the hooked bill knife over and over in his hand.

It made no sense for Allenwood to have killed Lisa Lemon, he thought. Unless she, for some reason, had threatened to blow his whole operation to the police, he would have no reason to silence her. He thought about her missing tongue. That was certainly a message regarding her willingness to inform; but a message to whom? Who needed to see it? Who ultimately saw it, other than the police?

Hatchett picked up the phone and called Lucy Leopold at the Coroner's Office.

"I just wanted to go over with you the wound in the Melinda Boatman case."

"Refresh me," she said. Her tone was disinterested.

"The prostitute that was beheaded."

"Oh, yes."

"The wound, could it have been made by a smaller blade?"

"No, as I recall, we're looking for a long, heavy blade; maybe an axe, a machete, or a, a hatchet, if you'll excuse the term."

"No offense taken."

"Oh, by the way, the wood between the victim's toes; it was from a monkey fruit tree."

"Really."

"The information just came in today."

Hatchett hung up the phone and called Vincent O'Leary. He could hear him eating on the other end of the line also.

"You know anything about a coke ring running loads in by eighteen-wheeler?" Hatchett asked.

"Are you kidding? There's probably only about fifty of 'em."

Hatchett took a deep breath and exhaled. "Okay, well, have you got anything on a Whitey Sansome?"

"Spell it."

Hatchett supplied him with a reasonable spelling of the man's last name. O'Leary repeated it back to him.

"His name doesn't ring a bell. But we get names every day; by tips, and through fliers from the feds." He paused. "Who does this guy drive for?"

"I don't know. It wouldn't surprise me if he was on owner operator. He only holds for about six months out of the year."

"What's his play?"

"He picks up dope, I don't know where, and brings it into Alabama where a guy named Allenwood picks it up and gets it to a mule. The mule takes it across the southeast to users and distributors."

"Now, this Allenwood I've heard of. Have you talked to him?"

"Yeah. He works at a tree farm over off the Vandalia Highway. He and I just recently made contact."

"Made contact, hunh. I hope you made contact with a boot in his ass."

"He'll remember our visit every time he looks in the mirror."

"Good. I'll see what I can get for you on this Sansome guy. You think this is a big operation?"

"Could be. I've already identified three links."

"Three? I heard Sansome and Allenwood, who's the other?"

"Lisa Lemon."

Hatchett hung up and leaned back in his chair. So Lisa Lemon was a drug mule trying to retire.

In Hatchett's mind, he had quickly sized up Allenwood and pronounced him not capable of the rage it would take to slice off the woman's head. As it was, he hardly put up a fight at the tree farm. A bullet would be more his style; it would be cleaner and quicker.

The others in the organization were another matter. Dope dealers were notorious for their message killings. If others in the chain had more to lose, then they might very well be capable of this murder.

The man at the top wouldn't do it, but he might have it done. But, Hatchett thought, it might be a while before he was able to pull enough threads to unravel this organization all the way to the top.

CHAPTER 15

Two weeks passed without a clue. Hatchett once again went over to visit the Boatman's in Waynesboro. He did it partly to let them know how he'd been spending their money, and partly in an effort to gin up another lead.

Mrs. Boatman met him at the door on a Thursday afternoon and ushered him to the kitchen table. Hatchett sat down in the picturesque room that smelled of chocolate cookies and strawberries. She offered him a cup of coffee, which he declined.

"I'm sorry I didn't make it to the funeral. I suppose the police were there."

Actually, Hatchett didn't like funerals and never had any intention of attending this one.

Mrs. Boatman sat down at the table across from him and folded her hands. "Yes, they were there, takin' pitchers, and copyin' down tag numbers. They was more of a nuisance than anything else." She paused and looked away. "But I guess we outghta' be thankful. If it hadn't been for them, there wouldn't been too many people there."

"Anybody there you didn't recognize?"

"No. There was just a few family."

"Didn't Mindy have a lot of friends here at home?"

She shook her head. "I think she'd lost touch with everbody she went to school with. This ain't a real big town, and the kids that grow up here usually just want to get out."

"How about old boyfriends."

"You know she didn't have any boyfriends in high school. Mindy was kind of an ugly ducklin'. She was a late bloomer, you know. But, I think there was one boy that took up with her some when she was a senior, but he was just as hard up as her, and I think he only wanted her for a prom date."

"He still around?"

"I don't know."

"If you could get an address or something, I'd like to talk to him; just to see when he saw her last."

Mary Boatman got up from the table walked over to the kitchen counter, near the wall phone.

She pulled open a drawer and fumbled through some papers and found an address book. She brought it back to the table and sat back down.

"His mama was married to one of the Meeks over near State Line. Let's see."

She turned pages in the book and ran her finger down columns until she found the name she was searching for.

"Here it is. Her name is Margie Meeks. Her boy is named Harold, Harold Meeks. I've got a note here that he's down in Pascagoula. I'll have to call her to find out his address."

Hatchett jotted down the name, then looked at Mary Boatman. He knew of no other way to tell her the things that he had learned about Mindy than to just do it.

"I'm finding out some things about Mindy that maybe you ought to know about now; so you won't be surprised later . . . like at a trial, or in the newspaper."

She sat up straight and folded her arms. Hatchett saw her clench her jaws. She nodded her head.

"Do you think Mr. Boatman ought to be here for this?"

She shook her head. "No. He don't want to know it. I think he disowned her in his mind a long time ago. He just acts like he cares for my benefit."

"Okay. Well, Mindy danced at clubs; you knew that. But she was also a prostitute."

"Oh." She unfolded her arms and began to rub her hands.

Hatchett thought he saw tears in her eyes. It was hard for him to believe that the thought had never crossed her mind.

"She danced at clubs throughout the southeast, you knew. But she would also make private gatherings and that's where she sold herself."

Clearly, the information was painful to Mary Boatman. Maybe, this reaction was the worst of it, he thought.

"One time, when she was in Mauvilla, she got hooked up in a drug ring. From what I've been able to piece together, she picked up drugs and delivered them while she was on her circuit. She was what they call a 'drug mule'."

Hatchett looked at her. She appeared to take this news a lot better than she did the other.

"And you think these people might have killed her?"

"I don't know yet. I'm told that she was trying to get out of the loop, and if that's true, then they might've been afraid that she would tell on them; though I don't know why. Usually, if someone wants out of this kind of thing, they want to get as far away from it as possible, and they don't have any intention of going to the police."

Mary Boatman nodded her head. "So she wanted out of it?"

"That's what I understand."

"Well . . . at least that's something."

Hatchett and Mary Boatman talked on. He answered every question she had about how her daughter died. She asked him to be graphic - a fact that he found surprising - and he was.

"What do the police tell you?"

Through her tears, she took a deep breath and exhaled. "They don't have much to say, really. They say, 'they're pursuing every lead,' but they didn't tell me about the things you said."

"Some of them they don't know about. You should keep this information to yourself."

She shrugged and nodded.

Hatchett cleared his throat. "Well, I should be going. You think you can get that address for Harold Meeks?"

"Sure. But I think you're barking up the wrong tree."

"How so?"

"Well, if memory serves me right, this boy grew up and has done right well."

"Oh?"

She nodded. "I think he's a doctor now."

CHAPTER 16

Mary Boatman supplied Hatchett with the office address of Harold Meeks, MD, who ran a small storefront clinic on Market Street in Pascagoula, Mississippi, about thirty five miles west of downtown Mauvilla.

Hatchett found the office right at quitting time that same day and waited in the Merc, parked at the rear of the building, until a tall, thin man with brown hair walked out of the back door. He pulled a stethoscope from around his neck and was just slipping out of his short white coat when Hatchett stepped out of his car and started toward him.

"Dr. Meeks?"

Meeks stopped short just as he was about to grab the door handle of his eight year old Mercedes. He acted defensively, perhaps thinking that Hatchett was an armed robber.

"Yes?" His tone was apprehensive.

"My name's Hatchett. I'm a private detective from over in Mauvilla. I'd like to talk to you."

"Did my ex send you?" His tone had changed to one of disgust.

"No. I wanted to talk to you about Melinda Boatman."

"Who?"

"Melinda Boatman, Mindy. I think you knew each other from high school."

He paused then seemed to collapse against the front fender of his car. He smiled and shook his head slowly.

"Mindy? Oh, man, I haven't thought about her in years."

Hatchett watched him closely, trying to gauge his initial truthfulness.

"What about her?"

"When's the last time you talked to her?"

He looked up into the air and whistled. "Oh, I guess it's been ten years ago, now; right after we left high school. I got a scholarship to Ole Miss, and she was going to junior college, I think. As I recall, we ran into each other over the Christmas holidays a couple of years out of school." He shook his head and smiled. "Man, I haven't thought about her in years."

"You haven't seen her since?"

"Is something wrong?"

"Well, she's missing, and I'm helping her parents run her down. Would you have any idea where she is?"

"No, I wouldn't." He shook his head.

Hatchett paused. "Tell me about you two. Did you guys ever materialize?"

"Ha. Not really. We both went to Wayne Consolidated High and were in the same class. I was the class nerd and never had a date. She was an 'okay' student, but she wasn't what you'd call a knockout. When the spring of our senior year rolled around, my mother made me get a date to the prom. I asked a couple of people, but got turned down. I think Mindy was about fourth on my list, after the cute ones. She said 'yes' and we went." He paused and looked up. "I remember I wore a black and white tapestry tux with a white ruffled shirt. She had on a white dress." He nodded his head. "It was really a pretty good night."

Hatchett eyed the doctor up and down and tried to spot a lie. At that point, his story sounded believable, although he hadn't mentioned how their meetings had gone at the Christmas get-togethers. He decided on another tack.

"So, what kind of practice you got here, Doc?"

"Oh, it's a combination really. We treat the inner city poor, and we also do some work in the area of drug rehabilitation."

"How's business?"

"With what we do? Jumping. Our waiting room's full every day."

Hatchett nodded. "You know, I heard that Mindy had a little bit of a habit."

"I think I heard that too. That's too bad."

Hatchett noticed his slip up but decided to let it pass. There was nothing left to do but leg work.

"Well, Dr. Meeks, here's my card. If you should happen to see her or hear from her, give me a call. Her parents are pretty worried."

Meeks reached and took the card. "Well, okay, but it's not gonna happen." He paused. "I mean, I'm pretty sure our paths aren't going to cross. It'd really be a surprise if they did."

"Hey. You never know."

The next morning, Hatchett contacted Tom Jensen in Tampa. It was shortly after nine, his time, and he was at his desk.

"I gotta name to run by you: Harold Meeks, MD. Can you check and see whether he's had any trouble?"

"Sure," Jensen in the middle of a yawn. "He one of those 'doctor's gone bad' you were worried about?"

"Could be. He runs a methadone clinic over in Pascagoula, Mississippi; the kind'a place you'd work at if you couldn't hang out your shingle somewhere a bit more respectable - or lucrative."

"Ever consider that he just might be a quack?"

"Maybe, but that's not the vibe I got."

"Well, if you didn't get the quack vibe, did you get the killer vibe?"

"No, I didn't get that either. He didn't look like a guy who has gotten his hands bloody. He looked more like a man who gave the wrong pills to somebody with a lawyer."

"That'll do it, too."

"Just let me know about his past."

"Got it."

Hatchett hung up and put his head in his hands. Peters, Watkins, T-Bird, Peahead, Hart, Allenwood, Sansome, and now Meeks. Shit, he thought. Any one of them could've killed her.

With her past, Lisa Lemon's killer could have been anyone from anywhere, with almost any motive.

The next morning, Hatchett got a call from Vincent O'Leary. He sounded excited.

"Whitey Sansome is an owner operator. He usually contracts with a company called Big Time Transport out of Charleston."

"What do they haul?"

"Dry goods mostly; textiles, paper, and the like."

"Have you talked to them?"

"Just got off the phone."

"Where is he?"

"He'll be coming through town day after tomorrow."

"I owe you one."

"I'll put it on your tab."

CHAPTER 17

Two days later, Hatchett was in his Merc, parked under a tree, in the northwest corner of the parking lot at the Belle Bay Auto Truck Stop on the north side of Interstate 10, at the west end of Manipi County, four miles from the Mississippi state line. It was one of the largest truck stops in the southeast, and Hatchett could reasonably expect that Sansome would stop for food, gas, rest, or just to take a piss break.

O'Leary had provided him a description of Sansome's cab and trailer. It was a red Peterbuilt with a dual sleeper and white lettering on the door that announced that Whitey Sansome was the owner. The trailer was a sixty foot aluminum that was distinguishable because it was so shiny.

Not knowing when or if he would arrive, Hatchett took up the position under the shady oak tree at eight in the morning. He was parked where he could see both entrances and the scales. He alternately read, listened to the radio, and ate, as what looked like twenty or thirty trucks an hour entered the huge, thirty acre lot.

The truck stop had been in business for about twenty five years; since the heyday of highway transport began when gas was much cheaper and the economy was just beginning to boom. The lot was clean and well policed, especially after the airing of a network news report that had exposed the fact that a large number of prostitutes used it as a kind of a concrete brothel. Pimps in passenger vehicles rode the interstate five miles either side of the exit and used citizen-band radios to set up tricks for the truckers passing through. The girls monitored the traffic on hand held CB's and were there to meet the drivers as they drove onto the lot. The tricks were turned in the backs of the sleeper cabs.

The Sheriff at the time, a moralist who saw the national news report on television, later made it his personal mission to knock out the eighteen wheel sex trade and clean up the stop. The station's management, who saw no net gain or loss in business when the girls were in operation, had no opinion about the cleanup and was happy to have the Sheriff make a show of force. It kept down the theft and the gas drive offs, and, oddly, the restaurant food actually improved.

It was close to eleven when Hatchett spotted Sansome's bright crimson semi-truck come down the interstate ramp, turn onto the access road, and make its way onto the lot. The big rig made a right turn and drove pass the diesel pumps, around the scales, and into the back side of the lot where the other vehicles were lined up in two long rows from south to north along the back fence.

Hatchett changed positions to the far northeast corner of the lot where he could watch the truck. He took out his binoculars and focused in on the man as he exited the driver's door of the shiny machine.

Sansome, or the man believed to be Sansome, was tall, though he didn't look it. His beer gut hung over the belt of his jeans so far that the buckle was invisible. He was bald with a bushy mustache. His red, short sleeved t-shirt accented his huge arms, and when he walked in his saddle type cowboy boots, his bowlegged gait looked just as if he'd gotten off a horse after a long ride.

Hatchett watched him as he waddled toward the rear entrance to the restaurant. How and when to make a move on the fat man was Hatchett's next problem. He decided to wait and play it by ear.

As he watched, it occurred to Hatchett that the sleeper might make for a good place to kill a prostitute. The subsequent dismemberment, however, would have to take place somewhere else; but with his constant travel, finding a secluded spot to behead her would not have been a problem. At some point in their conversation, Hatchett had to find a way to get a look into the cab.

It was forty minutes later when Sansome walked out of the restaurant accompanied by a much shorter man. The second man wore slacks and a dress shirt and didn't have the look of an over the road trucker. They both walked to the cab and got in, the shorter man on the passenger side.

Hatchett adjusted his glasses and watched as the two men talked. Sansome then reached behind him and came out with a package. He gave it to the short man, who, in turn, handed Sansome an envelope.

That son of a bitch, Hatchett thought. He's making a drop right here, in front of me.

The short man got out of the cab and walked with the package under his arm back inside the restaurant. Hatchett watched as Sansome sat in the cab looking at and writing in a book. He did that for five or ten minutes, then got up from the driver's seat and struggled, with great effort, over into the sleeper portion of the cab. He pulled the curtain closed, and Hatchett could see him no more.

His next move would have to be well thought out. Apparently, Sansome was tucked in for a while, so Hatchett would have some time the think. If the fat man was following ICC rules, he would have to be asleep for eight to ten hours. That would put him back on the road just about dark.

That theory was plausible for one huge reason. If Sansome's sole source of income was hauling freight, he would no doubt be willing to skirt federal regulations. However, since he was hauling dope as a sideline, and thereby increasing his income, then he would feel much freer to follow the government's guidelines. Either way, Hatchett felt he could count on a few hours out of the car.

Inside the restaurant, Hatchett took a seat in a corner booth and scouted the room. It contained a wide assortment of truckers: a tall one with a cowboy hat; two short, thin ones with jeans and checked shirts; a very, very fat one, fatter even than Sansome; and a dumpy, older woman with stringy hair who was shortly joined by a gray haired man with a 'CAT' hat, no doubt a husband and wife team.

A young, dark haired, jeans-wearing waitress, whose hips were poured into the garment, smiled as she took Hatchett's order of coffee and a glass of water. She turned to walk away, no doubt relieved that she wouldn't have to bring him food.

As she did, the short man with the tan slacks walked into the restaurant, empty handed, and sat down at the counter. He smiled as the counter girl brought him a cup of coffee also.

Hatchett's waitress, whose name tag identified her as 'Sherry,' returned to the table and set the cup of coffee in front of him. Hatchett nodded toward the man at the counter.

"Sherry, who is that guy over there? The one in the slacks?"

She looked that direction. "Oh, that's Mr. Fitch. He's the day manager."

Hatchett nodded. Sherry put down a ticket for an overpriced cup of coffee and left. Hatchett took two sips of the hot liquid and leaned back. He took two more sips, laid down two dollars, then walked from the booth to the counter.

"Mark Hacker. Appalachian Transport," Hatchett said putting out his hand.

"Allen Fitch." Fitch smiled showing straight teeth.

"My company is going to be running a new route through Alabama, from Texas to Jacksonville, and I was wondering if you guys had any kind of deals when it comes to fuel."

"We do have a revolving charge plan for diesel. I can get you an application."

"That'd be great." Hatchet paused. "We're also looking for alternate carriers, you know, for overflows. I noticed a Whitey Sansome truck outside, and the name caught my eye. Don't they have a fleet that makes a regular run through here?"

"Oh, no," Fitch said as he took swig of coffee. "He's an owner operator with just the one truck. He handles only one or two contracts."

"Oh, that's too bad. I thought I might approach him while I was here."

"Well, you could if you want, but like I say, Mr. Sansome is a one man show. I don't think he'd be interested."

Hatchett nodded. What he had just heard had confirmed that Sansome was outside asleep in the truck.

"Okay, then. Well, I'll just pick up that application for a fuel card, and then be on my way."

The two of them walked out of the restaurant, into the general store portion of the business, and then past the showers and locker room to a small office in the back. Inside, Hatchett saw the brown package sitting on Fitch's desk.

"Just fill this out and get it back to me, and after a credit check, we'll get you all set up."

Hatchett took the paper. "I'll do it." He paused. "Hey, there's one other thing. We have a lot of trouble at these stops with prostitutes running the lots. You guys got that problem here?"

Fitch chuckled. "Oh, no. We ran the girls out a couple of years ago." He grinned. "But, if you want a joint, you might not have too hard a time finding one."

Four hours, a hamburger, and two cups of coffee later, Sansome's vehicle hadn't moved. The curtain between the driver's compartment and the sleeper hadn't moved either. It was getting toward dark and Hatchett decided that he had to make his move soon. All he wanted from the fat man was a look at his sleeper and to find out who his connection was. Working this dope angle back to its source might be the only way that he could find out who wanted Lisa Lemon dead.

Right after sundown, Hatchett got out of his car and walked to the red Peterbuilt. When he got to the driver's side, he stood on the gleaming aluminum step and banged on the door. He heard a cough and movement. In a minute the door opened.

The fat man coughed and rubbed his face. He was in white boxers and a tightfitting t-shirt.

"Yeah?"

"Hey, you Mr. Sansome?"

"Who wants to know?"

"Mark Hacker, of Appalachian Transport. I wanted to talk to you about a deal."

The fat man shook his head. "Ain't interested." He tried to pull the door closed.

Hatchett yanked the door with his left hand, shouldered his way past it inside, and punched the fat man twice in the face with a stiff right fist. Sansome grabbed his face and fell back onto the passenger seat. Hatchett hoisted himself in and quickly closed the driver's door.

Blood was coming from the big man's nose, and he looked down at what had drained into his hands. Hatchett expected him to be quicker, but he was slow in reaching for the baseball bat lodged in between the two front seats. It had been trimmed down into a club about twenty inches long, and the knob end was taped with electrical tape. Hatchett saw it and grabbed it first, and held it away from him, back toward the driver's door.

"Now, calm down. This ain't a stick up. I just need a little information."

Denied his weapon, Sansome nursed his nose while rotating to his right and settling himself in the passenger seat. When Hatchett saw him eyeing the door handle, he hit the auto door locks on the driver's side and spoke in calming tones.

"Don't even think about it. This'll only take a minute."

"Who are you?"

"Let's just say I represent a co-worker of yours."

His face turned blank. "What?"

"Lisa Lemon."

"Who?"

"Lisa Lemon. She was one of the mules in your operation."

His face reanimated with recognition. "She the whore that got her head chopped off?"

"Right. Tell me what you know."

"What I know? What I know is what I read in the papers."

"She transported for you and your buddy Allenwood. So, what went wrong?"

He shook his head. "Look, I don't know what you've heard, but I didn't know this Lemon broad." He wiped his nose with his shirt. "And I don't know what she was transporting."

His answer incensed Hatchett. With a quick motion he hit Sansome with the barrel end of the bat. He heard the man's nose crack.

"Awwww! Fuck!"

"Look," Hatchett said. His tone was calm. "I hate a liar. Now, I know you move dope across the southeast, and I know you get it to Fitch, Allenwood, and probably a dozen others. I'm not interested in all that. What I want to know is who killed Lisa Lemon?"

"Okay, okay. Shit, man, you didn't have to do that. I think you broke my nose."

"So, I'll call you a doctor. Now, tell me about the girl."

"Look, all I know is what I heard." His voice was nasally, as if he was pinching his septum together. "I saw Allenwood for our regular pick up. I said somethin' to him about the girl, 'cause I'd seen it in the paper, and I said, like, wasn't it a bad thing. So, he says she used to be one of his mules. I said who did her? And he said he didn't know."

"Bullshit." Hatchett drew the bat back again preparation for another strike.

"Wait, wait. No, now. That's all I know, really." His tone was pleading.

"You just casually mentioned to him about a seemingly random murder?"

"Okay, okay. He had told me before that he had a dancer workin' for him. I thought it might'a been her."

"What made you think that?"

"'Cause the papers said she danced around the southeast, and I just figured . . ."

"What else did Allenwood tell you?"

"Nothin'. He just said now he had to get another girl and make her a star."

"What'd he mean by that?"

"You know, to get her dancin' around the country; so she could make the drops."

The words struck Hatchett. He took a deep breath and exhaled. If her work as a dope pusher is what got her killed, it was plain now who was behind it.

Hatchett looked at Sansome. "Get out." He flipped the door lock switch.

"What?"

"I said get out."

"But, but, my clothes."

"It's only for a minute. I just want to look at the sleeper."

He was reluctant, and he moved slowly, but Sansome opened the door and stepped out of the cab and onto the asphalt and gravel parking lot. Hatchett chuckled as the fat man did a little dance on the sharp stones. He locked the doors behind him.

Hatchett pushed opened the curtains and got on his knees in between the front seats. He took a small flash from out of his vest pocket and turned it on.

The place stank, and Hatchett didn't want to mess around in it any longer than he had to. He started at the foot end and slowly ran his light around the walls and ceiling, then across the filthy bed sheets. The pillow case was so greasy it looked as if it hadn't been washed in years. Hatchett lifted up the mattress and found a thirty eight caliber revolver. He opened the cylinder and emptied the chambers, and then threw the rounds onto the floorboard. After he copied down the serial number and the make, he put the gun back where he found it.

Three minutes later, he opened the doors, and Sansome climbed back in. He was still wiping his nose.

Hatchett looked at him with dead eyes. "Did you kill Lisa Lemon?"

"No. Shit, no. I may move a little blow, but I ain't gonna kill nobody over it."

"Well, then, there really is only more question?"

Sansome was silent.

"Where do you get your stuff from?"

He shook his head violently. "Oh, no. You want me to wind up like her?"

Hatchett patted the bat against his palm. "You tell me or things get painful."

Sansome had seen how easy it was for Hatchett to hurt him. He knew he'd do it again.

"Look, all I got is a number. I call the guy every week, and he meets me and gives me the stuff."

Hatchett knew the fat man knew more, but frankly he was bored with talking with him. He took another deep breath and exhaled again.

"Okay, give me the number."

Sansome moved hesitatingly and picked up an address book out of console between the seats. He thumbed it until he found the page. He showed it to Hatchett.

Hatchett took the book, ripped out the page, and threw it back at the fat man. He put the page in his vest pocket.

"Mr. Sansome, if you find out who killed Lisa Lemon, I suggest you hold onto that information."

"Why?"

"'Cause when the police bust you for moving dope, you'll need a chip to cash in."

CHAPTER 18

The next day, Hatchett dropped by the Police Department's Narcotics Bureau in order to forward along the information that he had gotten from Sansome. O'Leary was at his desk in the back, next to the Bureau's file room.

O'Leary had been with the department for more years than Hatchett could remember. He had worked deep undercover for about three years infiltrating a drug ring, while on loan to the state police in New Mexico. It was said that he had gone in so deep that he had once forgotten his own name, birthdate, and where he was from. When he returned to the department, the higher ups put him in charge of the narcotics intelligence section and, wary of his mental state, had let him keep his thick black beard. They had also given him an office in the back, away from the public and the office's day to day operations.

Hatchett found O'Leary reading a book on estimating the time of death of buried remains. He sat down across the desk from the hairy man and waited for him to look up.

"Hi ho, Hatchett. What brings you to my little corner of the world?"

"Just wanted to let you know how things went with Sansome." He nodded toward the book. "You transferring to homicide?"

O'Leary looked down. "Oh, this? I just had a notion, that's all." He paused and grinned. "Just tryin' to set up my alibi."

"Don't even joke like that."

He grinned again. "What did you find out?"

"I got a couple of names for you. One is Fitch, Allen Fitch. He's one of Sansome's connections. The other is Mike Allenwood. I told you about him. He works over at the tree farm and nursery on the Vandalia Highway. They both pick up from Sansome. Fitch gets his at the truck stop where he works. I witnessed their connection. I don't know where Allenwood's drop is. My guess is it's not far from the Platter, over on the north side.

"Now these are mid-level guys. Lisa Lemon was a lower level, along with who knows how many others. I'm trying to work my way back to whoever gave the order to kill."

O'Leary wrote fast. Hatchett could see that he was preparing the beginnings of some kind of table of organization.

"Anything else?"

"Just this." Hatchett reached in his vest pocket and pulled out the number from Sansome's address book. "I got this phone number. Sansome said he gets his dope from this guy."

O'Leary took the paper and looked at it. "Well, it's a Texas phone number; looks like Fort Worth, 817."

"Could you run that down?"

He nodded. "Sure."

"And, before you guys hit it, I'd like a crack at this guy."

O'Leary looked at the numbers and names that he had recorded. "You sure this is the right thread to solve your murder?"

Hatchett looked him in the eye. "No. There are other ways I can go. But this one is the most probable, right now."

O'Leary nodded. "Okay. I'll get with the feds. Whatever they do is going to take a while, but when they hit, they hit all at once. I'll try to give you a two or three day heads up."

"I'd appreciate it."

One hour later, Hatchett was in McRae's office in the basement of the county courthouse. The lieutenant was reviewing reports and drinking coffee behind a large stack of files in the cramped office.

"Lieutenant."

"Hatchett. What brings you here?"

"I just wanted to see if you had anything new on the Lemon case."

"Are you kidding? We've had two more murders since then. Her case is on the back burner. You still working for the Boatmans?"

"They send a check, religiously, every week." He paused. "They pay, I work."

"You got anything more?"

"Not really. Looks like she was into the drug scene pretty heavy. That means it could'a been anybody that killed her."

"You got anymore names?"

"Just one. Harold Meeks. He's a doctor over in Pascagoula. He knew the victim when they were in school. I understand he might have a shady past."

McRae jotted down the name. "Where'd you hear that?"

"My gut."

McRae chuckled. "Okay. I'll get the name to Ward. I've passed the case along to the staff. Anything else?"

"Just a few names for the narcotics people to check on. Nothing I can link back to her just yet."

McRae looked at him. "I suppose you've been doing your usual bang up job."

"You haven't had any complaints, have you?"

He shook his head. "No. But, I suppose with the clientele with which you're dealing, they wouldn't complain that much."

"Until someone starts to squawk, I'll keep doin' what I'm doin'. I've gotten some results."

McRae looked at him. "You do run with a tough crowd. Just keep it toned down."

"Look, I'm not gonna meet these folks singing in the Baptist church choir. So what if I have to remind them of what pain feels like to get their attention. We're not looking for a jaywalker here. The guy that carved up Lisa Lemon is an animal."

McRae looked at him seriously. He didn't necessarily like Hatchett, but he didn't want to see him get hurt.

"As a matter of fact," McRae said, "why don't you give Joe Ward a call. Maybe you two can keep each other out of trouble."

"I'm not interested in a partner."

"I know. I know. I just think you're gonna get yourself killed one day."

"You let me worry about that."

"I hope I don't have to worry about it," he said waving Hatchett out of his office.

CHAPTER 19

One week passed, then two, and no new information surfaced on the Lisa Lemon murder. Hatchett received checks from the Boatmans on a regular basis, and he spent his time making phone calls and hitting up informants trying to get a handle on who may have killed the young woman with the high risk lifestyle and the most unfortunate taste in business acquaintances.

One of those informants was a snitch named Larry. Larry Pettibone was an overage trust fund baby, who was also an alcoholic and a borderline sex addict. But most of all, he was slow. He was not retarded; he could function, but he was not real quick on the uptake and his drug and alcohol usage didn't help matters.

He hung out at all the strip clubs in town, fawning over the dancers, dropping heavy tips, and begging for dates. He had money, which gave him access to plenty of dope and all the lap dances he wanted. He had it all, really, except for three things: he was fat, dumb, and needy; the three things that women are least willing to tolerate in men.

Hatchett met Larry five years ago in the parking lot of Babe's, a downtown club, two blocks from his office. He was walking home late, after meeting a client, when he spotted Larry pissing on the sidewalk. Hatchett shook the drunk man down, found cocaine in his pocket, and an informant was born. In his intoxicated state, it made no difference to Larry that Hatchett was not an officer. He was an authority figure who had manhandled him and caught him in a compromising position. That was enough. It was later that he had learned that Hatchett's business was private in nature, but Larry hung on because being an informant - he never wanted to be called a 'snitch' - fit the persona he was building in his own weak mind. Larry halfheartedly tried to buy Hatchett off a couple of times, but Hatchett recognized the value of having a dimwitted man who hung out at clubs, so the coke stayed in Hatchett's safe, and the partnership remained intact.

They usually met in an underground garage between Second and Third Streets, near the Veteran's Auditorium, and they did so this evening, a Friday. Hatchett picked it because all the business people who usually parked there were gone from downtown shortly after six. It was hot, and Larry was sweating liberally.

"Hey," Larry said.

He liked to think of himself as a spy, so he looked from side to side suspiciously. There was no one else around.

"Hey, Larry. What'chu got for me?" Larry had called Hatchett at three that afternoon and said he had big news.

"Yeah, so you're workin' on that headless woman case, right?"

"Yeah."

"Well, so I was in the Platter the other night, and a guy came in, and he was askin' about Lisa."

"So?"

"Well, so nobody talks about Lisa anymore. So when this guy brought it up, it was, like, you know, unusual."

"What did he say?"

"He says, like, well, who you think killed her? And so Mac, behind the bar, he says, well, he didn't know. And, so this guy says, well, you know, he thought it was about dope, you know, that she was killed over drugs."

"And?"

"Well, that's it. This guy said she was killed over drugs."

Hatchett nodded. If he'd had something else better to do that night, it would have been a waste of time. But talking to Larry always amused him, so the evening wasn't a total loss.

"So, what'd this guy look like?"

"He was black, and he had a real thin mustache."

"Fat or thin?"

"Kinda thin. Hey, have you seen that new girl at the Platter?"

"What else, Larry?"

"Uh, oh yeah, he had an earring."

"Which ear?"

"Left, no, right; no, left, I think."

"What else did he do?"

"He had a couple of drinks and, you know, he just hung out."

"Did he talk to anybody besides you?"

"Oh, he didn't really talk to me. He just talked to Mac, and, well, nobody, really."

"You just overheard him?"

"Yeah, I was sittin' at the bar, and I just heard him." He paused. "She's got some really big tits, you know?"

"Who?"

"The new girl at the club."

"Oh, yeah. What's her name?"

"Oh, it's Jewel. Whenever she comes out, the DJ always plays that song about diamonds."

"'*Diamonds are a Girl's Best Friend*'?"

"No, the other one."

"Oh, right." Hatchett nodded, though he could think of no other song about diamonds.

"So, tell me more about this black guy with the thin mustache. What was he wearing?"

"Just normal clothes. He had on a blue shirt. It was real shiny."

"How'd he sound?"

"What'chu mean?"

"Well, did he talk loud or soft?"

"I don't know, kinda medium; loud when the music was on."

"He have an accent?"

"I don't think so."

Hatchett wondered if Larry knew what an accent was. "What else did he say about Lisa?"

Larry closed his eyes and looked up. "Just that she was killed about drugs; over drugs, I mean."

Hatchett looked around and decided he'd had enough of Larry. "Okay. You got anything else?"

Larry shook his head. "No. That's it. But that helps, right?"

"It sure does, Larry."

"So, I did good, right?"

"Yep."

"Well, so when will I work off that coke?" His brows were raised and his face was hopeful.

"You gotta long way to go, Larry. You know I can still hang you on it if you don't come through."

A smile crept over Larry's lips. He wanted to make it sound as if he was nervous about being arrested for possession of drugs, and he was trying to get out from under Hatchett's thumb, but really, he wasn't. Being the informant for an actual detective was rapidly replacing being a stripper groupie as his new identity.

"Okay, so, I'll keep my ears open, right?"

"Right, Larry."

"And, maybe you can throw that dope out, right?"

"You'll need a lot more good information to get that off your back."

"I'll keep listenin'." Larry grinned, looking somewhat relieved.

"You do that, Larry."

Two days later, Hatchett heard from Tom Jensen. His voice was laconic, as always. Hatchett was in his office.

"I've got something for you on your Dr. Harold Meeks."

Hatchett scrambled for a pad and pen. "Go."

"It seems that the good doctor has a past. He had a first marriage, and apparently he and his ex went at it pretty hard."

"How bad?"

"Bad enough for him to do a short stretch in Parchman." He was talking about Mississippi's notorious state penitentiary.

"How short?"

"Two years."

"Whewww. He must have hurt her pretty bad. How'd he keep his medical license?"

"Well, that was part of the deal. She didn't push it, as long as he'd do some time. He was willing to spend some years in the pen so he could still keep his job. I think they let him work in the dispensary while he was up."

Hatchett wrote. "What was his weapon of choice?"

"Knife."

"Any other criminal history"

"None that I can find."

Jensen provided Hatchett the name and address of Meeks' ex-wife, who lived in nearby Hattiesburg, Mississippi. Hatchett decided it'd be worth a trip over to see her. At that moment, he had little else.

CHAPTER 20

It took ninety minutes to get to Hattiesburg, a small city of around twenty thousand located about fifty miles from the Gulf Coast. It was home to the University of Southern Mississippi, a bunch of retirees, and little else. Janice Hopkins Meeks lived in a small ranch house off US 11, about three miles outside of town in a new subdivision called, descriptively, Tall Pines.

Hatchett stopped his Merc in front of the correct residence and looked around. At ten AM the neighborhood was deserted. There was a breeze off the Gulf, and thick cumulus clouds rolled by.

The door was thick and oak. Hatchett used the knocker, and in a minute, he saw a face look out of the bay window in the front room. A voice spoke from behind the door.

"Yes? Who is it?"

"My name's Hatchett, ma'am. I'm a private investigator." He took his credentials case out of his right hip pocket and held it. "I've got ID."

The dead bolt on the door sounded. The door opened about three inches, the chain keeping it secure. Hatchett held up the leather wallet and displayed his state issued license.

The woman looked at it. "What do you want?"

"You Janice Meeks?"

She nodded. "I'm Janice Hopkins."

Hatchett could see she was a slight woman with long, straight, dark hair. She looked her supposed age of thirty. Hatchett caught a glimpse of a scar on the side of her face.

"I'd like to talk to you about your ex. I'm working on a case."

"That bastard. I've got nothing to say about him." She started to close the door.

"Wait, wait. I think he may have cut another woman."

The door stopped, and Hatchett watched curiosity overwhelm her.

"What are you talking about?"

"One of Harold's old girlfriends was killed. Whoever did it used a knife."

"Who?"

Hatchett looked around. "Is there someplace we can talk?"

Janice Hopkins looked around also. "Wait just a minute."

She closed the door, and Hatchett waited. In another two minutes she was back. She unhooked the chain and motioned for Hatchett to come in. He walked into a fashionably furnished, paneled, living space.

"Have a seat on the couch."

Hatchett settled himself and looked around. The only thing amiss was the fact that the phone receiver was off the hook. She probably had someone listening in on their conversation, he thought.

Janice Hopkins sat down in a club chair facing the window. She was wearing jeans and a red polo shirt, and she was barefooted.

"Now, what's this about Hal's girlfriend?" She spoke with a slight southern drawl.

"She's deceased. Her name was Melinda Boatman. I wanted to ask you about your, ah, incident. How did he come to cut you?"

She took a deep breath and exhaled. Hopkins was a thin woman with a small nose and dark eyes. Without the scar, she would have been considered attractive, perhaps beautiful.

"We met each other up at Ole Miss, in school, and got married when Hal was doing his residency, in Jackson. He used to have to work long hours at the hospital and well, you know, there were nurses there, and . . ."

"He was cheating on you."

"I was never completely sure, but, yeah." She paused. "I was jealous, I guess. That part of it was my fault. If he didn't have someone else, I may have driven him to it. When he'd come home, we'd fight about it. Then, one night, he just lost it. We were at the dinner table, and he had a steak knife in his hand. He took a swipe at me, and, well . . ."

She shrugged. When she did, her hair fell away from her face and Hatchett could see the full length of the scar. It was bad, but he'd seen worse. It started at her temple and ended on her mandible, about halfway between her ear and the point of her chin.

"How long had the two of you been married?"

"Two years."

Hatchett nodded. "What happened then?"

She pursed her lips. "After it happened, he looked kinda' like he was sorry, you know? He got up and called the ambulance, and when the police got there, well, they took him off."

"You pressed charges?"

"Yeah, well, the DA did. He told me I didn't have to testify, cause I was his wife, but that it really didn't matter; he could make a case without me. Don't get me wrong, I was mad enough, but, well, you know. I guess I coulda' been talked out of pressin' it."

"He got jail time?"

"He did two years at Parchman. I told'em I wanted him to go to prison. Like I said, I was mad."

"But you let him keep his medical license."

"Well, yeah. That was part of the deal; he went off, but he could still be a doctor when he got out."

"When did you divorce him?"

"I called a lawyer the day after it happened."

Hatchett nodded and was silent. Right then it occurred to him that Meeks' medical license might have been a valuable commodity when the subject of alimony was being discussed. He was also beginning to get the feeling that Meeks wasn't the man he was looking for.

"Ms Hopkins, do you think your husband is capable of murder?"

"Murder?" Her brows went up. "Well, I don't know." She looked away.

"Why do you think he cut you?"

She paused. "I guess, it was like I said, he just lost his temper."

"Is that something that happened often?"

"No, not really; I mean, he yelled sometimes, and we'd argue, but that was the only time he really hurt me."

"Never struck you with his hands?"

She shook her head. "Oh, no. He'd just yell, sometimes." She paused. "You say his old girlfriend was killed?"

Hatchett nodded.

"How? Why?"

"Don't know why, but she was decapitated."

She went white. "Are you kidding?"

"No, ma'am."

They both sat in silence for thirty seconds. Finally, Hopkins spoke.

"He didn't do it. He couldn't have." Her tone was a confident 'matter of fact,' as she shook her head.

"Why do you say that?"

"'Cause, when he cut me it was . . . kinda' like in the heat of passion. He just lost his temper. He couldn't'a cut nobody's head off." She shook her head. "Nope."

Hatchett knew immediately what was happening. Janice Hopkins was in the middle of convincing herself that the man she had slept beside for two years was not a psychopath. If he was, she would lose all faith in her judgment, and at that point in her life, she couldn't let that happen.

In this case, Hatchett believed she was right. Meeks, apparently, had no history of violence; he had used a weapon of opportunity; and according to Jensen, he had been a good boy ever since.

Hatchett let his eyes linger over the scar on her face and thought about what it meant to her to be marred permanently in that way. It had been a while since it had happened, but in his mind, she still hadn't gotten over it. She had no doubt been a confident young woman, educated, married to a doctor, secure in her looks. Now, she was hiding behind locked doors and wondering about the man to whom she had been married. Wondering if, for the years they were married at least, she had ever really known him at all.

"Did your husband frequent nude dancing establishments or did he have an inordinate interest or addiction to pornography?"

"I never knew it if he did. He always went to work and came home - came home late, but he came home. He always claimed he was working late, but I think sometimes he was with someone else."

"Pardon this question, but did he ever want to try anything unusual in bed?"

"Oh, no. Hal was vanilla all the way."

"Would you describe him as someone who was, say, unusual in any way at all?"

She thought. "No, not really. I mean, everybody has their quirks, but Hal was nothing out of the ordinary."

Hatchett looked around the room trying to think of what to ask next. He was just about dry.

"Ever know Hal to spend any time in Alabama for any reason?"

She paused to think once more. "Not that I remember. I think he may have gone over to Montgomery once, for some medical conference, but other than that, no."

Hatchett nodded. "Okay, well, I think that's about it."

"Why ain't the police working on this case?"

"Oh, they are; and you may hear from them in a day or two."

"Who are you workin' for?"

Hatchett paused. "Let's just say the dead girl's family would like to find out who killed her as soon as possible." He rose and started toward the door. Hopkins rose also.

"Have you seen Hal? Talked to him?" she said folding her arms.

"As a matter of fact, I have."

"How's he doing?"

"He seems to be doing well. He runs a clinic down in Pascagoula."

"Yeah, I heard that."

Hatchett opened the door. Hopkins stood aside as he crossed the threshold.

"Hal didn't do this."

"How do you know?"

"Well, cause he's a real gentle person at heart; a healer."

Hatchett reached and lifted the hair away from the side of her face exposing the blemish that was a permanent reminder of Meeks' gentility.

"Yeah," he said softly. "I know. I've seen his work."

Back in Mauvilla, at his office, Hatchett sat down and put his feet up. It was midafternoon, and the sun shined through the only window in the room, a small one, near the ceiling. The sunbeams caused him to feel drowsy.

As he thought over the case of the murder of Lisa Lemon, he saw three tracks. The first was that someone from her personal past had come back to kill her. That included Harold Meeks, among others, who in Hatchett's mind was no longer a good suspect, at least not at that point. Delving into whether he had an opportunity - where he was when the murder occurred - was a job for the Sheriff's Department.

The next track was the drug angle. In his mind, it had yet to play out. O'Leary had not let him know when the big bust would happen; the bust that would shut down Allenwood, Sansome, Fitch, and their cross country cocaine caravan.

Finally, the other possibility was a that someone affiliated with Lemon professionally, perhaps someone for whom she'd danced at one of the many clubs and parties where she'd entertained, had developed a nefarious interest in her; a misplaced obsession, a psychotic fixation.

Hatchett's head hurt. He closed his eyes and visualized meeting her killer face to face. He was of average height, with dark hair. Hatchett couldn't see his face and couldn't discern his race, but that didn't matter. Hatchett saw himself raising his .45 to eye level, aiming directly between the man's eyes and squeezing the trigger. The man's head exploded and blood and brains showered down on both of them. The man fell forward and his nose landed right on Hatchett's shoes.

When he came out his trance, he considered his next move. He didn't really want to, but Hatchett decided he would contact this detective down at the Sheriff's Office, this Ward, the new detective assigned to the investigation. Maybe he would have some new leads.

CHAPTER 21

Hatchett waited at the back corner booth at Walt's Diner at breakfast time the next day for Detective Ward to meet him. It was a rainy morning and cars sloshed water off the streets and onto the sidewalk outside the plate glass windows of the restaurant as Hatchett spooned a cup of coffee. There were two other people in the diner: a young woman in a booth near the front, and an old man with white hair seated at the counter.

His attention was drawn to the front door as a young woman of Asian descent walked in. She was short and slim, with dark brown hair pulled back in a ponytail. She wore tan pants and some type of heavy shoes, almost boots, as well as a blue oxford shirt. Hatchett thought about how her shirt and boots looked like those he had seen worn by workers in Communist China.

Also, there was a blue steel, snub nosed revolver in a holster on her right hip and a star clipped to her belt. She walked up to Hatchett's booth. He looked up at her tanned face, a face devoid of makeup.

"Yes?"

"Are you Mr. Hatchett?"

"Who wants to know?" His tone was not contemptuous.

She looked frustrated. "Me. I'm JoAnn Ward." Her voice had a slight southern accent, but it was educated and articulate.

"Detective Jo Ward? From the Sheriff's Office?"

"Right."

She slid into the booth across from him, took a napkin from the holder next to the window, and wiped down the table in front of her. Hatchett said nothing as he noticed the lack of a ring on her married finger.

"You're speechless," she said.

He snorted. "Well, let's face it. You don't really fit the profile."

She smiled. "I know, but he wants the case solved. That's why he sent me."

He smiled. "Confidence. I like it. I just haven't seen a woman working full time on homicide cases."

"It happens."

"Well, this is Alabama, and I'm wondering how much good you can do around all these rednecks and good old boys."

"You mean, am I qualified."

"I mean can you handle the lack of respect you're gonna be shown."

"I'll deal with it."

He took a sip of coffee. "By the way, are you?"

"Am I what?"

"Qualified."

"I have two Bachelor's degrees; one in criminal justice and the other in accounting."

He nodded and chuckled. "Waiting on the FBI, are ya?"

She smiled but said nothing.

"Be honest, you're the product of some political favor, right?"

She smiled. "Okay, you're right. The boss is paying off a chip. I know it. My father's a cardiac surgeon, and he once operated on the Sheriff. But don't be fooled. I know what I'm doing."

"No, I'm sure you're able. I just mean, will people give you the respect that you think you deserve; you being female and Oriental and all."

"I can do my job."

She paused and looked him in the eye. He stared back at her almond shaped brown eyes and high cheekbones. She didn't look half bad, he thought.

"Besides, we want to be called Asian now."

"Pardon me. Where are you from?"

"Atlanta."

"That's a long way from Peking."

"My mother's from Shanghai, and my father's from Baltimore."

"So you're only half inscrutable."

"What?"

"Nothing." Hatchett smiled.

"Look," she said, "I think we can be of help to each other. I've got easy access to information, and you, well, Lieutenant McRae says that you're good at what you do; a little rough around the edges, but good."

He weighed his options internally and, though he wouldn't let her know it, he agreed with her. With her badge, she could make getting information much simpler. Also, some men let go of what they know a little easier when they're talking to a female.

Hatchett took a deep breath and exhaled. "I've been working on a lead. Harold Meeks, a doctor who works over in Pascagoula, is a former boyfriend of Lisa Lemon. He also has a history of cutting his wife with a knife. I gave it to McRae. Did he pass it along?"

Ward took out a pad and pen. "He did. Have you talked to this guy?"

"Only briefly. I didn't question him directly. You'll need to find out where he was when the murder happened."

She nodded. "I'll look into it."

"What have you been working on?" Hatchett said.

She leaned back in the chair. "Not much. Two of our people went and interviewed this Nicholas Peters in Nashville, and he filled us in on a few of the private parties at which Lisa had danced in the past year. Most looked pretty legit, however there was one group that stood out." She flipped pages in her notebook. "It was the . . . Society of Southeastern Sociologists; the S.S.S."

"Southern Sociologists? What kinda' bunch is that?"

"Mostly social workers. I think they're leftover sixties hippies; 'free love' kooks and drug users that are still trying to 'change the world.' They meet once a year, they say to talk over new techniques for raising the standard of living in the inner cities and in rural America; but my sources tell me that they mostly drink, look at strippers, and do drugs. They met last year in Birmingham."

"Your sources?"

"My ex-boyfriend. We still talk."

"I see. What makes them stand out?"

"Oh, I don't know. Hippies, dopers; they could pretty easily let things get out of hand." She paused. "Call it women's intuition."

"What kind of dope do they do?"

"The usual: cocaine and marijuana."

Hatchett nodded. "I guess McRae told you about Lisa Lemon's sideline."

"He did."

He paused. "Do these hippies have a chapter in Alabama?"

She smiled. "Only one. In Montgomery."

Hatchett decided, reluctantly, that he would run out this one lead with his new, albeit temporary, partner. The next morning, they left the city early and were in Montgomery by ten. They rode in Hatchett's Merc.

After the obligatory stop at the Sheriff's Office to let them know they were in town, they found the address of the Montgomery District Community Action Office on Cleveland Avenue, at the Jeff Davis Avenue intersection, south of Interstate 85, in a predominately black part of town. Ward had supplied the location from her notes. Hatchett parked his Merc in the parking area on the south side of building, a single story, brick structure with a screen door and burglar bars on the windows.

A Volvo, a Toyota, and a Datsun also populated the lot.

Ward led the way into the three room office. There was a desk immediately in front of the door and offices on either side. An enormous female with an Afro wig and what looked to be two inch, glued-on fingernails sat behind the desk talking on the telephone. She wore a polyester shirt and stretch pants and was using a finger and a thumb - with her pinkie extended - to pick up a piece of coffee cake. She looked up when her visitors entered but seemed in no hurry to end her conversation.

"Um hmm. Girl, look here, I gotta go. Some folks jus' come in. You know I'm gonna call you later." She paused to listen. "All right, now." She laughed loudly. "Girl, please. I got ta go."

She hung up the receiver and looked at Ward. "How ya'll doin?" She smiled broadly.

"Fine, ma'am. My name is Ward." She showed her star. "I'm from the Sheriff's Office in Manipi County. This is Mr. Hatchett. We're trying to locate Laurence Axlerod. I believe he works here."

Her smile vanished, and her face took on a look of suspicion. "I'll see if he's in."

After a short phone call, she ushered them into the office on the north side of the building. Axlerod rose from his desk.

"Come in. Have a seat," he said motioning to two chairs.

Axlerod was tall and slim. He had long brown hair that was graying and tied in a ponytail that hung almost to his shoulders; much longer than Ward's. He wore jeans and a red and blue t-shirt with 'Give Peace a Chance' emblazoned across the front.

"What can I do for you, folks?"

"My name is Ward, this is Mr. Hatchett. I'm from the Sheriff's Office in Manipi County. We'd like to ask you about a case we're working on."

Hatchett let Ward take the lead. He didn't like the look of Axlerod and felt a sudden urge to clock him; and would have done so with the slightest provocation.

She cleared her throat. "Are you a member of the Society of Southeastern Sociologists?"

"Yes," he said sitting back down. "I'm the chapter coordinator." His voice was devoid of accent, but Hatchett thought he detected something very slight from the northeast.

"Is that like the president or something?"

"Well, we don't call it that. It sounds a little too egalitarian for us."

"What do you do here?"

"We organize the community for political action; better housing, daycare, after school programs, that sort of thing. We get residents in the neighborhoods to actively petition their government for assistance."

"Do you work here alone?"

"Well, I've got a secretary and one administrative assistant, but I'm the only professional – I say that, a couple of the instructors at the University assist me as part of the community/University cooperative program."

"I see. Well, would you be the person in charge of the arrangements for the winter conference in Birmingham last year?"

"Well, yes, part of them. What's this all about?"

"Do you remember contracting with a Nicholas Peters in Nashville for a dancer named Lisa Lemon?"

His face went white. He cleared his throat and shifted in his chair.

"Well, now, you see, some of the guys wanted some entertainment on the last night of the conference."

"Did she show up?"

"Uh, yes." She waited for him to continue. "Is there a problem?"

"Ms Lemon is deceased."

"Oh." His eyes were wide, and he sounded a little surprised.

Hatchett watched his mannerisms closely. He didn't have the look of a violent killer; the blood left his face a little too quickly when he was under stress.

"What exactly did she do at your party?"

He cleared his throat again. "Well, you know, she came out and, uh, there was music, and, uh, and she danced a little and, uh, you know." He paused. "That was it."

"Were there any problems?"

"Problems? Well, no, I mean, how do you mean?"

"Anyone have any trouble with her? Anyone seem to crave a little more of her attention than she wanted to give? You know. Anyone seem a little obsessed?"

He looked away toward the window and shook his head. "No, no. Everyone was on their best behavior."

"Who hired her?"

"Hired her? Well, I guess I did."

"How did you come to get her name?"

"Ah, one of the guys had dealt with her manager in the past. He called him, and Peters set everything up."

Ward looked down at her writing pad and made a couple of notes. Hatchett had seen about enough. He spoke up in a way that startled the female detective.

"Okay, Axlerod. It's time to cut the bullshit. I've heard about all I can stand."

"Wh . . ."

"So you had a stripper at your little shindig. It sounds like it was all very progressive of you and your pals. Now, she's dead, and I'm getting tired of you doing your little toe dance around the truth. We'd better get some straight answers from you real quick or things might just get a little bit uncomfortable for you."

Axlerod paused and said nothing, but he looked relieved. His shoulders slumped, and he took a deep breath. He acted as if he now had an excuse - Hatchett's implied threat - to tell the truth. Ward sat with her mouth agape.

"Did Lisa Lemon bring you guys a load of coke?"

Axlerod nodded. "Yeah. Peters said she'd bring drugs if we wanted them. He said it was part of the price of the gig."

"How many of you guys were at the party?"

"Fifteen or twenty."

"How many did she bounce?"

He looked down and rubbed his forehead with four fingers. "You mean sex? I don't know; four or five, I guess."

"You?"

He nodded his head.

"So, who couldn't get enough of her and didn't want to see the party end?"

"I don't know, maybe Glenn. He seemed a little possessive. When he finished, he really didn't want anyone else to be with her."

"Was he high?"

He nodded. "Yeah, and drinking too."

"Glenn who?"

"Come on. He's got a wife and kids."

"Glenn who? And where can we find him?" Hatchett's voice gained intensity.

He took a deep breath and exhaled. "Out at the University. He teaches. His name is Cabot."

"So how'd you feel when the party was over?"

He shook his head. "Come on. This was just a thing. I don't get like that."

"Are you married?" Ward said.

Axlerod looked at her and nodded his head slowly.

Ward seemed to be getting back into the game. "Where were you the first weekend in April?"

"April? Well, here, at home. My wife can verify that."

Hatchett leaned forward and looked Axlerod right in the eye. "Did you kill Lisa Lemon?"

"No," he said emphatically.

"So, who else?" Hatchett said.

"Who else what?"

"Who else at the party could've killed her?"

His eyes widened and he shook his head. "No, no. You got it all wrong. We had a good time and all, and maybe we did overindulge some, but," he shook his head again, "nobody got so into it that murder was a possibility." He paused. "We just got together to relax and let off a little steam. We've done it before."

Hatchett pressed. "Anybody get rough?"

"No, no. We wouldn't have let that happen."

"Did you talk to her?"

"No. Well, yeah, a little."

"About what?"

"I don't know, where she was from, how long she'd been dancing. Nothing, really."

"Did Glenn talk to her?"

"Yes. He seemed to spend a lot of time with her."

"How'd she leave things? With him, I mean."

"It looked like everything was okay. She was kinda smilin' when things broke up."

The room was quiet, and Ward looked at Hatchett. He leaned back in his chair and waved a hand in her direction.

"Well, I think that's about all for now, Mr. Axlerod. If we need you again, we'll call you."

He rose from behind his desk. "Okay, well, look, now you won't tell Glenn I mentioned his name, will you?"

Ward spoke. "Not if we can help it."

Hatchett looked him in the eye. "By the way, how much did her services cost you guys?"

Axlerod blinked. "Five thousand dollars."

Hatchett shook his head. "For the children, right?"

Ward and Hatchett parked the Merc on Jeff Davis Avenue, around the corner from Axlerod's office and waited. It was Hatchett's idea. If Axlerod left to pay a visit to anyone and notify them of their presence, they would be waiting to follow.

"What was that you said in there?" Ward said.

"What are you talking about?"

"That veiled threat you made to Axlerod."

He looked at her with his right eyebrow raised. "Wouldn't you like to know."

"Lieutenant McRae warned me about you." She paused. "Would you have hit him?"

"Not with witnesses."

She smiled, but suspicion was in her look. "Look, I've got a pretty good career going here. I don't want anything to mess it up. So, when you feel the urge to give somebody a smack, just bite your lip, or something."

Hatchett exhaled deeply. "Well, I don't know what your almighty criminal justice education taught you, but you need to know something about positive and negative reinforcement. If you let people get away with lying and manipulating the flow of information - or lack of it - without punishing that negative behavior, they'll do it all day long. Sometimes all we've got to rely on to make cases is what people tell us; and that's not worth anything if it's not the truth."

"Still . . ."

"If you start to feel a little queasy, you don't have to look."

She sat in silence looking straight ahead.

"Besides," he said, "didn't old Axlerod open right up when he found out we meant business?"

She shrugged. "He did seem a bit more forthcoming after your . . . what do you call it?"

"Just call it, 'Jesus in the Temple.'"

Their conversation was arrested by the sight of Laurence Axlerod exiting the front door of the office and getting into his silver Volvo. Hatchett started the Merc.

The Volvo turned north on Cleveland Avenue, went over the freeway, and took Mildred to Perry Street. He followed Perry to Madison; then Madison west, to Court Street, where they turned north and went all the way to the University on the north side of town, off the North Boulevard.

Hatchett, who was familiar with the city, kept at a safe distance and was sure that Axlerod hadn't made him by the time they had reached the campus. Axlerod left the Volvo in a faculty parking spot close the building marked, 'Liberal Arts,' and Hatchett put the Merc in the student section between two large pickup trucks.

"Think he's going to see Cabot?" Ward said.

"Nope." Hatchett paused. "I think he's here to warn someone else. Unfortunately, we won't know who until we talk to Cabot."

"Why not Cabot?"

Hatchett shook his head. "Too obvious." He paused. "I think there's someone else involved. My guess is that it's someone connected to Peters; somebody with a dope angle. You know, a college campus is the perfect place for a drug supermarket."

"So Axlerod lied about Cabot."

"Absolutely not. Cabot probably did have a thing for Lisa Lemon. Axlerod wouldn't cover up for him if he's a killer. But, he would want to keep a coke pipeline, and the money that accompanies it, wide open."

"So he's in the building keeping his dope connection viable and not warning off a killer."

"That's my theory. Axlerod wouldn't protect a murderer. Even he has some scruples."

They sat in the car and watched the front door of the building. The tennis courts were close by – immediately to the east – and a class was practicing.

Students came and went from the building, and cars entered and left the parking lot. The large trucks on either side of them left at the top of the hour. A campus police officer happened by, but Ward badged him, and he went the other way.

It was close to an hour before Axlerod exited the building. He walked to his Volvo, got in, and scratched his tires as he backed up and drove quickly out of the parking lot.

Hatchett and his partner slid down in their seats as he went by, made the loop around the parking lot, and drove west down the main road.

Hatchett looked at Ward. "You ready?"

"Who are we going to talk to?"

"Cabot, of course."

"Let's go."

In five minutes they were on the third floor speaking with the Sociology Department secretary, a pudgy, twenty-something with brown hair and a big smile. The young woman directed Hatchett and Ward to the office of Glenn Cabot, PhD, in the far northeast corner of the floor, amidst several other instructor offices.

Cabot's name was burnt into a wood plank and fastened to the door. Underneath the plank, taped to the door, was a typewritten office schedule. Ward rapped twice, and the door opened quickly.

"Dr. Cabot?" Ward said.

"Yes?"

Cabot was a middle aged man with a naturally curly mop of brown hair that featured a few flecks of gray. He was less than six feet tall, with a pronounced spread, and a clean shaven face. He smiled broadly as if happy to have someone with whom to converse who was not nineteen.

"My name is Ward. I'm from the Manipi County Sheriff's Office. This is Mr. Hatchett. We'd like to talk to you." She displayed her badge and credentials.

He lost his smile quickly, stepped aside, and motioned toward chairs across from his desk. The two detectives sat down.

Hatchett looked around the room. Cabot's 'I love me wall' contained diplomas from Vanderbilt University, two photographs of him shaking hands with what looked like congressmen, and a Certificate of Merit from the American Genealogical Society. The rest of the room was choked with books and papers. A typewriter was prominent on his desk.

"What's this all about?" Cabot said taking a seat in a leather chair.

"We'd like to ask you about the Sociologists Society meeting last winter, in Birmingham."

He leaned back in his chair and folded his arms. The message was unmistakable. Even Ward should be able to get the truth out of this guy, Hatchett thought.

"What, what, is anything wrong?"

"We understand you spent some time with a young woman there, a dancer named Lisa Lemon. Is that correct?"

He looked from side to side. Then he took a deep breath and exhaled. "Is something the matter with her?"

"Please, Dr. Cabot. This will go much faster if you answer the questions instead of ask them," Ward said.

"Yes, I spent some time with her."

"We understand that you liked her a lot. Is that correct?"

"We got along well. She seemed like a nice young woman; a good personality; easy to talk to." He paused. "Do I need a lawyer?"

"Not if you haven't done anything wrong. We understand you slept with her, and that maybe when it was over, it was a little hard for you to let her go. Is that correct?"

He became slightly animated. "Okay, that's enough. What's this all about?"

"Ms Lemon is deceased."

"What? How?" His arms unfolded and he leaned forward.

"She was the victim of a homicide. We're talking to anyone who came in contact with her."

He leaned back, looked to the ceiling and said nothing. He closed his eyes. Hatchett watched him closely to see if what he was doing was an act.

"Dr. Cabot. What was your relationship with Lisa Lemon?"

He opened his eyes and shrugged. "She danced at our convention. I slept with her, and . . ." He paused. "I fell in love. She was kind, soft spoken; she was a good listener, and . . ."

"You knew she was a prostitute?"

He nodded. "I know. But, I found my soul mate."

"How'd you feel when she took turns with the other men?"

He exhaled loudly. "I won't lie. I was angry; but at the others, not at her."

"After the convention, did you see her again?"

He shook his head. "No. We talked before she left. She was nice, but she said she knew I was married, and, you know, she was who she was, so it wasn't going to work. We parted on good terms." He looked down. "I tried to get in touch with her a couple of times afterward, but the guys in our chapter knew what I was trying to do, and they wouldn't give me her agent's number." He looked away and shook his head. "I haven't stopped thinking about her."

Ward looked down and made notes. Hatchett sat with his arms folded.

"Dr. Cabot, who else in your department, here at the University, was at the convention?" Hatchett said.

He licked his lips. Hatchett thought he was about to lie.

"Just Matt Huntleigh. He's the only other member of the Society who works here."

"Is he here today?"

"No." He looked at his watch. "Well, his office hours ended about an hour ago. He usually leaves pretty quickly.

Ward wrote the name down. Then she turned to Hatchett. He cleared his throat.

"Where were you around the first of April of this year?"

Cabot sat up straight, as if somehow indignant that the question had even been asked.

"I was here, teaching school, I think, and home with my wife and children. I'd have to check my calendar to be sure."

"Do that and call us," Ward said. "Can they attest to your whereabouts?"

"Of course."

"You sound certain. What kind of relationship do you have with your wife?"

"She would have no reason to lie for me or about me. I love my wife, and she loves me."

Hatchett nodded. "Right. Nothing says, 'I love you,' like bangin' a prostitute."

CHAPTER 22

Outside in the Merc, Hatchett and Ward settled in and contemplated their next move.

"What do we do now?" Ward said.

"Why don't we call the Police Department. See if you can get hold of one of their detectives and have them check the street directory to see if they can find an address for this Matt or Matthew Huntleigh."

Hatchett started the Merc, and they left the student parking lot in search of a pay phone. They found one at a filling station near US 231.

Ward got out, made the call, and was back in five minutes. She had written the address in her notebook.

"The investigator, a guy named Mobley, said that Huntleigh lived not far from here, in a place called Arrowhead on the east side. He gave me directions."

Hatchett found the house in short order. It was a sprawling ranch style home with a brick veneer and a manicured lawn, located at the head of a cul de sac. They parked on the street.

"Let me talk to this guy," Hatchett said.

Ward nodded, though he could see the apprehension in her eyes.

Hatchett walked up to the front door and pushed the bell. Ward stood behind him, her badge and sidearm clearly visible.

The door opened a minute later. The man who answered was fortyish, maybe fifty, thin, with shoulder length hair and a beard, and modern clothes - polyester shirt and bell bottoms.

"Yes?" the man said.

"Dr. Huntleigh?" Hatchett put his foot on the threshold and leaned in.

His gaze met Hatchett's then shifted to Ward. When his eyes hit her waistline and the badge clipped to her belt, he reached and shoved Hatchett in the chest.

Had he been in better shape, he might have forced Hatchett back out onto the porch. As it was, he was neither strong enough nor fast enough to do the job. Hatchett used his left hand to grab his arm at the wrist. Then, with his right hand, he bent the wrist back. Hatchett pushed him backwards into the house while continually pressuring the joint. Ward followed.

"Detective Ward, what did you see?" Hatchett said over his shoulder.

"I saw the occupant of this house commit battery on you, at which time you were forced to defend yourself."

"That's what I thought." He looked at the bearded man. "Now, once again, are you Matthew Huntleigh?"

"Ahhhh, yes. Let go of my arm."

"Not so fast. This lady is Detective Ward from down in Mauvilla. We're investigating a homicide." Hatchett paused to gauge the effect of his words. "Tell me about Lisa Lemon."

"Who? Ahhhh!"

"The stripper who danced for you up in Birmingham."

"What about her? Oh, come on, man!"

"Who killed her?"

"How should I know? She was okay when she left the party that night."

Hatchett gradually eased up on the man's wrist until he finally let go. He didn't enjoy inflicting pain on Huntleigh, but seeing the bearded man in distress didn't make him at all uncomfortable.

"If you think you can stop shoving me, we can talk like adults."

"Sure, sure, man," Huntleigh said rubbing his wrist. "I think you broke my hand."

"Don't be a sissy."

Hatchett looked at him and their eyes met. Huntleigh had disgust in his. Intensity radiated from Hatchett's.

"So tell me about the party. It was you who called Peters up in Nashville, right?"

He nodded as he sat down in a chair in the foyer, just inside the front door. "I knew him from college. I knew he was an agent. Some of the guys wanted a dancer, so I gave Axlerod his number."

"Axlerod said you called him."

"Maybe, I don't remember."

"You knew he was into something else, right?"

He tilted his head in confusion. Hatchett tilted his head threateningly. Huntleigh shrugged.

"Yeah, okay, I knew he could get us some coke." He paused and looked at both of them defiantly. "Hey, it's harmless. It ought to be legal."

"And, it makes the sex better, right?"

"Well, sure."

"You had a go with Lisa?"

"Well, yeah. A few of us did."

"So, anybody fall in love? Maybe didn't want to see the night end? Get a little possessive?"

He thought for a moment. "I don't think so, I mean, I was pretty drunk. I guess if it was anybody, it was probably Glenn, Glenn Cabot. He got kinda mad when I went in to her."

"How'd that end?"

"You know, he cooled down and, I . . . well, she and I . . ."

Hatchett nodded. "Sounds very sophisticated."

"Look, we were just blowing off some steam. We do it every year. Hey, my wife knows all about it."

"She knows you're screwin' around?"

"Sure. She understands."

"Sounds like a very accommodating woman," Ward said.

She had heretofore been silent, but Hatchett could see that all the salacious talk of orgies and adultery had offended her female sensibilities. He decided to change the subject.

"And she was the one who brought the dope, right?"

He nodded. "Yeah. Peters said he would send it along with her. It was included in the price."

"Is he your regular supplier?"

Huntleigh looked from Hatchett to Ward and back again. He was silent.

"That's right. We know what's going on. But, lucky for you, we're from out of town and our only interest is the dead girl."

"That may be, but . . . I think I need a lawyer." He bowed his head.

Hatchett nodded. That was all he needed to know. "Well, okay. It was certainly nice meeting you Mr. Huntleigh."

Ward and Hatchett turned and walked out the door. Ten minutes later, Ward was on the phone to Mobley at the Police Department laying out the connections that kept the local University as high as a kite every month.

On the highway back to Mauvilla, the two rode in silence until Ward finally spoke up just outside of Greenville, thirty miles south of Montgomery.

"You really like hurting people, don't you," she said turning her head his direction.

He looked at her, then back at the road. "Thirty miles, and that's all you've got to say about what I think has been a very productive day?"

"Yeah, we got some things accomplished, but that thing back there with Huntleigh. What was that all about?"

He shrugged. "He just needed a little persuading."

"Was it necessary?"

"Well, you saw the results." He paused. "Besides, you were pretty quick to back me up."

Now, Ward was silent; caught in her implicit consent to Hatchett's methods.

"Look," he said, "the best way to train these people is with physical punishment - like children."

"How do you figure?"

"Well, when you catch a three year old doing something wrong, you give'em a swat, because they're too young to understand the consequences of what they're doing. You use a small amount of physical discipline in order to train them not to do something that could cause them a larger amount of pain."

"But Huntleigh isn't a child."

"Oh, but he is. Huntleigh has a moral age of three or four. He doesn't see the need to obey the law, and because he doesn't, he might very well one day find himself on the wrong end of it; in jail, or maybe worse."

"And you think you're keeping him out of trouble."

"Maybe, maybe not. But at least he knows that some things are illegal and that existing in that atmosphere could cause him pain; maybe not physical pain, but he knows that he is in danger of losing his freedom, his job, or maybe even his family."

"He got all that from that elementary 'come along' hold that you used, and thirty seconds of pain?"

"Okay, so maybe he's already thought the consequences through, and he's ready to take the gamble. But, for our purposes, we did get some useful information."

She nodded, not wishing to seem ignorant of the value of what they had learned from Huntleigh.

"We confirmed that Peters, up in Nashville, is either the head, or least a major player in a pretty widespread drug ring, of which Lisa Lemon was a small part." Hatchett didn't tell her that he already knew that about Peters.

"We confirmed the story about Glenn Cabot, his relationship with the victim, and, I think, for now at least, eliminated him as a suspect.

"And, you were able to buy a little good will with the PD up here, just in case you need them in the future."

She chuckled. "All that from bending that poor slob's wrist back."

Hatchett was no longer conciliatory. His voice took on an edge.

"Matthew Huntleigh is a drug dealer. If that doesn't make you just a little angry, then maybe you're in the wrong line of work." He paused. "I hate drug dealers."

The tone of his voice told her he was serious, and she did not speak. They rode in silence for another fifty miles. Finally, she could take the solitude no longer.

"So, how'd you get in this business?"

He looked at her. Hatchett wasn't used to being quizzed about himself, and he certainly would never consider volunteering to her any information about his background. He debated in his mind whether to do it now. After a minute, he spoke.

"Well, let's just say I had to make a living, and this seemed the best way to do it at the time."

"What? Are you an ex-con?"

He shook his head. "No. In fact, I was once a cop, like you."

She too debated within herself, on whether to pry deeper. Finally, her native curiosity won out.

"What happened?"

"I decided there was a better way."

"To?"

"To make my world a better place."

She could tell that he didn't want to talk about it. That was fine.

CHAPTER 23

Ward and Hatchett were back in Mauvilla at eight that night. Hatchett dropped her at the Courthouse then stopped at his office to check his messages. He was bone tired and flopped immediately into his chair.

After a short – fifteen minute – cat nap, he called his answering service.

"Hey, Peaches. Hatchett. Anything for me?"

"Hey, good lookin'. I'll look and see."

"Tell me something," Hatchett said, "how do you know I'm good looking? To my knowledge, we've never met."

"Oh, sweetie, you forget what I do for a living. It's in the voice. I can tell just by listening that you're hot."

Hatchett chuckled. If she only knew, he thought.

"Let's see, looks like a couple of things: Mary Boatman called and said she wanted an update; and O'Leary at the Police Department called to let you know he had more information on that operation that you put him onto."

Hatchett scribbled the names on the legal pad on his desk. "That's good. 'Cause I've got more information for O'Leary."

"Is this Ms Boatman important?"

"Not right now. I'll call her tomorrow morning."

Hatchett heard the phone ring on the other end of the line. Marilyn the operator said her goodbyes and hung up.

Hatchett rubbed his face and contemplated sleeping at his office. He closed his eyes and let his whole body relax.

A picture of Lisa Lemon exploded on his mind's eye, again. He started at the dead woman's feet and moved slowly up her naked legs, passed her pale buttocks and back, but stopped abruptly at her neck, a bloody stump.

Instead of recoiling at the sight, Hatchett mentally lingered over the wound. Dried blood seemed to have been caught in mid drip as it fell from the pointed end of her exposed vertebrae. Shards of flesh hung over the rim of the laceration and blood dripped from there also. Her hands were relaxed, that is her fingers were bent only slightly and were flat against the ground. It was an ugly sight, but Hatchett had seen much worse.

Far from being appalled, the sight made him angry. It wasn't the pain and grief that her family felt; nor was it the fear that a pathological killer was operating about in the city. It was just the abnormality of it all; the stress of it, the fact that somehow the universe had been upset by the violence of it. It grated on him.

When he opened his eyes, it was eleven o'clock. He decided to walk home to his downtown apartment some three blocks away on Grand Avenue at 2nd Street, near the River. It was warm and humid and a breeze was blowing off the water. Downtown was deserted except for an occasional taxi cab that trolled by looking for a drunk walking out of one of the bars that were interspersed amongst the tall office buildings that lined the city's streets.

He was within a half a block of his building when it happened. The car rolled slowly toward him down Grand, so slowly that it didn't attract his attention. He only looked over when it stopped as it reached a location next to him.

As the barrel of the rifle protruded from the driver's rear window, Hatchett managed to duck behind a thick lamp post as fire issued from the muzzle of the fully automatic weapon. He heard some rounds ricochet off the light standard behind which he was standing, and others travel past his head and into the plate glass window behind him. The glass crackled, then fell to the concrete sidewalk where it shattered.

Thirty or forty rounds later the vehicle scratched away, west bound on Grand. Hatchett, from his knees, attempted to retaliate with his forty five. He didn't know if he hit the vehicle or not as it was a half a block away when he fired. The whole incident was over in less than thirty seconds.

He rose to his feet and looked around. The rifle rounds had taken out the window of a shoe repair shop. There was a pay phone across Grand Avenue, so he walked, pistol in hand, to it and dug for change in his pocket. He took two deep breaths to calm himself and then called the Police Department. He gave them the location, and in three minutes the downtown scout car was pulling up to the scene. Two young officers got out.

The officers surveyed the area. "What happened here?" one of them said.

The speaker was a tall thin officer with close cropped blonde hair. He wore his revolver hung low on his right side in a motorman's, low rider, swivel-type holster.

Hatchett stood up straight after brushing the urban dust off of his trousers, and pointed to the broken window.

"A couple'a goons in a silver gray Chevy Caprice tried to kill me. They missed me and hit the glass." He pointed over his shoulder.

"Where were you standing?" The second officer said.

He was shorter and very muscular. He had kind of a Mediterranean look with curly, black hair and a dark five o'clock shadow.

"I was behind the lamp post trying to make myself about thirty pounds thinner." He pointed at the post. "See, some of the rounds hit the pole."

The short officer walked around to the side closest to the street and nodded his head at the other. The rounds had gouged several holes into the light standard. It was only then that the two officers fully believed Hatchett.

The tall officer took out a pad and pen. "Can you describe the car?"

"It was a silver Caprice, four-door, occupied by at least two males. One of them was armed with what looked like an M-16 or CAR-15. They were last seen westbound on Grand about ten minutes ago."

"Did you see what color they were?"

"Not really. It happened fast, and I was on the move pretty quick, but my sense is that both were white."

"How about a license plate?"

"It looked like it was white with black lettering. The first two letters were 'E' and 'D'. I think there was a '2' and a '7' in the number half."

"State?"

"Couldn't tell, but my guess it was Tennessee. You might include in your BOLO that they're gonna be north bound on the freeway that direction." He paused.

Hatchett didn't say why he thought the shooters were from the north. "I took a shot at them, but I don't know if I hit'em."

The blonde officer went back to the squad car and sat down on the passenger side of the front seat. Hatchett could hear him relaying the description to the dispatcher.

He showed them both his driver's and his PI licenses, and they started a report. As he stood, waiting for the two to complete their investigation, Hatchett noticed blood dripping on the ground. He looked down to find his right pants leg saturated. He looked closer and found a wound on the outside of his calf. He didn't feel the sting when it happened initially, nor did he feel any pain afterwards. But the ache in his ankle had become acute as he stood and talked to the officers.

"Hey, buddy, looks like your hurt," the dark haired officer said. "Want me to call you an ambulance?"

"No. I can get there."

"Okay," tall blonde said, "we'll be on the road looking for the Caprice. Call us back if you need some help."

Hatchett nodded. He looked both ways and started limping back toward the parking deck below his office, to get his car.

In twenty minutes, Hatchett was in the emergency room of Mercy Hospital. The triage nurse found all of his vital signs stable, diagnosed him immediately, and then had him removed to a treatment room shortly after he walked in, probably because he was continuing to drip blood on the otherwise clean floor.

Hatchett hoisted himself up onto the examining table and watched as the nurse came in and pulled the curtain behind her. She was a short woman with brown hair, who wore green scrubs and a pair of tennis shoes. She washed her hands, pulled on rubber gloves, and when she turned around, she smiled and picked up a pair of scissors.

"What are you gonna do with those?" he said.

"I'm gonna cut your trousers off."

He shook his head. "No, no. Wait. I'll take'em off. Pants aren't cheap."

She stood back as he unbuckled his belt and slipped the tan slacks over his hips and then past his shoes. In a moment they were in a heap on the floor.

The nurse, whose name tag identified her as 'Betty,' looked at his outstretched right leg and wrinkled her nose.

"How'd this happen?"

"Somebody tried to kill me."

"I'll have to notify the police."

"Don't bother. I've taken care of that."

She cleaned the wound of dried blood on both sides and succeeded in getting it to start bleeding again. The hydrogen peroxide stung.

"So," Hatchett said, "what's a nice girl like you doin' in a place like this?"

She looked up from her work and smiled. "I ask my husband the same thing every night before I go to work. He tells me I'm supposed to be earning a living. I tell him I want to have babies."

Hatchett was slightly disappointed for Betty was a reasonably attractive woman; slim, with a stout chest and hips, and a kind face.

"So, have'em."

"He says we can't afford kids right now. So, I come here and save my money."

"Don't be in such a hurry. Kids are highly overrated."

"How so?"

"They can't do anything for themselves for about three or four years, then, when they get old enough, they think they can do everything for themselves, at the expense of everyone else."

"Is that what this is about?" she said pointing to his leg.

"Nope."

"Jealous husband?"

"No; knife-happy psychopath."

She made a face and was just about to ask a question when in walked the doctor. He was a tall, broad shouldered, graying man with the name 'Cobb' stitched on his white coat. He picked up a clipboard and started flipping the pages

"Well, let's see here, Mr. Hatchett. Gunshot wound to the right calf; apparently through and through." He looked down at the wound and had Hatchett roll over so he could inspect the back of his limb.

"Are you in any pain?"

"Not much. It aches a little."

"Can you wiggle your toes?"

"Oh, yeah. I tell you it's not serious."

Cobb nodded his head. "Okay, we'll just give you a tetanus shot and a couple of stitches on this larger hole, here in back, and you should be good as new in about a week." He nodded at Nurse Betty then left the room.

"So," she said as she prepared the hypodermic needle. "Is this psycho anybody that I should be worried about?"

Hatchett rolled over and presented his buttocks to the needle. "Not unless you moonlight as a dope mule, or a prostitute who dances nude in clubs." He paused as she slid the needle in his hip. "But, I guess that kind of life wouldn't fit in with your long range plan."

"It seems to have altered yours just a bit, too," she said with a smile.

CHAPTER 24

When he got home, Hatchett took two of the pain pills that were prescribed for him by the ER doctor, and filled for him at the hospital pharmacy, and thereafter slept soundly. He enjoyed the feeling of being under the influence of pain meds. They kept him from dreaming.

He got to the office at ten the next morning, and the answering service had ten calls awaiting him. One was from McRae at the Sheriff's Office. He decided to call him first.

"So you had a little trouble last night, did you?" McRae's tone was sarcastic.

"Nothing I couldn't handle. Any lead on who did it?"

"Well, we found the Caprice abandoned at the Airport. They were from out of town; whether it was Nashville or not, we don't know yet."

"Was there a Nashville flight around that time?"

"No, but they could have flown to Atlanta and gotten a connection. I've got JoAnn looking into it. How are things working out with you two?"

"I work alone, Lieutenant. But, she seemed to get the hang of what I was trying to do."

He paused on the other end. "Don't get her hurt, Hatchett. There are a lot of people that want to see her succeed."

"Then you better get her away from me. What was it you said? About 'a red trail?'"

"I know, I know. But she seems to think the two of you can do some good together."

"Is this really why you called?"

"As a matter of fact, yes."

"Well, being stylish was never my strong suit. If she can't protect herself, maybe you better keep her away from me."

"Just be careful, will ya?"

Hatchett hung up and immediately called Mary Boatman in Waynesboro. She sounded tired and hopeless.

"Do you have any news?" she said.

"Well, yes and no. We've eliminated about a half a dozen people who potentially had a motive to kill Melinda." Hatchett always called the victim by her real name when talking to her mother.

"But, the trouble is that she had such a wide circle of acquaintances that we might have to eliminate the whole southeast before we get to the man who did it. It's just going to be a numbers game." He paused. "It may take some time."

She was silent on the other end. When she spoke it was low and slow.

"My husband doesn't want to pay you anymore. He thinks you'll never find out who killed her."

Hatchett paused. "He may be right."

She was silent again. "Well, I don't think he is. I think whoever done this is somebody she knew, and if ya'll just talk to enough folks, you'll find out who."

"I don't disagree with you, ma'am." Hatchett did not want to pile on a grieving mother, so he played along.

"But that's not what I called you for. I wanted to let you know I can't send you what I was sending you before, moneywise, I mean. My husband said not to. He said just let the police handle it."

"I understand."

"But I ain't gonna listen to him. I can only send you a little bit, but I'm gonna keep sendin' it. 'Cause I think you can find the man that killed my baby."

"I'm trying, Ms Boatman. I'm trying."

She paused on the other end. "I just got to thinkin' the other day, that there was somethin' she said a couple of years ago that might be of help."

Hatchett was silent on his end of the phone.

"She said, 'If anything ever happens to me, 'check the heart.'"

"'Check the heart?'"

"That's what she said."

Hatchett quickly scribbled the words on a notepad in front of him. His mind raced back to the autopsy and his conversation with Lucy Leopold.

"Did she ever have any kind of heart trouble?'

"Not that I know of. But . . . well, if you say she was doin' drugs, well, then, she may have."

Hatchett said nothing.

"Anyway, I just wanted to let you know, about the money an' all. I'll do what I can."

"I appreciate it, Ms Boatman. And I'll let you know as soon as I hear something."

She hung up, and Hatchett picked up the notepad and pondered the words: 'Check the heart.' Could she have meant her own heart? Someone else's heart? Louis Hart?

Hatchett picked up the telephone and called the Coroner's Office. He spoke to the secretary, and in three rings Dr. Leopold was on the line.

"I just had another question regarding the Melinda Boatman case; you know, the headless prostitute."

"Oh, sure. You still working on that?"

"Still working. I was wondering whether you found anything in the victim's heart."

"Like what? You mean, disease?"

"Like anything."

"I'll have to check my notes, but I don't think so. She was a relatively young woman and any type of cardiac ailment would certainly be an anomaly." She paused. "But, I'll look again and give you call. You get a lead?"

"Just a cryptic message from the victim: 'Check the heart.'"

"Hmmmm."

"Could you tell how much coke she had in her?"

"At the time of death? No. But her liver still had traces of it when she was found, so she must have ingested quite a bit in the hours before she died. Cocaine is the usually the quickest drug to break down. My opinion is that she was heavily under the influence."

Hatchett paused and took a deep breath. "Okay, well, listen, if you think of anything else about her heart, give me a call."

Hatchett hung up and leaned back. His leg hurt, so he popped a couple of pain pills and washed them down with coffee.

He closed his eyes and tried to fall asleep, but the ringing phone caused him to jump ten minutes later. It was O'Leary from the Police Department.

"Well, I've got some good news and some bad news," O'Leary said.

"Gimme the bad news first."

"The bad news is the Feds haven't broken up the dope ring, yet."

"The good news?"

"The good news is I've uncovered another link in this coke chain. I thought I'd give you a crack at him first, because of your murder."

Hatchett picked up a pencil. "Shoot."

"His name is Alonzo Jermaine Toussaint. He's a mid-level distributor in New Orleans. I'm told he's one step from the top."

"You got an address?"

O'Leary supplied a location in, oddly, the Garden District, on St Charles Avenue.

"Apparently, he's doing pretty well. That St Charles Avenue is pretty high rent," O'Leary said.

"Can you tell me anything about him?"

"Cajun; came from over near Baton Rouge, near the Mississippi state line; short and fat, with greasy black hair, according to his jail records. They say he carries a forty five."

"Does he have a gaggle?"

"He's got two or three around him all the time. You should assume they're armed too."

"Okay. You got a phone number on him?"

"Just the one you gave me."

"That number was his? I thought it was from Fort Worth."

"The number is; the owner is not. He's got some way he reroutes his calls from Texas back to New Orleans."

"Just how heavy a player is this guy?"

"He's not at the top, but he's close. He keeps a pretty low profile, but he moves dope throughout the southeast. I'm told that he gets his orders from the top, up in Nashville."

"From a guy named Peters?"

"No. Peters is connected, but he's not Mr. Big. Toussaint is probably two steps below. He's a mover, living off the weakness and misery of others." He paused. "He ought to be killed."

"Maybe that can be arranged."

That afternoon, Hatchett met JoAnn Ward at her office, a small cubbyhole in the northwest corner of the Manipi County Sheriff's Office, inside the basement of the courthouse.

Ward's office was tiny, but immaculate. Hatchett looked around her desk and saw only a clean blotter, a Cross pen, and a notepad. Files were hidden, the trash can was empty, and typewritten reports were in a basket on a small table next to the office door.

One metal chair sat across the desk from her. Hatchett sat down in it just as she hung up the telephone.

"I'm glad you came. I did some work on Harold Meeks; you know the doctor in Pascagoula."

"Right."

"We can put him in Pascagoula at the time of the murder, we think."

"How?"

"Mostly phone records. He lives alone and apparently, he's quite the chatterbox."

"So, you've eliminated him?"

"Not completely, but I've looked at the police reports of the assault on his wife. I don't think he's got it in him to cut off a woman's head, do you?"

Hatchett felt the same way, but he wanted it to be her conclusion. "Unless something new surfaces, you're probably right."

"It just seems to me that the incident with his wife was a, I don't know, just kind of a heat of passion thing; like he just lost his temper."

Hatchett nodded.

"Are you working on anything else?"

Hatchett was tempted to tell her about Toussaint in New Orleans. But, at the last minute, it occurred to him that if he made contact with the man, he might have to do some things that he did not want her to see. He decided to give her something else to run down.

"Yeah, I've got a name for you: Mike Allenwood. He works at a tree farm on Vandalia Road, Abner's Tree Farm. An informant of mine told me that he had a relationship with Lisa Lemon."

"Who is this informant?"

"One of the dancers at a club here in town."

"I don't suppose you'd care to name her."

"Not right now. But she'll be available if you get anything on him."

"You know anything about him?"

Hatchett shook his head. "Not really. All I've heard is he's a low level dope dealer."

Ward wrote the name and the rest of the information on her notepad. She looked up at Hatchett, her eyes wide.

"Do you want to be involved in talking to him?"

He shook his head. "No, I've got something else I'm working on. But, if you go out there, be careful. I've heard he does carry a knife; a hook bill knife that he uses to prune trees."

"I'll be careful."

CHAPTER 25

Hatchett went back to his office to blueprint his trip to New Orleans. He fell into his chair and turned on a small fan that sat on the corner of his desk.

His visit with Toussaint would have to be meticulously planned and carried out. Hatchett's mark would have to be separated from anyone that could conceivably protect him, taken to a remote location, and then questioned. Then, he thought, well, he'd just have to see.

He picked up his note pad and started making a list of the things he would need to in order to apprehend and control a short fat man armed only with a forty five caliber pistol; but a man who was likely to have a mean streak.

Shortly, he laid the pad down, closed his eyes, and began meditating on just how the operation would go; the beginning, the middle, and the end. In minutes he was fast asleep, again, sleeping the sleep of the peaceful.

The next Sunday, in the early morning hours - six AM - Hatchett was in New Orleans, seated in the Merc on St Charles Avenue, a half a block from the residence of Alonzo Toussaint. There was no movement around the home, a three story Victorian with a wrought iron fence along the front. There was little traffic on the street. The house looked deserted. Hatchett watched through binoculars for a hint of movement in the curtains, but saw none.

He had been in town for two days studying Toussaint's movements and the comings and goings around his house. He was just as O'Leary had described; curly black hair, a black mustache, and darkly tanned skin. His stomach looked to be about fifty inches around, and his legs and arms were short and stubby.

Toussaint kept a predictable schedule. By the activity around the residence, it appeared as if he arose around seven AM each morning. He let the dog out and walked out to the street to pick up his copy of the Times-Picayune. At around ten, two of his goons arrived in a Cadillac to pick him up. Hatchett tried to follow him one day, but lost the car in traffic. He guessed that they were going to a bar, a restaurant, or some small neighborhood store where they could make phone calls and meet criminal consociates without comingling them with his home. They returned to the house at six each evening, after which the bodyguards left, and Toussaint entered the front door, alone. Hatchett had watched for two days, and there appeared to be no women or children at the residence.

He had formulated his plan based on Toussaint's alone time each evening, and in the early morning. There was a pay phone at the end of the block in front of a small grocery store, and he had chosen Sunday as the day to set things in motion. Prior to moving, however, he had changed out the barrel in his .45 with a new one; one without lands or grooves.

At six thirty, Hatchett parked the Merc in front of the store, got out, and dialed the Fort Worth phone number. It rang three times.

"Yeah."

"Mr. Toussaint?" Hatchett said frantically.

"Who's asking."

"You need to know that the there's a bomb in your house."

"Who is this?" His voice rose in tone.

"Look, the boys in Nashville are looking to cut out some dead wood. You need to get out of your house, right now." Hatchett hung up.

He jumped in the Merc and drove down the street and stopped in front of Toussaint's residence. In ten seconds, the Cajun ran out of the front door wearing a bathrobe and slippers. He stepped spritely down the sidewalk to the front gate and stopped. Then he looked from side to side, as if he didn't know what to do next.

Hatchett got out of the car and stood next to the driver's door.

"Mr. Toussaint, come quick. Come with me." Hatchett's voice was urgent, and he beckoned him with his arm.

"Who are you?" His accent was pure Cajun.

"Peters sent me. Hurry up, before it blows. They're after you." Hatchett kept waving his arm, and he spoke in a loud whisper.

Toussaint hesitated, looked back at his house then trotted toward the Merc. He opened the passenger front door and got in.

Hatchett dropped the car in gear and took off.

"Where are we going? And who are you?"

"I'm gettin' you outta here. They'll be by after the house goes, and if you're still alive, they'll finish you."

Hatchett drove the Merc away from downtown toward Audubon Park at a high rate of speed.

Toussaint sat nervously on the front seat, his head on a swivel. He rocked back and forth in his seat.

"Wh, what'd I do?" He said.

Hatchett looked toward him. "Peters got the word from up above that they want you gone. They think you've been skimmin'."

"No, come on, now. I've been taking my cut, but I've been sending the rest along like clockwork."

"That's not what they think up top. Peters said they're cleaning up. They took out that whore over in Alabama, and now they want you."

Toussaint looked down. He seemed to be running all the possible scenarios through his mind. Hatchett looked over at him and tried to gauge his willingness to talk.

Hatchett found a side road that turned south off St Charles, about five blocks from the park. He was looking to get down to the waterfront and into the myriad of warehouses that would be deserted this time of the morning. He was seeking privacy; a place where he could lean on Toussaint and find out who killed Lisa Lemon.

They were at the riverfront in five minutes. Toussaint had ridden in silence since he found out what was up. As they got closer to the warehouse district, he began to look around again, this time with his head swiveling more urgently.

"What are we doing down here?" he said.

"We've got to get you away from you house for a while."

"But, down here?"

"It's quiet, and it'll give us time to think."

Toussaint nodded and seemed to relax. He took a deep breath and exhaled.

Hatchett slowed the car considerably as he reached the warehouse district and looked for a deserted place to park. Owing to the weekend, few cars and trucks passed them.

"This looks like a good place," Hatchett said.

They parked in between two long cold storage buildings, behind the corner of the truck loading dock. A railroad track, overgrown with grass and weeds, stretched from one end of the building to the other. Hatchett backed the car up until it almost touched the tall concrete platform and, after putting it into park, turned off the motor. He looked over at Toussaint. The fat man was wringing his hands and chewing his tongue.

Without another word Hatchett got out of the car and walked around to the passenger side. He looked all four directions, and seeing no one, reached and grabbed the door handle.

Toussaint's face contorted in surprise as Hatchett took him by the collar of his robe and pulled him out of the vehicle. He fell on the concrete and did a half roll as Hatchett kicked him in the ribs. The fat man grunted.

"Hey, wha's goin' on?!"

"Get up!" Hatchett kicked him once again.

"Owwww! Stop! I'll get up!"

He struggled to his feet and reached down to dust himself off. When he thought Hatchett was off his guard, Toussaint brought his arm back and tried a long roundhouse right that Hatchett ducked. Hatchett counterpunched to the ribs. Toussaint doubled over and tried to get his breath.

In two minutes he was breathing more normally. "Who are you?" he said gasping for air.

"That's not important. What's important is who killed Lisa Lemon?"

"Who?"

"Lisa Lemon. You know who."

He said nothing as he rubbed his belly. Hatchett couldn't tell if he knew and was just not talking, or if he was being honest.

"Come on coon ass. Who killed her?"

"Look, I don't know who you're talking about." He was upright now.

Hatchett looked left and then right before he kicked Toussaint as hard as he could in the groin. The fat man doubled over again.

"Owwwww!"

"Now, listen, Alonzo. I can do this for hours; and, frankly, I want to. To me you're just a dirty little maggot that peddles blow and brings misery into the lives of a lotta people. But, I'm really here to find out who killed Lisa Lemon. She was a dancer over in Alabama. She worked in your organization, and somebody cut her head off two months ago. Now, I want to know who killed her."

Toussaint was still rubbing his crotch when he once again stood up straight.

"Look, whatever your name is, I don't know this Lisa Lemon, and I certainly didn't kill her. What was she your ole lady or something?"

Hatchett punched him in the nose with a straight left hand, thereby drawing blood for the first time. Toussaint turned away and wiped his nose.

"Owwwww!"

"I can go on all day, Alonzo. Who killed her?"

"I don't know, all right? Just don't hit me no more."

"You're lucky I don't kill you." He reached around to the small of his back and produced his .45. "As a matter fact . . ."

Hatchett's thumb engaged the safety, and he pointed the gun at Toussaint's head.

"Now, I'm only gonna ask one more time."

"Wait a minute, wait, now. Hold on, hold on." Toussaint's tone was frantic, and he held up both blood covered hands toward Hatchett in a defensive manner.

"Okay, okay. I've heard of her. I think she was a distributor. I didn't have any direct contact with her. She, she, I think she moved stuff directly to the street."

"You're not telling me anything I don't already know, Alonzo." Hatchett stepped forward.

"Okay, okay. Peters. It was Peters, I think. He usually makes those decisions."

"Is he at the top?"

Toussaint licked his lips. "I don't think so, no. There's someone above him."

"What's your chain?"

"I work for Peters. Some guy in a truck brings me the stuff. I don't know his name. I get it to a couple of broads here in town. They distribute and collect."

"Who are the two goons that I saw at your place yesterday?"

His brows knitted. "Those guys work for me. Business is good, so I can bring on extra help."

Hatchett exhaled hard and lowered the gun. He didn't believe that business about Peters killing anyone – a contract would probably come from the very top – but neither did he believe that Toussaint killed her. He just seemed a little too prissy to get that bloody.

"Did you kill Darla Hedrick?"

"Who?"

Hatchett took the .45 and hit Toussaint on the right side of his forehead. It staggered the fat man.

"Ohhhhhh! No!"

"Did you kill Darla Hedrick?"

"No, no! Ohhhhhhh! She used to work for me, but she got strung out, so I let her go. I don't know who killed her."

"Who does Peters' hits?"

Toussaint thought. "I don't know. He's never had anyone hit before, that I know of."

Hatchett was getting tired of talking with the fat man in the flowing silk robe and brown slippers. He raised the pistol to Toussaint's eye. Toussaint gasped, but calmed when Hatchett lowered the gun. Quickly, Hatchett pointed the weapon at his brown slipper and pulled the trigger striking him in the right instep. The loud report echoed off the brick buildings. Toussaint sat down hard grabbing his foot. Hatchett reached down and picked up the spent casing and put it in his pocket.

"I better not find out that you've lied to me."

Toussaint rolled over to the fetal position while at the same time moaning loudly. Hatchett got into the Mercury and scratched out of its parking spot. In seconds he was gone.

It was late that same afternoon when Hatchett got back to Mauvilla. He held up in his office until late into the night thinking about what he had really accomplished.

He learned that someone whose name he didn't know ran this particular drug operation. Underneath him, perhaps directly underneath, was Peters in Nashville. The truck driver, Sansome, was one of probably many who delivered the goods to distributors, like Allenwood, and Fitch at the truck stop, throughout what was probably just the southeast but what could be the entire country; after which they are given to poor slobs like Lisa Lemon and the girl in New Orleans who had also been relieved of her head. They took the product to points of sale locations, like the one in Birmingham with the happy professors.

As he went over these facts in his mind, Hatchett of course had no idea how they were a part of Lisa Lemon's death. Undoubtedly, some unknown factor in her relationship to this as yet unnamed cartel of narcotics peddlers got her killed, but he didn't know what it was.

It was still Hatchett's opinion that any hit on Lisa Lemon most probably had to have come from the very top. Lower level operatives, except in cases of extreme stress on the system, usually didn't take it upon themselves to sanction anyone, for a couple of reasons.

First, most or all of the functionaries in a drug organization who were involved in the enterprise solely for monetary remuneration, were unwilling to take on the punishment that would inevitably come with a murder conviction.

Second, they realized that killing someone who had gotten out of line was better left to a professional who was experienced and less likely to make a mistake and get caught. There was a move afoot to make murder in the course of a drug enterprise a capital offense in the federal system, a system that tended to carry out sentences with a bit more alacrity than state corrections systems, therefore no one wanted to chance an arrest and conviction.

Hatchett rubbed his temples and closed his eyes. If Lisa Lemon's death was a result of her activity in drugs, then he needed additional information. His next call would have to be back to O'Leary.

CHAPTER 26

The next morning, Vincent O'Leary answered his extension on the third ring, and Hatchett could hear him slurping coffee on the other end. He coughed twice before speaking.

"Yeah."

"O'Leary, this is Hatchett."

"Yeah, yeah. What's up?"

"I just wanted to give you an update on the information you gave me."

O'Leary was silent.

"Don't worry, I didn't do anything. He might walk with a limp for a while, but that's all."

O'Leary laughed. "Is that all? I was hoping he was no longer in the game."

"No. I just couldn't swing it." Hatchett's tone was resigned.

"Well, did you get anything out of him?"

"Not really. He said that Peters in Nashville was not the top man in the organization. He laid out his chain. He said he works for Peters, gets his dope from a guy in a truck, somebody like Sansome, and the girls get it out to the street."

"Well, shit, we knew all that. Did he just give all that up to you?"

"It took a little persuasion, but I think he said most of what he knows." Hatchett paused. "He did let one thing slip. He said business was so good that he was able to take on a couple of guys that work for him. My guess is that he's either planning to go out on his own, or he's skimming. Either way, it might be valuable to keep that in mind. It's why I was able to get him away from his house so easily. He thought the organization was coming after him."

"Ingenious."

"Anyway, I was hoping maybe I could get an audience with the Drug Enforcement people working on this thing. Apparently, if I'm going to get to someone who knows anything about Lisa Lemon, I'm gonna have to go a little higher up the ladder."

"Sure. His name is Joey Hernandez. Their office is on High Street, a block south of the

Medical Center. It's the brick building, two story, no windows, with the parking lot in the back."

"Thanks, Vince. Call me if you need me."

It was ten AM when Hatchett parked the Mercury in the rear parking lot of the non-descript building on the south side of the two hundred block of High Street. It was just as O'Leary had described it, and Hatchett found it without difficulty.

At the front door, he rang the buzzer and heard a female voice ask him what he wanted. He told her who he was and that he wanted to see Joey Hernandez. The buzzer sounded and Hatchett pulled open the heavy metal door. He entered and sat down in one of two vinyl upholstered chairs opposite the entrance. A photograph of a smiling Jimmy Carter hung on the west wall. Hatchett turned sideways so as not to have to look at the face.

In five minutes, a short Hispanic man with a Freddie Prinze haircut and a thick mustache walked in the door on the east side of the room. He wore a brown print polyester shirt, matching polyester pants, and brown stacks.

"Mr. Hatchett?" His accent was not heavy, but it was noticeable.

"Agent Hernandez." Hatchett extended his hand to shake.

"Come on back."

They walked through the door and down a short hall to an office in the southeast corner of the building. Hatchett followed close behind but stopped short in the threshold of the opening.

Seated with her back to the door was JoAnn Ward. Hatchett was surprised but not stunned.

"Do you know Detective Ward from the Sheriff's Office?" Hernandez said.

"I do." Hatchett took a seat next to her across the desk from Hernandez.

"O'Leary at the PD told me you were coming. I think you and Ward are working on the same case, no?"

Hatchett looked at Ward. "The Lisa Lemon murder, yes."

"Right. And you both think there's a drug angle, right?"

Ward and Hatchett nodded.

"Well, we've been working on this drug connection for about two years now. We call it the Confederate Connection because they operate in the thirteen states of the old Confederacy. It's headquartered in Nashville, and they deal strictly in cocaine; powder and also something new. They're calling it crack."

"Crack?" Ward said.

"Right, it's cocaine boiled down into cookies and smoked in a pipe. It's a great high, they tell me."

"So, Agent Hernandez, do you know of anything that can help us?" Hatchett didn't need all the details of the narcotics ring.

Hernandez sensed Hatchett's impatience and cleared his throat. "The bottom line is, we haven't heard anything about Lisa Lemon's death, or who may have ordered it."

Hatchett looked at Ward. He wasn't willing to let it go at that.

"Do you have a line on the guy that runs it all?"

"It's two guys. One is a fellow named Chet Winterbush. He used to be pretty high up in the music publishing business in Nashville. The other is a musician, Tommy Leon. He was with a couple of groups in the sixties but fell on hard times. The word is they got together and scraped up a few dollars, took a trip to South America - Columbia, we think - and came back with some powder cocaine. That was three or four years ago. They established a route through Mexico, into Texas, and on to about half a dozen labs throughout the South. They cut it, package it, and then get it out to the customers. We learned from you that Lisa Lemon was involved." He paused. "They call themselves the 'Music City Mafia.'"

"Catchy. Any reason for her to be murdered?"

"Not that we've heard."

"Was she snitchin' to anybody?"

"Not to any of our people, and I've talked to O'Leary. He says they didn't know her, and he's usually got a nose for things like that. I put her name out on the teletype and nobody responded."

Hatchett exhaled loudly. Ward spoke up.

"What about personal relationships? Ever hear of anything between Lisa Lemon and Peters, or any of the rest?"

"No. Of course, we might not hear of anything like that." He looked at Hatchett. "You're a little more up close and personal with it. You'd hear about it quicker than we would."

"How about hit men? Do they have anybody that they've used in the past?" Hatchett said.

Hernandez shook his head. "To my knowledge, they haven't had anyone rubbed. It could happen at any time, but so far as we know, it hasn't yet."

Ward and Hatchett exchanged looks. Hernandez could see their frustrations.

"Look, I know how you two feel. Mr. Hatchett, all you've talked to so far are low level people that wouldn't have any knowledge of whether or not anyone had been knocked off for business reasons." He paused and a smile began to cross his lips as he looked at Hatchett. "And, from what I've heard, if they had known anything, you certainly would have found out about it."

Hatchett was not amused. Ward was wide eyed.

"Agent Hernandez, do you guys have an informer inside?" Hatchett said.

Hernandez looked at him. "I think you know I can't tell you that."

"Just so, if I run into him, or her, I wouldn't want to get too active."

He took a deep breath and exhaled. "I see your point. The answer is yes."

Hatchett nodded.

"Look, just because these people haven't killed yet, doesn't mean they won't, if you get too close," Hernandez said.

"I understand. But, it'll be someone else before it's me."

"How do you know?"

"Alonzo Toussaint. I think he's trying to break free and start a competing network. Keep your eyes on it."

Hernandez nodded. "Good to know. Good to know."

Thirty minutes later, Ward and Hatchett adjourned to Walt's Diner for lunch. Hatchett sprang for a pair of BLTs and some iced tea.

"How'd you manage to wind up down at Hernandez's place today?" Hatchett said.

"Well, I knew, like you, that the DEA would have the best line on the structure and layout of this dope organization that Lisa was involved in. He'd at least be able to identify a few more of the players, and maybe a suspect." She paused, smiled, and tapped her temple with her index finger. "Not just a hat rack."

"I don't know. You always work a conspiracy from the outside in. The key to finding out who ordered her to be killed is to find out who did the actual murder. Then you pressure that person to put a finger on the people at the top."

"I'm beginning to think maybe Lisa Lemon wasn't killed by her drug friends," Ward said.

"Why do you say that?"

She shrugged and took a drink of tea. "No motive." She paused. "And, just because."

They ate in silence. "What do you propose to do, now?" she said.

"I don't know just yet, but I think it'll involve a trip north – again."

The waitress refilled Hatchett's glass of iced tea, and when she walked away, he looked at the young Asian woman as he munched on a French fry.

"So, what's a nice girl like you doing in a place like this?" he said.

"What, in police work?"

He shook his head. "In homicide."

She shrugged and continued chewing. "I guess I just always liked puzzles. It seemed a great way to do what I enjoy most."

Hatchett snorted. "I guess you're good in math, being Chinese and all."

"Ha. All Asians aren't good at math; and some of us can even drive. I've never had a ticket, and I never got past algebra. I just like the crosswords, and the jumble, you know. My dad is a surgeon and mom's a schoolteacher. They both put a lot of emphasis on education. I just spent a lot of my childhood reading."

He nodded. She seemed comfortable with him; willing to open up to him – if that was what he wanted.

"How about you? Why do you do what you do?"

He chuckled. "I hate the crosswords. I do, however, like to eat. I work for the money."

"Were you in law enforcement?"

He looked at her with a deadpan expression. It was clear he had no desire to be as open to her as she had been to him.

"You working on anything else besides this?" he said after taking a swig of tea.

She paused, cognizant of the evasion of her question.

"Just a couple of naturals and a suicide; the lieutenant's got me on this thing pretty much full time."

He studied his sandwich before taking another bite. "You know, this just might get a little dangerous; it might not be just another puzzle. If a guy's willing to cut a head off, he'll do just about anything."

She nodded. "I know." She paused and looked at him. "I'll be careful."

"Please do."

He didn't mention why he was concerned, but it was plain to him that a woman as small as she, trying to apprehend a man as vicious as the one who killed Lisa Lemon, could potentially be in a tremendous amount of peril.

At that moment Hatchett put down his tea glass and looked up to see Wiley Hairston walking toward their booth. Hairston was a Vietnam vet who took his mustering out pay and decided to do what he had done in the service - cook. He owned Walt's, named after his last company commander in the Army, and had for five years. His white apron was splotched with ketchup, and he wiped his hands as he neared their table. He was not smiling.

"Hey, Hatchett. Your answering service is lookin' for you."

Hatchett put down his sandwich and wiped his mouth with a white paper napkin. He started to rise.

"You can use the phone in my office." He jerked his thumb over his shoulder.

Hatchett walked behind the counter, into and through the kitchen, and into a small eight by eight office in the rear, near the open back door. The smell of garbage hit him as he sat down at the wooden desk and picked up the black receiver.

"Hatchett."

"Mr. Hatchett?" It was the voice of Martha, an older woman who sounded like everyone's grandmother.

"Hey, Martha. What's up?"

"Need you to call a woman named Jasmine, as soon as possible." She supplied the number, a local exchange.

Hatchett hung up and immediately dialed the number of the dancer with whom he had talked at the Silver Platter Lounge.

"This is Hatchett."

"Please, come!" The voice was frantic and sobbing.

"Jasmine? Is that you?"

"Please come! It's Lindsey!" she said through her tears.

"Who's Lindsey? What's wrong?"

"That guy, the one with Lisa, was here. He give her something. She got sick."

"Allenwood? Did you call an ambulance?"

"It's on the way. Please come!"

Hatchett picked up a pen off Hariston's desk. "Where are you?"

"At home!"

"Well, where's that?"

"Hunting Lodge Apartments; number 931."

"Alright. I'll be right over."

He hung up the phone, then picked it up again and dialed the Police Department.

"Operator." The female voice was middle aged and bored.

"Yes, ma'am. Do you have an ambulance going to the Hunting Lodge Apartments, number 931 for a possible OD?"

"Yes we do. Do you have information about the case?"

"This is Mark Hatchett. I'm a private investigator. You should get a homicide detective over there. This may be related to a county murder."

"Which one?"

"Just send someone. I'm on my way."

Hatchett hung up quickly. He knew that the dispatcher wouldn't let him leave if he didn't. It was a combination of the woman's curiosity and her duty to try to get as much information as possible, but she would keep him on the line for hours if he let her.

He walked quickly back through the kitchen into the dining area and back to the table where Ward was just finishing the last of her meal. He laid a five on the table and took a long draw from his water glass.

"Come on. Let's go."

"What's up?" Ward said, wiping her mouth.

"I don't know, exactly, but it sounds bad."

In the Merc, Hatchett drove at high speeds away from the river, north on the freeway, toward Highway 6. The Hunting Lodge Apartments were in the city limits, but two miles west of the highway, in a wooded area that backed up to a golf course. They arrived in twelve minutes. An ambulance and a marked patrol car were parked in front of building nine.

On the way, Hatchett had filled Ward in on his relationship with Jasmine. When they arrived, they bounded up the stairs quickly but were met by two ambulance attendants exiting the door of 931. A tall male and a short dumpy female were struggling to get the stretcher down the steps and out to the waiting van whose engine was running.

Hatchett and Ward stood aside until the gurney had passed and then walked through the open door of the apartment. Jasmine was seated on the couch talking to a uniformed officer, an older male with silver hair, who had removed his cap and was writing on a report pad. The officer looked up. Jasmine put her hands over her face and rubbed back and forth.

"Who are you two?" the officer said.

Ward flashed her star, and he relaxed noticeably.

"I'm Detective Ward at the Sheriff's Office. This is Mark Hatchett." She nodded at the young woman. "Jasmine called us."

"How is she?" Hatchett said, directing his question to the officer and jerking his chin over his shoulder toward the ambulance outside.

He said nothing but shook his head slightly, almost imperceptibly, back and forth. They knew what that meant.

Hatchett sat down on the couch next to Jasmine. She turned to face him.

"What happened?"

She wiped her face again. "He came over to see Lindsey with some coke. She said she was going to work for him. When he got here, she said she wanted to try some, 'cause she never had before. He told her 'no,' that she wasn't supposed to use the product. But she just kept on, wanting him to show her how to do it. So he opened up a package and showed her how to snort it up her nose." She paused and took a deep breath. "She inhaled real big through a straw and did a whole line. Then something happened?"

"What?"

"I don't know. She just fell out, just like a stone."

"What did Allenwood do?"

"He grabbed up the rest of the packages and run out." She began to cry. "I run over to her and shook her and slapped her face and shook her again. But nothin' happened. So I called the ambulance; we keep the number on the refrigerator. Then I called you."

"How do you know it was Allenwood?"

"I remember him from when he used to come in and see Lisa."

Hatchett sat back. The officer, whose nametag identified him as Walters, was just finishing up the narrative portion of the report. He sat back also.

"Do you have a detective coming?" Ward said.

"Yeah, but it don't sound like you got a homicide here. Just sounds like a plain old overdose."

Hatchett nodded. "That's what it was: a plain old overdose." He spoke softly and quietly.

Jasmine, wearing pink shorts and a blue tank top, slipped her feet into a pair of flip flops. She wiped her face again and looked at Hatchett.

"Will you take me to the hospital?" she said as a tear rolled down her cheek.

Hatchett rose from the couch and nodded. "Sure."

He used the phone to call the ambulance company and found that they had taken Lindsey Allison Haines to Mercy Hospital in the middle of town, not far from Walt's Diner.

Jasmine rose and picked up her purse from the coffee table in front of couch. She started for the door.

"Are you going to stay here?" Ward said to Walters.

He nodded. "I'll lock up when we leave."

Downstairs, in the Merc, Jasmine, a large, but well- proportioned young woman, folded herself into the backseat. She alternately cried and then wiped her face.

"What happened to her?" she said.

"Cocaine will do that to you, in large doses. It'll just stop your heart," Ward said.

Hatchett looked over his shoulder into the backseat. "By the way, Detective Ward from the Sheriff's Office, this is . . . what's your real name, Jasmine?"

"Becky, Becky Arnold."

He spun his wheels as he left the parking lot enroute to the hospital emergency room.

Hatchett left Ward at Walt's to get her car and then drove Becky Arnold on to the ER. He parked on the circular drive, right behind the ambulance, and the two walked quickly through the sliding glass doors.

They were directed to an examining room off the main hall where a doctor and three nurses were busy around a young woman's naked chest. Hatchett and Becky stood back and watched for three minutes. Then, the doctor stood up straight, looked at the clock, and said:

"Alright, that's it. Time of death is thirteen seventeen." He turned to Becky Arnold.

"Are you the next of kin?"

She shook her head then ran crying back out into the hall, away from the examining room and the body of her dead friend.

Hatchett looked at the doctor whose white coat had the name 'Radcliffe' monogrammed over the left breast pocket. He was sixty with thinning gray hair.

"That's her roommate." Hatchett said.

"I understand." Radcliffe said.

Hatchett nodded toward the dead girl, a girl he had never met. "Any reason to believe she died from anything other than cocaine poisoning?"

Radcliffe was writing on a chart. He looked up.

"And you would be?"

"Mark Hatchett. I'm a private detective. I'm with the roommate."

Radcliffe cleared his throat. "No, not really. But I'm going to save anything else I know for the police, if you don't mind."

His tone was not smarmy, but resolute. Hatchett knew he would get nothing else out of him. He nodded.

"Okay. Well, thanks for all you did."

He looked around. "This kind of thing happens all too often these days." He took a deep breath and exhaled. "She's really just a child."

Hatchett nodded and walked past him, into the hall, to look for Becky Arnold.

He found her walking out of the ladies room off the main waiting area near the front door, where she sank into an upholstered chair near a large picture window. Two elderly volunteers sat behind a circular desk and spoke in hushed tones as Hatchett took the seat next to her.

At first he was silent. Hatchett knew himself and knew he didn't do grief very well.

"Hey," he said finally, "it's gonna be okay."

She sniffed. "It's just so unfair."

"How long you known her?"

"About a year. We met when she started at the club."

"She was a dancer?"

She shook her head and wiped her nose with a paper towel. "Waitress. She wanted to dance but she couldn't 'cause she wasn't old enough yet. She was gonna get her card and start dancin' next month, when she turned twenty one."

Hatchett nodded. "Did you call her family?"

"She was from outta town. I don't know 'em. She never mentioned'em. I think she just run away. If she's got anybody, she never talked about'em."

They sat in silence for a minute. Finally, Becky Arnold spoke.

"Is what that policeman said right? Ain't there somethin' that can be done to this Allenwood guy?"

Hatchett looked away toward the exit. "You know, he's probably right. There isn't really much that the law can do." He paused and looked down. "But, these things have a way of working themselves out."

CHAPTER 27

It was two days later, as Hatchett sat at his desk, when the phone rang. It was Ward from the Sheriff's Office.

"Hatchett, what are you doing?"

"Contemplating my existence."

"Well, hold onto your hat. Mike Allenwood is dead."

"Go on."

"Found shot, out at the tree farm."

"Get out."

There was a pause on the other end of the line. "This is not a surprise to you."

"On the contrary, it is a complete surprise."

Another pause. "By the way, where were you last night?"

"Detective Ward, am I a suspect?"

"Are you?"

He chuckled. "I was at home. Alone."

"I thought as much."

"Any leads?"

"Nothing hard. Just a blue car parked by the side of the road near the scene."

"What a coincidence. I have a blue car."

"Yes, you do."

He paused. "Either you don't really think I did it, or you're glad I did, else I'd be downtown in handcuffs right now."

He heard her snort. "Right again."

"Do you know who did it?" His tone was harder.

"No, actually. The medical examiner said that he was shot with a .45 calibre round." She paused. "That's why the questions. The lieutenant knows you carry a forty five."

"Well, set his mind at ease, and yours, too. If you want, I'll bring my piece in and you can test fire it."

"It won't do any good. The bullet was broken up too badly to compare. The evidence guys only knew the caliber due to the weight."

"Well, I'm just tryin' to be a good citizen." He paused. "I do have a name for you."

"Go ahead."

"Take a look at a man named Whitey Sansome. He owns an eighteen wheeler and moves dope across country for the same organization as Allenwood."

"And you know this how?"

"I talked to him. He might have gotten the impression that Allenwood ratted him out."

Silence on the other end of the line. "Okay. I'll pass it along, but, frankly, this investigation doesn't figure to get high priority. I'm still assigned to the Lisa Lemon case. And by the way, there's now a fifteen thousand dollar reward for information leading to the arrest and conviction of the perpetrator."

"Interesting."

"How so?"

"That the Sheriff would think this a valuable enough case to put up a reward for it."

"Actually, the state is putting up the money. The Sheriff just asked for it. He sees it as a high pub case that can help him at election time. He wants someone putting some serious time in on it. Besides, everyone knows who Allenwood is, or was, and what he did for a living." She paused. "Any new ideas?"

"As a matter of fact, I was thinking of a short visit to Nashville."

"I'll clear it with the boss."

The next morning they were on the highway north to Tennessee. Ward drove a county issue, four-door, yellow Plymouth Satellite. Hatchett was not wild about the situation, he usually liked to be in complete control, but he acquiesced in deference to his fuel budget.

In fact, he didn't expect the trip to bear fruit. Hatchett considered it busy work, with two goals in mind. He wanted to keep law enforcement personnel harassing the drug dealers, and he wanted to see if he could find out who shot him.

He had become convinced that someone else had killed Lisa Lemon. All the motives that the drug dealers had for offing her, in his mind, had fallen apart. This trip was to tie up the loose ends.

If she was stealing product and using it herself - a likely prospect, for half the year, at least - there was no evidence that anyone even cared.

And, if she was snitching, the question was to whom? She didn't work for the DEA; she didn't inform for any of the local agencies; and there was no evidence that she was in bed with any rival organizations.

Money, revenge, and love or sex. Those were the three motives for murder, and as of yet, Hatchett had been unable to hang any of them plausibly on the Music City Mafia.

"Just who are we going to see up here?" Ward said as she piloted the county-issue Plymouth north at a healthy rate. They were a hundred miles out of town, almost to the capital city.

Hatchett took a deep breath and exhaled. "First, I'd like to stop by the Police Department and see if we can find out what they know. Heck, they may not even have knowledge of this Music City thing, and it's happening right under their noses."

"Is that why you brought me?"

"That's one reason. Police tend to take a suspicious view of private investigators."

She grinned. "I understand."

He looked at her. Her eyes were straight ahead, on the road. There were other reasons for bringing her, of course. JoAnn Ward was a reasonably attractive woman. She had dark brown hair, dark brown eyes, and tanned skin. A thin belt accented her slender waist. Her small hands matched her feet, and Hatchett wondered humorously if they had both been bound. She seemed to be intelligent, but not obnoxiously so; soft spoken, but forthright, and not talkative; and, though she had not exhibited the traits of a crackerjack detective, she did seem to be a fast learner and a faithful 'lead follower'; and she had not shown a lack of courage when it came to confronting witnesses and suspects while being exposed to the dark side of detective work. In his mind, she was an asset.

"Also," he said, "I want to try to get the lay of the land when it comes to these two clowns running this thing."

Secretly, he felt that if he could get one or both of them alone, he could allay all his suspicions regarding their involvement in Lisa Lemon's murder once and for all. He hoped Ward would have the stomach for it.

"So, do you know Kung Fu?" Hatchett said, just trying to make conversation.

She smiled again. "Not all Orientals are Bruce Lee."

"I thought you guys wanted to be called Asian?"

"By whites. We can call ourselves anything we want." She paused. "But, in answer to your question, I have had some formal training. My father insisted upon it when I told him I wanted to go into police work."

"Bet that was kind of a shock."

"It was. He had hoped that I might give medicine a try."

"What a disappointment you've been."

"I guess. He wanted someone to whom he could pass along his knowledge, and his practice."

"You an only child?"

"The son he never had." She paused and looked away from the road. "So, what about you?"

"What about me."

"Well, where do you come from? Family? Background?"

He chuckled. "You don't want to know."

She smiled. "Sure, I do."

"Well, it's not a pretty story. I was born in Australia. At age two, a dingo came into my bedroom, kidnapped me, and dragged me into the woods. He had earlier in the day consumed a koala bear, so he didn't eat me, but he carried me off by the scruff of the neck to a benign Aboriginal tribe three miles from home. They raised me as one of their own. They taught me to fish, hunt, shoot a bow and arrow, and speak their native language. When I was thirteen, a shepherd traveling to market with his herd traded two lambs and goat for me in hopes that he could train me to assist him. But he beat me, so when we got to town, I ran away from the shepherd and was taken in by a benevolent prostitute. She cleaned me up, taught me English, and eventually took my virginity. Afterwards, I ran away again, hopped a tramp steamer to America, and joined the Army. I fought . . ."

"Okay, okay, I get it. You don't want to talk about yourself," she said through her chuckles.

"But how do you expect us to work well together if I don't know you."

"You've seen too many Starsky and Hutch episodes. I'm a single. I work alone. Right now, we're just together for convenience." He paused. "Our little team is supposed to be for both our benefits."

"Right."

"Remember, you bring along access and information I'd normally have to spend hours of surveillance trying to get, or else beat out of someone."

"That's what you get." She emphasized the word 'you.'

"And you get the credit when we solve this case," he said.

"When?"

"When. We're gonna solve this case. Besides, I need the money."

"Her mother still paying you?"

"A little."

Ward looked back at the road and took a deep breath. "I hope you're right."

"I'm right."

She said nothing for a quarter mile. Then she looked at Hatchett and grinned.

"Did the benevolent prostitute really get your virginity?"

At five that afternoon, they checked into the cleanest cheap motel in Franklin, Tennessee, about fifteen miles south of Nashville. The place was on a service road a couple of hundred yards from the highway, near several fast food restaurants. They chose a national chain for their evening meal.

"What do you want to do first?" Ward said.

"Let's stop at the PD first thing. They can give us information on the players up here. And, we can show them the courtesy of letting them know we're in town."

She paused to chew. "You're not going to do any of your tricks, are you?"

"Why, whatever do you mean?" His tone was sarcastic.

"You know, your persuasive techniques?"

He looked at her over his hamburger, and his eyes turned hard. "You're new to this business, but perhaps one day you'll see just exactly what kind of people we're dealing with out here. Then you'll understand."

She stared into his eyes, trying to get inside his mind. She had heard that he had killed several men, and the thought was in one way very exciting and in another very disturbing. The fact that he was able to handle any situation, even to the point of violence, made her feel very secure in his presence. It also made her doubt her ability to trust him. She wondered if he was capable of murder. Killing in self-defense, or even in judgment, was one thing. Killing for fun, by compulsion, or for profit, was entirely another.

"Guess I've got a lot to learn, huh," she said.

"I guess you do."

CHAPTER 28

The next morning, the two found the Metro Police Department's Narcotics Division in the basement of the Police Building downtown, a half a block from the Cumberland River. Ward presented her credentials at the front desk, and they were directed to the lower regions of the building by a middle aged woman who manned the information booth in the lobby.

Hatchett pressed the buzzer on the wall next to the locked metal door. A small window opened and one eye peered at them.

"Yeah?"

Ward held up her star. "My name is Ward. I'm from Manipi County, Alabama. This is Mr. Hatchett. We're trying to get some information about a murder case back home."

The eye blinked twice and the sliding window closed. They heard the lock disengage after which the door opened. The man behind it stood back and beckoned them in.

"You folks from Alabama?" the man said.

He was a young man of medium height with dark brown hair that fell over his ears. His mustache was thick and accented his overall borderline hippie image. He wore a tan t-shirt and jeans, with blue Nikes.

"That's right. JoAnn Ward."

She stuck out her hand and the officer shook it. His hands and forearms where heavily muscled, and he acted as if he was wary of hurting her.

"Henry Waggoner," he said. "Come on back."

"Waggoner? Like Porter Waggoner?" Hatchett said.

"No relation. I spell mine with two g's."

He ushered them down a barren hallway to a plain interrogation room to the left. There were three chairs and one large table, and nothing else. Each took a seat.

"How can I help you folks?"

"We're working on a homicide back home," Ward said. "A dancer/prostitute was beheaded and left naked in a field near the freeway. We've traced her movements and associations, and we've found that she was a client of a man named

Nicholas Peters from here in Nashville. She also worked in his drug distribution network. The DEA tells us that Peters is a part of a larger group that call themselves the 'Music City Mafia.' It's a drug ring run by a couple of country music rejects up here." She paused. "Does any of this ring a bell to you?"

Waggoner took a deep breath and exhaled. "Well, yes and no. Peters we know about. Who are these two 'rejects'?"

"The feds mentioned a couple of guys named Chet Winterbush and Tommy Leon. Both of them used to be in country music; Leon played in a band, and the other one was on the business side. When they didn't get rich in music, apparently they bought some cocaine and went another direction."

"Did the feds know where they were getting their dope?"

He spoke calmly, almost lazily. Hatchett got the impression that all Ward was telling him was old news, and since she wasn't offering him any help, they could expect little assistance from him.

"If they did, they didn't tell us."

"So, how can I help you?"

Ward looked at Hatchett. Her brows were raised as if she didn't know what to ask. Hatchett spoke up.

"We were wondering about a couple of things. One, have you had any intelligence about our murder? The victim's name was Lisa Lemon.

"Second, have you gotten any information about anyone getting picked off by this particular group? And if so, who took the contract?

"Thirdly, do you guys know of anyone up here who might take a contract for a hit like this?"

"Wow, Mr. Hatchett, was it? Just how are you involved in this case?"

Ward spoke up. "He's a PI working for the family of the dead girl. Even though their daughter kind of got off the straight and narrow, they still care about her. They're good people; country people from over in Mississippi."

Waggoner nodded. "I see. Well, in answer to your question, no, I haven't heard of anyone flaming a hooker in Alabama, and I'm kind of the intelligence man in our unit so I would know. As far as who might've done it, it's been our experience that these guys generally take care of business themselves." He seemed much more comfortable talking to Hatchett than Ward.

"Talking about Winterbush and Leon?"

"Right. Now, that may have just been on the way up. As their organization has grown, I don't know, maybe they've begun to farm out some stuff, but as far as anything this heavy, well, I don't know." He shook his head.

"Now, about a list of hit men in this area, I'm not sure that something like that exists. Sure, we've got our share of knuckle crunchers like anywhere else, but I think you're gonna be looking for someone inside their organization for this thing. I mean, this is a pretty serious crime."

There was silence for a minute. Hatchett was seeing that this meeting was getting them nowhere. There was only one course of action.

"So," Ward said, "nothing on the death of Lisa Lemon."

"I've never heard of her. Nothing's come across my desk about a beheaded prostitute."

"Nothing that could help us?" Ward was persistent.

Waggoner took a deep breath and expelled. "There is a guy here in town that's informed for us in the past. Name's W.C. Cox. He's been in the know on everything big that's gone down in the underworld here in Nashville for the past ten or fifteen years." He chuckled. "Funny, everybody knows he's a snitch, but they tell him stuff anyway. Anyway, if it happened, he prob'ly knows about it."

"Where can we find this guy?" Ward said.

"At a club on 7th Avenue a block off Broadway called Harriet's Hideaway. It's a disco. He'll be the big fat guy - and I mean, really fat - seated at the end of the bar. That's where he usually is."

"Interesting name for a club," Hatchett said. "Grind house?"

"Used to be. The broad that runs it is Harriet something, I forget her last name. She keeps a pretty tight rein on things around there: no drugs, no hookin'. Cox is an accountant, and he does the bar's books, so he hangs out there about twenty hours a day."

Ward looked at Hatchett. She shrugged.

"Okay, well, I guess that's it," she said. "Thanks for your help."

Ten minutes later, in the car, Hatchett's opinion still hadn't changed. They could spend some more time running down these dealers, but he didn't believe it was getting them any closer to the truth.

Ward consulted the city map and five minutes later, in mid-morning traffic, they were in the parking lot of Harriet's Hideaway. It looked to be closed.

"Let's don't hang around here waiting for this joint to open. Let's see if we can find this Tommy Leon."

"You got any ideas about where he is?"

"As a matter of fact, I do. Pull over."

They stopped at a phone booth, and Hatchett got out. He put in two nickels, and in five minutes he returned to the car.

"Head south," he said pointing toward the freeway. "Get off in Oak Hill."

"Who did you call?"

"I've got a PI contact up here. She had his address in two minutes. Remind me to send her a check."

"Impressive."

In fifteen minutes they were parked in front of a sprawling, ranch style, brick home off Tyne Boulevard a quarter mile from the Franklin Pike. The lawn was manicured and the house was thirty yards from the road.

"Wow, look at this place. We're in the wrong business," Ward said.

Hatchett didn't acknowledge her as the two exited the car and walked toward the front porch. They stood on either side of the door, and Ward hit the bell. As they waited, Hatchett said:

"Keep the badge hidden for a minute. Let me see what I can do," Hatchett said. Ward nodded assent.

In three minutes, a diminutive, middle aged domestic in a starched white uniform and white shoes, the orthopedic kind worn by nurses, opened the front door.

"Yes?"

"We're here to see Mr. Leon."

"Who shall I say is callin'?"

"Just tell him, Mr. Peters sent us."

The woman looked at them suspiciously and closed the door. Ward looked at Hatchett.

"What are you going to tell him?"

He held up his hand. "Just follow my lead."

In two minutes, the woman reopened the door. "Follow me," she said and led them into a sitting room off the foyer. It was a large space with early American furniture and a fireplace, and a large bookcase choked with books.

As the woman exited the room, a middle aged man, medium height with blonde hair passed her in the threshold. She closed the sliding doors. The man wore a white terry cloth robe over his expansive middle, and he was barefooted. Ward and Hatchett looked up as he cleared his throat.

"What can I do for you folks?" Hatchett saw that his hands were in his pockets.

"Mr. Leon, my name's Mark and this here's JoAnn. Nicky Peters sent us; thought maybe you had a job for us."

"What kind of job?"

"Well, I'm a driver and pretty good with my hands, and JoAnn here is a pretty hot little dancer." Hatchett smiled and put his arm around her shoulders.

Ward looked at him with eyes wide and brows raised but kept her tongue. Leon eyed her lecherously.

"Why'd Peters send you here?"

"He said you had to approve anyone that he wanted to hire."

Leon looked at the floor and then up at the two. In a flash, he pulled his right hand out of the pocket of his robe and pointed a small revolver at them. Ward took a step back. Hatchett took a step forward.

"Who are you two?"

Hatchett smiled. "What gave us away?"

"Peters never calls himself 'Nicky.' And, he approves all the low level hires. Now, who are you?"

Hatchett inched two feet closer. "My name is Mark, that's true. This is JoAnn. We're from Alabama." He was clearly stalling for time until he could get closer.

"So you're from Alabama. So what? What do you want?" His tone was not yet angry.

Hatchett had sidled to within four feet of the man. "We wanted to ask you about . . ."

At that, Hatchett pivoted on his left leg and sent Leon flailing backwards with a quick flying sidekick to his midsection. The revolver flew out of his hand, and Ward moved quickly to pick it up.

Leon's head hit the sheet rock wall and cracked it. He was not unconscious, but he was stunned. He threw his arms over his grimacing face and rolled from side to side. He closed his eyes tightly.

"Please, don't kill me," he whimpered.

Hatchett knelt next to him with his right knee on the man's chest. "Calm down, calm down. We're not going to hurt you. We just came for information."

"Ohhhh, my head!" Leon continued to roll back and forth.

Hatchett grabbed Leon's hands and pulled them away from his face. "Look, calm down. We just want some information." Hatchett slapped him on the cheek twice, hard.

Ward walked toward the two and stood. She unloaded the gun and put the rounds onto a table, but held onto the weapon.

"Listen. We're from Alabama. We're looking for information about one of your girls, Lisa Lemon."

"I don't know her."

"Yes, you do. Somebody cut her head off and left her on the side of the road."

"Ohhhhh, I don't know her, I tell ya." He talked as if he was in pain, but Hatchett could tell otherwise.

"Look, Tommy, Peters hired her as part of your distribution network. Now, I know you're not hurt. But that can change."

"Peters does all the hiring and firing. I don't know who you're talking about."

Hatchett took his thumb, found the sensitive spot under the chubby man's left mandible, and began to press hard. In a second Leon was hollering.

"Does Peters report to you?" Hatchett said.

"Owwwwww, yes!"

"Anybody between you and him?"

"Ohhhh, No!"

There was a knock at the door. "Everythang alright in there, Mr. Leon?" It was the voice of the nurse.

Hatchett released his pressure, pulled his .45 and showed it to Leon.

"Yes, Mavis. It's fine. I just slipped. These folks are helpin' me," he said.

They were all silent for a minute as they heard footsteps walk away from the door. Since he was getting answers, Hatchett released the pressure on Leon's chest.

"Where does Winterbush fit in with all this?"

"Oww," Leon rubbed his chin. "He handles the money end."

"You're in operations?"

"Yes, yes."

Hatchett engaged the thumb safety on the pistol and turned it flat in his hand. He used the muzzle to tap lightly on the top of Leon's head.

"Tommy, do you feel that tapping?"

He nodded.

"Well, you just think about how much it's going to hurt if I hit you as hard as I can. Now, if you're in operations, I expect you to know a little something about operations. I'm gonna ask you some questions, and I best begin to get the truth."

Leon was breathing heavily. "Okay, okay. Yeah, I heard about the broad down in Alabama. Peters told me. He said he hired her through a punk down south in, what's the name of that town down there, Mauvilla? He said she was real good. She hit all the big conventions and parties on the circuit for him. He said he was sorry to hear about her."

"Did he say who did it?"

He shook his head hard. "No, no. Look, we don't go in for rough stuff."

"Yeah, I can see that." He nodded toward Ward and the revolver. "What do you call that, a lollipop?"

Leon's eyes cut to the small Colt in Ward's hands. "Say, who are you guys, anyway? Cops?"

"We're friends of Lisa Lemon. We want to know who killed her." Ward said.

Up until then she had been a silent partner. Half of her could see her career flashing before her eyes as Hatchett's brutality sucked her in deeper, but the other half was curious as to what they were going to get out of the burly man in the white robe.

"Look, I don't know, I swear."

"Well, here's something I bet you do know. Who took a shot at me out on the street corner back in Mauvilla?"

He was dumbstruck. His eyes widened, and his mouth fell open.

"That was you?"

Hatchett took the pistol and laid open a gash on the top of Leon's head. Blood began to flow down his forehead. He closed his eyes tightly and tears began to seep from the corners.

"That's right. That was me."

"Look, I didn't know," he blubbered. "Peters came to me and said he needed to send a message. He wanted a couple'a grand. I told him that sounded like a lot. He said he thought it would help, that he found out somebody was . . ."

"Was what?"

"You know, getting' a little close." He wiped his face with his right hand, looked at the blood, and grimaced again.

"He wanted to kill me?"

"No, no. He just wanted to send a message; just to say, you know, 'back off.'"

"So, it was Peters' idea."

"Yeah, yeah."

Hatchett was silent. He looked at the floor and then up at Ward. She shook her head. He looked back down.

"Where's Peters now?"

"I don't know, at his office, I guess."

He reached for a phone on the end table next to a couch and handed it to Leon.

"Call him. Tell him to wait for you at his office."

Tommy Leon pushed himself to an upright, seated position on the floor with his back to the busted wall. He took the phone and dialed a seven digit number.

"Yeah, this is Leon. You're at your office, good. Wait there for me. I'll be over in fifteen minutes."

He hung up the phone and Hatchett took it from him. Then Hatchett took out his pocket knife and cut the phone wire in two places.

The fireplace was on the wall opposite the door. Hatchett motioned for Leon to get up. They walked to the hearth and Hatchett directed the fat man to his knees, facing away from the fireplace.

Then he took the robe sash, cut a small portion of it, and used it to gag Leon's mouth. Hatchett then used the rest of the sash to tie his hands behind him, and took the phone cord, looped it around the bindings of his wrists, and tied it to one of the fire irons, effectively securing his movements. He moved everything away from the big man, thereby preventing him from making any noise.

"This is just until we can get to Peters," Hatchett said to the struggling man. "We don't want you tipping him off. We'll tell the nurse you're napping in here, to check on you in forty five minutes. That should give us enough time." Hatchett left the bound man with a wave.

Outside in the car, Ward drove away quickly. Her hands shook as she tried to hold the wheel.

Hatchett looked at her. "Intense, hunh."

She looked at him. It was obvious she was incensed. Her brows were knitted, and her mouth was in a tight line.

"We'll be lucky if we don't get arrested," she spit the words out.

"Are you kidding? Leon call the police?" He laughed out loud.

"What's funny?"

"He'll never tell anybody he snitched on his partner. It'll ruin his tough guy image if it gets out that some guy and a broad from Alabama put a couple of holes in him. And he'll certainly never invite the police into his home. I bet Waggoner's been looking for a way to get in that house and into his life for months."

"You sure?"

"Just head downtown, quick."

In fifteen minutes they found a parking place in front of Nicholas Peters' office on Broadway, in downtown Nashville. Ward slid the Plymouth in between a van and a pickup truck and put the vehicle in park.

"Wait a minute, before we go in," she said.

Hatchett froze. "What's up?"

"Just what's going to happen in there?" She nodded toward the office.

"Well, nothing, if we don't hurry. We don't know how long Leon's going to be in his predicament. He may already be loose."

"No, I'm talking about, what are you gonna do to Peters?"

He shook his head and looked toward the Opry House. "I knew you wouldn't have the stomach for this. This jackass hired somebody to shoot me, and I'm gonna find out who it was that did it. If you don't want to be a part of it, feel free to stay in the car."

Ward looked forward out the windshield and took a deep breath. She exhaled and shook her head.

"Let's go."

At the top of the stairs, he and Ward found the door to Peters' office and took positions on either side. Hatchett knocked lightly.

"Come in," a voice said from inside.

Hatchett motioned for Ward to stay put. Then he reached up and turned the knob slowly. He pushed the door open then snuck a peek around the corner.

Peters was seated in his chair, his hands invisible. Almost immediately, they heard the report of a shotgun and part of the door facing by Hatchett's head blew away. He and Ward both stepped back and produced their handguns.

"Come on now, Nicky. We just want to talk." Hatchett's voice was soothing.

"That you, Hatchett?"

"It's me, Nicky."

"I heard how you talked to Tommy Leon."

"Now, we didn't hurt Tommy. We just got his attention. Besides, what are you gonna do? Kill us?"

Peters was silent. Undoubtedly, he had not yet thought through his plan. Hatchett looked at Ward and whispered directions to her.

"Go downstairs and find a phone. Call the cops."

Ward looked around her side of the door jam and saw Peters reloading his now visible shotgun. She darted past the door and back down the stairs and into the street.

"The cops'll be here soon, Nicky. Just put the gun down and we can talk."

"What have we got to talk about?"

"Two things: tell me who cut the girl's head off in Alabama."

"I told you before, I don't know."

"The police are on the way, Nicky."

"I can't tell you what I don't know."

"Okay, well, who shot me?"

He was silent. "They hit you?"

"They sure did. It wasn't serious, but I still want to know who it was. I understand why you did it, but I want to know who it was."

"What's in it for me?"

Hatchett thought for a minute. "Well, maybe we just forget that you tried to kill me just now."

"I wasn't trying to kill you. I just wanted to scare you off."

"You knew that wasn't going to work."

Silence again from inside the room. "Look, forget about the shooting, and I'll tell you who it was."

Sirens began to sound in the background.

"All right. Start talking."

"How do I know your word's good?"

"You'll just have to trust me."

Silence again as the sirens got louder.

"It was two guys from Birmingham. I don't know'em."

"How'd you find'em?'

"I got a number. I burned it."

Hatchett began to back away from the door, toward the stairwell. He was met on the stairs by two uniformed officers and Ward bringing up the rear. Hatchett stopped them in their tracks.

"Sorry to get you guys out, but Mr. Peters up here was just showing me his shotgun and the darn thing went off accidentally."

"What is your name, sir?" The speaker was a tall male with a mustache.

"Hatchett, Mark Hatchett."

"You say this is an accidental shooting? This lady here said some guy was trying to kill you two."

Hatchett chuckled. "She just got a little hysterical."

"But . . ." Ward said.

Hatchett held up his hand in a 'hold your peace' gesture. "We just came up so I could take a look at his gun. She was looking out the window when it went off and hit the door frame."

Hatchett looked at Ward with raised eyebrows. She frowned but said nothing.

"Let's go up and take a look at your friend."

The four marched up the steps and down the hall to Peters' office. They found him still seated in the chair. The shotgun was standing in the corner.

"What is your name, sir?" The tall officer said.

Peters was wiping his hands on his pants. "Nicholas Peters. This is my office."

The officer looked around the room while his partner, a shorter man with blonde hair examined the door jamb.

"What happened here?"

"Well, I, I was just cleaning my gun, and it went off. I guess I forgot to unload it. It scared me to death. Fortunately, the only property I damaged was my own."

The officer, whose name tag identified him as Stevens, looked all around the room. His facial expression indicated that he wasn't buying any of it, but there was no complainant and no property damage to anyone other than the owner, so, really, in his mind, 'no harm, no foul.'

"Okay, if that's the way you want it."

"Everything's fine here, officer," Hatchett said.

The two police officers nodded, exited the office, and were last heard tramping down the wooden steps.

Ward was angry. "What was that all about?"

"Calm down," Hatchett said. "Nicky's sorry, aren't you Nicky? We've got things to talk about."

"Stop calling me that. It's Nick."

"While you were outside, Nicky and I had a talk. He's going to get us a line on who took a shot at me."

Hatchett had moved to a position to one side of Peters, who had risen from his seat behind the desk. Ward walked to the other side.

"Okay, I held up my end of the bargain. Now, tell me more about these two in Birmingham."

Hatchett leaned on the side of the high backed chair.

"I told you, I don't know'em. I called them and told them I wanted them to put the fear'o God into somebody in Mauvilla."

"Who put you on to them?"

He took a deep breath and shrugged. "I don't know."

Hatchett grabbed Peters by the hair, pushed him down, back into the chair, and pulled his head back. In a millisecond, the switchblade in his right front pants pocket was out and extended. He put the blade to Peters' carotid.

"Hatchett, No!" Ward said.

"Shut up."

His voice was not loud, but there was a growl in his tone, as if he was in complete control, but like a dog, still enraged. It was a tone Ward had never heard before.

What she didn't know was that if Peters knew who killed Lisa Lemon, Hatchett intended to get it out of him.

"No, no!" Peters said. His tone was a whimper.

"Now, who killed Lisa Lemon?" He laid the steel to his neck. A single drop of blood appeared.

Peters hands began to shake. "I swear to you. I don't know. I loved her."

"Bullshit. Look, I'll cut your head off just like you did hers." He paused. "She was ripping off product, so the word came down, and you had to have her killed."

"No! No! I didn't, I swear it." He began to cry.

Hatchett pulled back harder on his hair. He put the blade right at Peters' Adams' apple. The scared man's bladder emptied onto the leather chair and, ultimately, the floor.

"Hatchett!" Ward said.

"She was doing everybody in the southeast, and you couldn't stand it. So you said if you couldn't have her, nobody would."

"No, no!"

"She was going to rat you guys out to the Feds."

"Nooooooo!"

Peters was crying profusely. Hatchett let go of the sobbing man's hair. He pulled the knife away from his neck and folded the blade, then slipped it back into his pocket. Peters bowed his head and put his face in his hands.

Hatchett had gone over all the possible motives for why Peters and the others might have had Lisa Lemon killed, and the crying man had denied them all. Hatchett was now absolutely convinced that her dope dealing friends had no part in her dismemberment. He stepped away and looked down at him.

"Okay, okay. Calm down. Now, just tell me who it was that took a shot at me. Where did you get that phone number?"

"From a guy named Cox. He hangs out over at Harriet's place here in town." His voice was muffled through his sobs. He wiped his eyes and tried to calm himself, and then he lifted each leg up off the chair to gauge the wetness of his pants.

"The accountant?"

Peters nodded. He took deep breaths and exhaled loudly.

Hatchett looked Ward and chuckled. "You got anything?"

She smirked. "Let's go."

"You're a son of a bitch, Hatchett," Peters said as they were walking out the door.

Hatchett stopped and turned back toward him. "The next time you send somebody to shoot me, Peters, you tell'em to make sure they do the job. 'Cause if they don't, I'm gonna come back up here and finish what I started."

CHAPTER 29

Downstairs, in the car, Ward was livid. She started the car and raced the engine four or five times.

"What are you trying to do?"

He looked at her and smiled. "Now, don't have a bitch fit. Everything's okay."

"That was assault and battery. By rights, you should be under arrest."

"First of all, you're a little out of your jurisdiction. Why don't you just leave the A & B collars to the local cops; that is, if Mr. Peters up there even wants to complain. Second, you know who that guy is, and what he does for a living. He deserved to be cuffed around a long time ago and a whole lot worse than what I just gave him. And third, we got what we wanted didn't we? We now know that Leon, Winterbush, and their organization didn't have anything to do with killing our girl." He paused. "I'm convinced. Aren't you?"

She drove in silence. Ward could think of no good responses to what he said. But she was a law enforcement officer, and her training told her that what she had just witnessed was wrong.

"That kind of thing can't happen again; not in my presence. It's just not right." Her tone was forthright, tough.

"It's not legal. But the morality of it, you're not sure about that, are you."

She was silent once again. When she spoke her tone was softer, not as judgmental.

"How about if I just turn you in?"

He looked at her with a face that was not shocked. "No, you won't. If you did, you'd have to answer for not doing anything about it before now." He paused. "Look, Peters knows who I am, but not you; Leon doesn't know either of us; and the police that we just met know only our names." He paused again. "Don't worry. You're golden. Just keep your head low and if there's any fall to be taken, it'll be mine. I've got a good lawyer and great insurance."

She drove in silence for three blocks. "Would you have done it?"

"What?"

"Killed him?"

He looked at her hard. Hatchett had killed, but never without thought and never without a good reason; either to save his life, or the life of someone else. Taking a life meant more to him than it did to the sociopathic thugs that populated the street. He was serious about his work, his life, and he wondered why no one could see his true purposes and motives. Then he spoke softly.

"Nawwww. Not with a witness."

She paused. "Just don't make things hard for me, Hatchett."

In twenty minutes, they were parked in the crumbling concrete parking lot of Harriet's Hideaway. It was early afternoon and only seven or eight cars, three of which were backed in so that their license plates were not visible, dotted the asphalt lot.

Ward parked and turned off the engine. She looked at Hatchett.

"Look, I don't know what you've got planned for in there, but please, don't go overboard again."

He grinned. "Okay, okay, I promise to be on my best behavior. Besides, if I know this smarmy bastard, he'll spill what I want to know pretty easily."

"What if he's not here?"

"He'll be here. He's got nothing better to do. He works for these people, and he's fat. The girls here are the only ones that'll give him the time of day."

A large bouncer guarded the front door. Hatchett paid him the cover charge - five bucks for himself, nothing for Ward - and they entered the darkened lounge. There was a lighted dance floor right in the middle of the room, and several tables broadcast about along the walls and up on a second level in the back. A long mahogany bar, easily the classiest and most expensive piece in the place, was immediately to the right. Hatchett stopped in the doorway and scanned the length of it.

A grossly obese man who could only be W.C. Cox sat perched on a stool at the far end. He wore a baby blue leisure suit, and his pink, ruffled shirt was open almost to the navel. A garish gold chain hung around his neck and lay on top of his hairy and globular abdomen. His face was round and red under slicked back, black hair.

Hatchett turned to Ward and nodded toward the man. They walked his direction.

"You Cox?" Hatchett said when they were within three feet.

"Who wants to know?"

"My name's Mark. I'm from Alabama. This is JoAnn."

"Well, hey, honey," he said nodding at Ward. She smirked.

"Nick sent us. We want to talk to you."

He chuckled. "What's my old buddy Nick up to these days?"

"Last time we saw him, he was so busy he was losin' his head." He looked at Ward and smiled. "He said you were the guy to see for information."

He looked around. "I am, if the price is right."

"Can we talk?"

He slipped off the stool and jerked his head toward a door behind him. "Come on."

The three walked into a small, dirty office. Cox walked around to the back side of a desk that was choked with papers and file folders. Hatchett and Ward took seats in wooden chairs across from him. A small oscillating fan was vainly attempting to cool the hot space, but beads of sweat almost immediately began appearing on Cox's forehead.

"How can I help you folks?" Cox said. He took out a handkerchief and wiped his brow.

"Just a name, W.C. Can I call you W.C.?" Hatchett said.

"Call me Billy. Everybody does." He paused and looked from one to the other. "How'd you folks find me?"

"Nick Peters. He told us where you were. What we want is the name of the folks in Birmingham. You know, the guys that do the 'special jobs.'"

He looked at Hatchett with raised eyebrows. He looked down at his desk and then back up.

"Now, what do want to know about them boys for?"

"Sure. See, JoAnn's got an old man that likes to beat her. We'd like to get that problem handled, you know? Nick said that they did a job for him, puttin' a scare into some guy down near the coast."

He looked at Ward and nodded. "I see. Well, we can't have that, can we now, little lady." He smiled at her, displaying badly stained teeth.

"So, what do you say, Billy?"

He looked at them again, ostensibly gauging their guilessness. Then he pulled a pen from his inside coat pocket.

"I can give you a number." He wrote it on a small piece of paper. "But, it'll cost you a c-note."

Hatchett looked at Ward. She shook her head. Then he reached for his hip pocket. He pulled out a leather billfold and extracted two fifties. He held them out. Cox did the same with the piece of paper. They exchanged them at the same time. Hatchett looked at the paper. On it was a phone number with a two o five area code.

"Now, you're sure these are the guys?"

"They can solve your problem."

"That's good." He paused and looked down at the number again. "We heard about another job they did down there."

He looked away. "You know, I really don't want to know."

"We heard they killed a prostitute down there; cut her head off."

He looked up. "I don't know nothin' about that."

"It was in all the papers."

He shook his head hard. "Nope. No, no, no, no."

Hatchett nodded then looked at Ward. "You see honey, I told you he could help." Ward smirked. "These guys'll take care of Louis, and then me and you can . . ."

Hatchett winked and grinned, then leaned in to nuzzle her. Ward backed away.

Cox grinned and all three rose from their chairs. "Ya'll take care now," he said.

In the car, Hatchett and Ward made the decision to start for home. It would be late when they arrived, but Ward had no desire to remain in Nashville any longer. Inside her, she was afraid of what Hatchett would do next. She drove the first leg.

When they were fifty miles down the road, Ward spoke.

"You think these people in Birmingham have something to do with Lisa Lemon's death?"

Hatchett was sitting in the passenger seat with his eyes closed. "I don't know. I just took a shot. His reaction sure indicated they were. Anyway, as far as I'm concerned, it was a pretty productive trip. I didn't think it would be, but it was."

"How do you figure?"

"Well, we know now that her drug dealings didn't get her killed. Peters and Leon were such weasels, if they'd had a part in it, they would surely have spilled it. Leon cried like a baby and Peters pissed his pants. They couldn't have kept it a secret if it was true."

"What about the other guy, Winterbush?"

"If he's the money guy like they say, he'd never know whether or not she was killed. Drug syndicates are pretty compartmentalized. Everybody at the top wants deniability."

"So what makes you think the guys Peters used to try to kill you might be involved?"

"Well, Peters didn't use them to kill Lemon, but that doesn't mean someone else didn't. These people sound a little like 'Murder Incorporated,' that bunch from the thirties, up in New York, who took contracts to kill. They eliminated problems and specialized in message murders, like Lisa Lemon's. What we've got to do is find out about these people and then find out who they know that knew our girl."

"How do we do that?"

"Well," he smiled at her, "we could use the direct approach: threaten them to within an inch of their lives and hope they tell the truth."

She smirked. "That sounds dangerous. And, besides, I'm still in the business of looking for evidence to make an arrest."

"Okay, okay. You're right. So, what we have to do is to work this from two angles. One, we've got to gather intelligence on whoever this is in Birmingham; and, two, we've got to continue to learn who had a motive to kill her and then try to connect them to these guys. That is, if the Birmingham Boys are involved in our case; and that's not for certain, yet."

Ward said nothing else, as they rode in silence. Even with all she had seen, she felt a sense of exhilaration mixed with her fear. Yes, his methods were wrong, but in a strange way they were just. The bad guys paid, and in ways that they might never otherwise. She had laughed within herself when Peters' bowels had let go and he had wet himself. Still, the tone of Hatchett's voice had given her a shiver when he told her to 'shut up.'

As they rode, Hatchett was thinking, too. He was thinking that, though it was Ward's job to gather evidence to make an arrest and prove a case, when he was found, the man that had cut off the head of Lisa Lemon would have to be killed.

CHAPTER 30

They arrived back in Mauvilla at midnight. Ward dropped Hatchett off at his office where he spent the night. It was the next morning before he showered, shaved, and otherwise purged himself of the trip.

Before he left her, Hatchett put Ward in charge of the Birmingham telephone number. She was to trace the number to a building or residence – if need be getting a subpoena for an unlisted exchange – and work up background information on the names of any persons connected with the number.

He'd spent the rest of the trip home lost in a silent brainstorming session about the case. If the Nashville drug ring was no longer a possibility, he had to gin up additional suspects.

It was only a hunch when he first mentioned it, but his theory that the fixers in Birmingham were somehow tied to Lisa Lemon's killing was stuck in his brain. If her death was a message killing, even something more personal, then it made perfect sense that someone who wanted her dead would hire a professional to have it done.

He picked up the telephone in his office the afternoon after his trip.

"Ms Boatman, Mark Hatchett. How are you doing?"

He heard a sigh on the other end of the line. "I guess we're holding our own. Is there anything new?"

"Well, the case is not solved, no ma'am. We don't know who killed your daughter. But we've eliminated a couple of people as suspects, and we've got a couple of promising leads.

"You sound confident . . . or hopeful, anyway."

"I'm trying not to sound either. These cases are like birthing a baby, Ms Boatman. The child comes when it wants to, not before. But when it happens, it usually happens quickly."

"I'm prayin' every day."

"Well, keep prayin', Ms Boatman. In the meantime, I want to ask you a little more about Melinda's past."

"I'll tell you all I can remember."

"Where did she go when she left home?"

"You mean, after high school?"

"Right."

"Well, she spent a semester in junior college; Lower Mississippi Junior College over in Greene County."

Hatchett was writing quickly. "What about after that?"

"After that, she called us from Jackson, said she had gotten a job as a secretary."

"How long was she there?"

"Oh, I don't know, only a little while. Six months, I guess; maybe less."

"Where'd she go then?"

There was silence on the other end of the line. "Memphis, I think."

Hatchett paused. "Any idea why she left junior college so quick?"

"No, not really. You know who'd know, though, is her friend Eileen, Eileen Woodard. She went off to school with her. They was roommates in the, uh, the, uh, dormitory over there."

Why hadn't he thought of this already. "You got a number for her?"

"Sure, well, I say sure, I got her mama's number. They live up the road about a mile." She recited a Mississippi exchange.

"Do you know who she hung out with up in Memphis?"

"No. To tell you the truth, I think that's where she started dancin'."

"Do you know anyone who knew her well?"

"Nobody 'cept the people she grew up with."

"Did she ever correspond with any of them?"

"I'm rackin' my brain, but I can't think of a soul."

Hatchett paused. "Okay, well, I'll give this Eileen a call."

Mary Boatman paused. "I need to know, Mr. Hatchett."

"I'm working as hard as I can."

"And, when you find him?"

"I know what to do."

Hatchett reached Eileen Woodard by telephone later in the afternoon. She was married and living in Brandon, Mississippi, just east of Jackson.

"Nobody lives in Jackson anymore," she said. Her voice was husky, and she had a pronounced southern accent.

Hatchett identified himself and told her why he was calling. She sounded open and receptive. Her last name was now Winters.

"When's the last time you talked to Melinda Boatman?"

Hatchett heard her sigh on the other end. "Wow, that's a name I thought I'd never hear again. We went to high school together."

"How about junior college? Didn't you guys know each other then?"

"You know, you're right. We did room together for a semester. I'd forgotten that."

"Tell me about her?"

"Well, I don't 'member much. Mindy was always real friendly with the boys. As I recall, she kinda filled out the summer before we went off, if ya know what I mean. At JC she had a lotta dates. She was real outgoin' and laughed a lot."

"Any boy in particular?"

"Not that I remember. She usually went with anybody that asked her. It was football season, you know, and she always had a date for the home games."

"Have any idea why she dropped out?"

"You know, I don't. She seemed to be real worried about a grade in some class or the other, and when she didn't do well, I think she lost interest."

"Which class was it?"

"Psychology, no, it was Sociology, I think."

Hatchett's heart skipped. "You wouldn't happen to know the instructor's name would you?"

"Now, let me see. I took the same class in the summer." There was silence on the other end. "You know, I really don't."

"Try, Ms Winters, this is pretty important."

He heard her exhale on the other end. "I think his name was . . . Cabot."

Hatchett was off the phone with Eileen Winters and on the phone with Ward within five minutes.

"Do we have enough to check a criminal history on Glenn Cabot?"

"Who?"

"One of the Sociology dudes we talked to in Montgomery, at the University."

He could hear her flipping through her notes. "Oh, yeah. Well, if we don't, I can get it."

"Check his record. We're looking for a history of sex offenses."

He paused while she wrote.

"What's this all about?" she said.

"I think we can connect Cabot to our victim when she was in junior college. And, I think something happened then that did two things: it turned her to the sex industry . . . and it may have gotten her killed."

Hatchett met Ward for coffee down at Walt's two hours later. She had some of the information he wanted.

"No criminal history on Cabot except a couple of speeding tickets, and one DUI. He's pretty clean."

"You got anything yet on the Birmingham people?"

"I'm still working on it. I've got a name for the phone number, but I'm still trying to locate an address." She paused and looked up from her notes. "What's this all about?"

Hatchett blew on his coffee and took small sip. He recounted his conversation with Eileen Winters.

"You think something happened between Melinda Boatman and Glenn Cabot when she took his class in college?"

"I do. Winters said that she was all happy as a clam until she started having trouble in this Sociology class. Winters thought it was about grades. I think he raped, or tried to rape her. After that, she lost interest, dropped out of school, and moved to Memphis. Her mother thinks she started dancing up there."

"And, . . ."

"And, if they did know each other, then Cabot would have a reason to both to fall in love with her again, and to ultimately shut her mouth."

"You think she threatened to expose him to his family?"

"Or, to the school," Hatchett said taking another sip.

"But who'd believe her, even if she did tell?"

"It wouldn't matter. She might just create enough of a stink to make life miserable for him."

"I wonder what could have set her off?" Ward said.

"I know what set her off. If all this is true, I bet when she saw his face, the clock rolled back, and it all came back to her. When he started babbling all that shit about 'bein' in love,' she lost it. That was all it took."

Ward's face was pensive. Perhaps there was an incident in her own past, Hatchett thought.

Hatchett took a bite of a cinnamon roll. "My guess is that when he saw her, he had a flashback to his younger days, too. Back then, he probably got all he wanted from those young junior college chicks. He probably thought she would fall for him like he thought she fell for him back then. I bet it never occurred to him that some of those girls didn't want to sleep with him."

"So everything he told us was a lie?"

"Well, probably not everything. But the part about them leaving on good terms was."

She took a sip of coffee. "So what do we do now?"

He took a deep breath and exhaled. "You know what I'd like to be able to do. I'd like to be able to connect Cabot to our boys up in Birmingham."

"You still think they're involved."

"I still think they can point us to the killer. What was the name you got from the phone number?"

She flipped through her notebook. "It was Raoul Harris."

Hatchett chuckled and shook his head. "Sounds made up to me."

"How so?"

"A guy named Raoul is the person that James Earl Ray said killed Martin Luther King. He was from Birmingham, too."

Ward raised her eyebrows and tilted her head. "Small world."

CHAPTER 31

In two days, Ward had additional information. She contacted Hatchett at his office by telephone.

"We're gonna need to get a subpoena for the phone number up in Birmingham," Ward said. "I'm working on the affidavit, but I'm wondering how we're going to connect our case with that phone number."

"We don't have to. We'll just use my assault case, and W.C. Cox as a cooperating informant. The PD in Nashville will attest to his veracity in the past and that should be enough."

"Okay, I'll use your case. It was a PD report?"

"Yeah. It happened the night we got back from Montgomery."

"Good. I'll finish up and call you back."

An hour later, Ward was back on the phone. "We've got a meeting at the DA's office in an hour. Can you make it?"

"I'll be there."

An hour and a half later, Hatchett and Ward were seated in the hall outside the office of Chief Assistant District Attorney Jill Murphy.

"When I was in this racket, all we had to do was tell the Circuit Clerk what we wanted, get the subpoena from them and go serve it. Why do we have to talk to this woman?" Hatchett said.

"She runs the Grand Jury. The DA has decided that the system is getting too clogged up with paperwork, and Murphy has to approve any requests for subpoenas."

"Sounds like she doesn't trust you."

"It's not that . . . well, maybe it is that. But mostly it's the need for control. I think a lot of officers were threatening people with subpoenas, and then once they got them, they were never returned, with or without evidence. The subpoena was kind of losing its power."

"Seems like kind of a waste of time, to me."

"Just humor her."

A secretary stepped out and beckoned them into the office. Murphy was writing when they sat down.

"I'll be with you in a minute," she said.

Hatchett and Ward took seats across the desk from her. Murphy was a short, thin woman with shoulder length, mousy brown hair who was dressed in pants and a white blouse. She had a turned up nose, gray eyes, and a business-like carriage. When she finished, she looked up. She was not smiling.

"So, you folks want a subpoena duces tecom."

Ward spoke. "Yes, ma'am. We'd like to get information about a telephone number up in Birmingham."

Murphy looked at Hatchett. "I've met Detective Ward. Who might you be?"

"This is Mark Hatchett. He's the victim."

"The victim?" She leaned back and took off her half-moon glasses. "Fill me in."

Ward spoke again. "Mr. Hatchett is a local Inquiry Agent. He was retained by the family of a murder victim to look into her case."

"Which one?"

"Lisa Lemon, aka Melinda Boatman, ma'am. She was a prostitute found beheaded just north of the city. Mr. Hatchett and I are sort of working this thing cooperatively."

"That's a little unusual, isn't it?"

"Not really. We have converging interests, and the family is from out of state. Truthfully, they just wanted someone over whom they had control to keep them informed."

Murphy looked at Hatchett with distaste.

"At any rate, after a recent trip to Montgomery where we interviewed several witnesses, Mr. Hatchett was shot at, and wounded, actually. The suspects were traced to Nashville, Tennessee.

"We went to Nashville, spoke with the Metro Police up there, and they referred us to an informant who has been reliable for them in the past. This informant gave us a telephone number of a kind of a syndicate in Birmingham that specializes in murder, or at least assaults for hire."

She paused and looked at Hatchett. Then she continued.

"The phone company gave me the name of the individual to whom the number is listed, however they refused to provide the address and other identifying information without a subpoena." She paused. "So, here we are."

"Who did the phone come back to?"

"A 'Raoul Harris.'"

"Hmm. Sounds made up."

"That's what we thought."

"And, who is this informant in Nashville?"

"His name is W.C. Cox. He is a known underworld character who is actually an accountant for several businesses up there."

"And he just volunteered this information?"

"Well, actually, Mr. Hatchett purchased it from him for a hundred dollars."

Murphy looked at Hatchett. "Is this true?"

"It is."

"So how does this all relate to the prostitute case?"

Ward spoke. "We know the men who shot Mr. Hatchett were employed by a man named Nicholas Peters. Peters was a consociate with Lisa Lemon; they were in the drug business together. We believe that knowing who these hit men are 'may' lead us to Lisa Lemon's killer, or at least to who may have hired them."

"Is this Peters a suspect?"

"Actually, no. Not at this time."

"Well, seems to me he'd be a pretty good one."

"It is entirely possible that he is, however, there are actually several people with a motive for killing her."

"Do any of them have access to these people in Birmingham?"

"We don't know."

"So you want this information to lean on this group in Birmingham in hopes they once you find them, they will tell you who their client list is?"

"Yes, ma'am."

Hatchett was sitting in the leather chair fuming. Why, he thought, did it take an act of Congress to get an address from the telephone company.

"Now, will the phone company give you this information?"

"Yes, ma'am." Ward's tone was completely deferential. "I have their commitment."

Murphy closed her eyes and appeared lost in thought for a minute. At least until Hatchett could no longer stand it.

"Son of a bitch!" he said.

He rose from his chair and began stalking around the room. "All we want is a fuckin' subpoena. Somebody shot me, and I want to find out who did it. Is that too much to ask?"

Murphy was completely shocked. Her eyes shot wide open, her brows went up, and her chin fell.

"If we knew all the answers we'd've put these bastards in jail already," he said. "Is all this debate really necessary?"

Murphy was stunned and speechless, for a moment. Then she cleared her throat and looked wide-eyed at Ward.

"Well, okay. I'll have my secretary type it up."

CHAPTER 32

While Ward spent the next two days securing the information in response to the subpoena, Hatchett had other ideas.

But first he met with Jasmine, or Becky Arnold, at a diner around the corner from her apartment. It was a greasy spoon, but Hatchett knew it had good coffee. He ordered some for both of them and took a long look at the young woman before he spoke.

"So, how are you gettin' along?" he said.

"Oh, fine, I guess." She paused. "You know, I'm out of the business now."

"Dancing?"

"Yeah. I went home and made peace with Mom and Dad. They want me to go to school, so I'm gonna enroll in junior college."

"You still living at the same place?"

She nodded. "For a little while. Well, not in the same apartment. The manager moved me over to a new one. I'll be there 'til the lease runs out. I couldn't stand to stay in there where Lindsey . . ."

Hatchett nodded and took a sip. "I can imagine."

He really couldn't. Hatchett had seen so much death the thought of staying where someone had died made no difference to him at all.

"Well, I think that's good; you gettin' an education and all." He paused. "You always knew that other thing wasn't permanent, didn't you? I mean, it was only going to last as long as your looks, right?"

She nodded. "Yeah. Well, I mean, it wasn't in my head all the time. It just seemed real glamorous like. Show biz, you know?" She looked away, out the window. "But it's really a pretty dirty business. I just hadn't seen how dirty, 'til Lindsey died."

Hatchett took another sip, and Becky Arnold looked down at the table.

"Well, so about why I called you. I need some information about Lisa. Did she ever say anything about dancing in Memphis? A club she worked at? Somebody she knew there? Anything?"

Becky looked up. "Yeah, I think so. She only talked about it once or twice. She said she'd started up there; said she'd worked at a club called, Grace's,

I think; said it was on the south side near Elvis's house."

"She talk about anybody?"

"Just the woman who ran the place; said her name was Chloe Grace."

Hatchett nodded. "Can you remember anything else that Lisa ever said about the business?"

Becky Arnold closed her eyes. "Just one thing."

Hatchett looked at her.

"She told me I ought to get out of it."

The next morning, early, Hatchett made his way up US 49 to Jackson, Mississippi, then north on the Interstate highway to Memphis. Graceland Boulevard ran east and west skirting the south side of town. Hatchett found Grace's about a mile east of Graceland on the north side of the highway. It was a cinderblock building with a pink neon sign just above the door that spelled out the name. Hatchett parked in front. It was right at noon, and the early shift was just starting.

There was no doorman on duty so Hatchett walked right in. Two women were putting food on a steamer table for the lunch buffet.

Inside, he found the middle aged bartender washing glasses at the far end of the bar. Hatchett sat down on the stool in front of the man, who had a round face and the bald head.

"Hey, is Grace available?"

"I don't know. Who's askin'"

"My name's Hatchett, from Alabama. I need to talk to her."

"You a cop?"

"No."

"IRS?"

Hatchett chuckled. They were obviously the two dirtiest words that the bartender could think of.

"No."

"What's this about?"

"Just tell her it's about Lisa Lemon."

He smirked. "I'll see if she's in."

He walked through an unmarked door to his right. In a minute he opened the door and motioned for Hatchett to enter.

Chloe Grace was seated at her desk writing in a ledger. She looked to be sixty, a wizened woman with gray hair and glasses held around her neck by a chain. A cigarette hung loosely from her lips, and she had a mole just off the right corner of her mouth. When he got closer, Hatchett saw one hair emanating from that mole. The bartender left the door open, and Hatchett made no effort to shut it.

"Sit down." Her voice was raspy and deep, and she coughed up phlegm.

Hatchett took a seat across the desk from her in the cluttered office and folded his arms.

She finished her writing and looked up from the ledger. "I don't believe I know you, Mr. Hatchett. Who's this Lisa Lemon?"

"I'm sure you don't, ma'am. I'm from Mauvilla, Alabama. I'm a private detective workin' on a case down there; the death of a girl named Lisa Lemon. You might know her as Mindy, or Melinda, Boatman."

She dropped her pencil, and her mouth fell open. "Mindy's dead?"

"Murdered."

"Who? Why?"

"Don't know who, and don't know why. I thought you might could help me. I understand this is the first place she ever danced."

The old woman shook her head. She was clearly stunned. Hatchett saw that her hands were shaking. She put out her cigarette and immediately lit another. Hatchett didn't speak. The woman leaned back in her chair and swallowed, then took a long drag, exhaled, and coughed again.

"Mindy was like a daughter to me. She come up here completely green; I mean she didn't know which end was up. I got her on stage, showed her how to dance, and she started makin' real money for herself. She ended up a headliner. She stayed here about two years and then lit out. I told her not to go, that she had a pretty good thing goin' on here, but she said she could make more money movin' about."

"She get along with everybody here?"

She paused. "I can't think of a single person she didn't get along with. Everbody liked Mindy."

"Anybody from outside, maybe?"

She shook her head. "You gotta understand we run pretty tight ship here. Yeah, we have trouble with drunks ever now and then, and we deal with it, but we don't 'low no drugs and such as that in here."

"Did Mindy just leave, or did somebody recruit her?"

"You know, I don't know. Prob'ly somebody filled her head with how she could do better, but I never met'em."

"How about lovers? She ever make it with anybody?"

"You know, now that you mention it, her and another one of the girls had a thing."

"Mindy was bi?"

"Well, not when she come. But she kinda' fell for one of the girls. Now, let me see, her name was . . ."

Hatchett got out a pad and a pen and prepared to write. A female lover, he thought, would sure be a longshot as a suspect.

"I think it was Tonya, uh, her name was, uh, Whitman, Janice Whitman."

"Any idea where she is today?"

"Oh, no, not really. I heard once she was in Pensacola, at a place call Sandy's, but I don't know for sure. She would be gettin' a little long in the tooth for dancin.' She wasn't a babe back then."

"What does she look like?"

Grace described a white female, about five two with big bones and very muscular. She said that a surprising number of men liked that look. As best Grace could remember, Whitman had an olive complexion and dyed blonde hair.

"She called herself Tonya, when she was here."

Hatchett nodded and finished writing. "Anything else you can think of that might help?"

Grace tilted her head and took a drag on her cigarette. She blew the smoke into the air.

"No, I just hate to hear that about Mindy. You know she used to come over to the house all the time, right after my divorce; helped me with the house work, even cooked a little. I was in pretty bad shape back then." She shook her head.

"She ever say what made her want to get into dancing?"

"No. She come from down in Mississippi, somewhere; and seems like she went to college somewheres but somethin' happened, and she had to drop out."

"She say what happened?"

"No. It was grades, I think."

"I didn't ask you this, but did she ever hook out of here?"

"If she did, I didn't know about it." Grace pointed her finger at him. "I don't allow no hookin' in here. We dance, sell drinks, we even got a buffet for lunch, but that's it. The girls know that when they come here." She nodded her head once, hard, for emphasis.

Hatchett thought for a minute what else he could ask. "What's your name Grace, if you don't mind."

"Presley."

Hatchett smiled. If she didn't want to tell, she didn't have to. "What name did Mindy use when she worked here?"

"Oh, Mindy called herself 'Olivia Orange.'"

Hatchett nodded while hiding a smile.

Hatchett was back in Mauvilla, and in his office, by nightfall. He sat down at his desk and began eating an apple he bought from the small grocer two blocks from his apartment that stayed open until midnight. Then he checked his answering service.

"Hey, Peaches," he said. "Guess what I'm eating?"

"Uhhh, an apple."

"How'd you know?"

"Women's intuition."

"Ha. Anything for me?"

"Yeah, Detective Ward called. And you got a call from Larry. He said he had something for you."

Hatchett noted the names on his blotter. He took down Larry's phone number.

"Larry say what he wanted?"

"Nope, but he did sound a bit agitated."

"Hmmmm."

"Somethin' big breakin'?"

"Probably not. Old Larry's too dramatic. He prob'ly just wants to tell me about the newest stripper that he's in love with, or some other such thing."

"I almost got into that once."

Hatchett's ears pricked. "Dancing?"

"Yeah. My boyfriend wouldn't let me. He told me it was a slutty job."

"You still got the boyfriend?"

"Oh, no."

"Well, then, the world's your oyster."

"Nope. This is a good job, and I'm working on something else."

"Well, alright. Spill it."

"Not yet."

"How about over dinner?"

"Ha, ha." Her laughter trailed off as she hung up.

Hatchett took a look at the two messages. Ward could wait until tomorrow. He'd call Larry tonight.

"What's up, Larry?"

"Hey, where you been?"

"Outta town. What's up?"

"Look, I gotta see ya. Can you meet me?"

"Is this important? It's not about some new girl at the club, is it?"

"Well, no."

Hatchett took a deep breath and exhaled. "Same place, in ten minutes."

Twelve minutes later, Hatchett got out of the Merc and walked over to the large pillar near the entrance to the parking garage. He leaned against the post and waited for Larry to stumble down the concrete incline. He arrived in about five minutes.

"Hey," Larry said. "You're here."

"I said I would be, didn't I?"

"Yeah, but I called earlier . . ."

"What'chu got Larry?"

"You know that guy that came into the club talkin' about Lisa?"

"Which one?"

"The black guy, a light skinned black guy; 'member, I told you about him?"

"Oh, yeah. The one that said she was killed over drugs?"

"Yeah, yeah. Well, he was back again."

"What'd he say?"

"He just keeps sayin' that Lisa was killed over drugs. He says that he's sure of it."

"You get this guy's name?"

"No, he never said. He was talkin' to one of the girls."

"Which one?"

"Jewel."

"That the one you like?"

"Yeah. You know, *'Diamonds are forever, forever, forever,'"* he sang the song lyrics.

"Oh, yeah."

I just might have to pay this Jewel a visit, Hatchett thought.

"So, you told me to keep my ears open, right?"

"I did."

"So, I did good, right?"

"Perfect, Larry."

"So, what'cha think about that coke?"

"Still not enough, Larry. Keep working."

As he drove back to his office, Hatchett thought about the light skinned black man who kept coming to the club talking about Lisa Lemon. It sounded a lot like Louis Hart, Lisa Lemon's old running buddy. It was clear that whoever he was, he wanted to plant a seed about the motive for her murder.

He rubbed his eyes and his temples. He was beginning to feel the stress of a case that was now dragging through its second month. Who knew how much longer it was going to last and how much more it was going to take out of him.

The whole case, in his mind, was getting completely out of hand. The suspect list was growing, not shrinking; and if the boys in Birmingham were somehow involved, there was no telling where it might ultimately lead, and how large it might get. Lisa Lemon knew a thousand people, any number of which might have a reason to kill her.

CHAPTER 33

Sandy's Lounge was located in the seven hundred block of Harper Street in Pensacola. It was a nice place, as those types of places went; so nice, the management had taken to calling it a 'gentlemen's club,' instead of a strip joint. Hatchett had departed home at about noon so he could arrive just at opening time. He wasn't sure what he'd find, if anything.

He had called Ward early in the morning, before he left town. She told him that the grand jury subpoena was on its way to the phone company, and she expected to get the information back before the close of business. In the meantime, she had touched base with the FBI in Birmingham, and they told her they had no knowledge of any hit squad doing business in Birmingham or anywhere else in the south. Hatchett told her he wasn't surprised.

Hatchett parked his car on the west side of the building and entered the front door of Sandy's at a little after one. The door man, a full bodied man with large arms, took the five dollar cover charge.

When he was inside, he found himself a small table on the upper tier overlooking the runway. There were only four or five men in the place, all of them middle aged, trying to pretend they were young again; trying to get that last erection before it was no longer possible, Hatchett thought.

A waitress who was attractive enough to be a dancer came to his table for the purpose of getting his drink order. She wore a very short skirt and a transparent blouse.

"What'll it be, sir?"

"A glass of orange juice and little bit of information." Hatchett held up a ten.

She took the money and slid it into the pocket of her skirt.

"I'm looking for a dancer named Tonya, real name is Janice Whitman." He paused. "Blonde, maybe a little older than the other girls."

"Jan? Yeah, she's in the back. You want her?"

"Yeah. Ask her to step out and talk to me."

"Sure. I'll get your drink."

Hatchett watched as she walked toward the bar. The bartender, another weightlifter-type wearing a yellow pullover shirt and jeans, looked his way and gave him the stink eye.

The waitress brought back his orange juice, and he paid her two bucks. She left, and Hatchett settled back for the show.

A young girl who couldn't have been much more than eighteen was walking back on forth on the stage while the rest of the room was enraptured. Hatchett's gaze was diverted when a mid-thirties blonde wearing a pink and purple dressing gown walked over to his table. She was just as Grace had described her.

"You wanted to see me?" Her voice was light and breathy without a trace of accent.

"You Janice Whitman?"

"Yeah."

"Sit down. My name's Hatchett. I'm a private detective from over in Mauvilla."

She took a seat, but the look of defensive curiosity that was in her body language - brows upraised, arms folded across her chest, seat on the edge of her chair - was noticeable.

"Did you work at a club called Grace's, up in Memphis back a few years ago?"

She leaned back and smiled. "Gee, I haven't thought about that place in years. Yeah, I did."

"Do you remember a girl named Mindy, Mindy Boatman; Olivia Orange?"

She swallowed hard and a blank look fell over her face. She looked away, at the floor, and spoke.

"Is Mindy in some kind of trouble?"

Hatchett leaned forward. "Janice, I'm afraid I've got some bad news for you." He paused, and she looked at him. "Mindy is deceased."

Janice Whitman sat stunned for a second then began to go to pieces. She put her hands over her face and began to sob convulsively. Hatchett sat back to give her as much time as she needed.

It was only a minute later when he felt a hand on his left shoulder. He turned to find the burly bartender standing behind him.

"All right, buddy. Let's go."

Hatchett looked up at him. "Get lost."

He felt the man's grip tighten.

"I said, let's go."

Hatchett spun in his seat and grabbed the man's crotch with his right hand, finding his testicles easily in his loose fitting jeans. The man froze.

"Look, Carl or Bubba, or whatever your name is, I didn't hurt the lady. I just gave her some sad news. Now, go on and leave us alone, or I'm going to yank out your reason for living."

The man nodded his head and relaxed. Hatchett did the same. He stepped back two steps, and Hatchett turned back toward Whitman.

It was only a second later, but Hatchett heard the bartender at his back and turned quickly to find him swinging a leather sapper. Hatchett ducked, narrowly avoiding the blow. In a millisecond, he caught the man's arm by the wrist with both his hands while on its follow through. He stood up, bent the man's arm back behind him, and pushed it upward, toward his neck. The man grimaced and bent over. Hatchett relieved him of his blackjack, and then pushed him forward so that he fell on the floor face first.

"Stop, stop!" Janice Whitman stood up. She was still crying. "Stop, I said! Leonard, it's okay. It's okay. He didn't do anything. Leave him alone!"

Leonard, the bartender, looked up. "You sure, Babe?" he grunted.

"Yes, yes. Go away, please."

The big man got up, dusted himself, and stalked back to his position behind the bar while rubbing his arm. Hatchett slipped the blackjack into his vest pocket and then sat back down, as did Whitman. She wiped her eyes and tried to compose herself.

"I'm sorry," she said.

"Don't mention it." He paused. "You loved her didn't you?" he said.

"Yes, I did. She was beautiful, inside and out."

"When's the last time you talked to her?"

"I don't know, maybe six or eight months ago." She looked at him with tear stained eyes. "What happened?"

"She was murdered." He said it fast to get it over with. There was no need to traumatize her with the details.

"But, who?"

"We don't know. Her mother hired me to work with the police to find out. Did you see her six months ago?"

"Oh, no. I haven't seen her since, well, maybe a year ago. But we wrote and talked on the phone."

"Do you know why she left Memphis?"

"She told me some guy from Nashville sold her on being a circuit showgirl, a headliner, rather than staying at one place. I mean, we all move around, but not on a weekly basis."

"Did she break it off with you, or vice versa?"

"She had talent; she left. I got no offers, so I had to stay.

"Did you ask her to stay?"

"I didn't want to stand in her way."

"Did she ever mention having trouble with anyone? Whether anyone was angry with her or wanted to hurt her?"

"Mindy was always complaining about the men she danced for." She paused. "But she did say that a guy that she had gotten into trouble with a few years ago had contacted her. It was some kind of thing, I don't know. She said she was a little nervous about that, but that he was really an all right guy, and she thought it would be okay."

"She say who this guy was?"

"No." She shook her head.

"She say anything about him at all?"

"No."

"Did you ask? Did she seem evasive?"

"I really didn't ask. I'm always just so glad to hear from her."

"Was Mindy into drugs pretty heavily?"

Whitman sighed. "Look, we all do a little something to get us through. Mindy used, sure. She said she wasn't hooked, but . . ."

"You think otherwise?"

"There was just something in her voice."

"Can you think of anything else that might help?"

She looked at the table and shook her head slowly. Neither of them spoke. Finally, she looked up.

"No. Nothing."

"Was Mindy bisexual, or, just . . . experimenting?"

He asked the question with a specific purpose in mind. Hatchett didn't think Janice Whitman had cut anyone's head off, but stranger things had happened. If you carry a torch for that long, anything's possible, he thought.

Whitman looked up with alert eyes. "She loved me. Whether she went that way or not, she loved me. She said so."

"I understand."

Hatchett slipped her his business card and told her to call if she remembered anything else. He rose from the table.

"I'm sorry to have to bring you this news, but I guess you'd've heard it from somewhere else anyway, eventually, hunh?"

She shrugged. He turned slowly and walked in front of the bar, past Leonard, and then out the front door, pausing only to drop the sapper in a trash can by the exit.

In an hour he was back in Mauvilla and in his office. Hatchett put his feet on his desk and tried to reflect on what he had learned.

This Louis Hart character was being more frequently mentioned. There was motive, but nothing else to link him to the murder. Just like everyone else.

There was Cabot, the college professor; Hart the criminal consort; Whitman the jilted lover; the hit for hire guys in Birmingham who could be working for anyone; and who knows who else that she danced for or just met on the side of the road who couldn't contain himself and just had to kill her.

In minutes Hatchett was asleep. The traveling and the late nights were taking their toll. He was fully gone when the phone rang loudly thirty minutes later.

"Yeah." His voice was groggy.

"Hey, it's Ward."

"Oh."

"I'm sorry. Were you asleep?"

"Yeah, as a matter of fact. What'cha got?"

"I got what we need from Birmingham. And, I was able to get some background on Cabot."

Hatchett perked up. "Yeah?"

"Apparently, he's got a problem."

Hatchett yawned and stretched. "Meet me at Walt's in an hour."

After finishing a little something of what he started, Hatchett stumbled into the diner ninety minutes later. Ward was seated in the corner looking peeved.

"Where were you?"

"Sleeping. I'm really tired."

"Well, while you've been sleeping, I've been working." She slid a manila folder toward him.

He opened the folder and looked at the papers. He scanned the pages quickly.

"So teacher's had a lot of pets," he said. "Is there a file here from the Mindy Boatman's junior college?"

"No, but I called around and there are files from a couple of other schools. You think Lisa Lemon knew about them?"

"I don't, but that doesn't matter. She knew what happened to her and whatever allegation she might have made would get this university checking into him, too." He paused. "If the college he works at now kept him employed after knowing what he's done, they could get sued. They might have trouble sweeping this under rug."

"You think she wanted to get him fired?"

"I think she wanted money."

"Blackmail?"

"Maybe."

"So, what do we do now?"

"We've got to think of a way to get him to admit what he did to her. That might give us cause to search his house, and, who knows what we'll find."

"I doubt that'll be enough."

"That what you learned in college? How to give all the breaks to the criminals?"

She smirked. "It's the law."

"Well, sometimes, the law stinks."

"It's all we've got, Hatchett."

"Not all."

They were both silent. "What if we could either confirm or debunk his alibi?" she said.

"That's another way to go."

Hatchett sipped a glass of water, and Ward looked out of the window. She knew what he was talking about. The name of Mike Allenwood was still in the back of her mind.

"So, what's your plan about the Birmingham thing?"

He spoke trying to include, but also to placate her. Her inexperience was not helping them. Clearly, this was a different kind of case and it would require unorthodox methods to solve it.

She took a deep breath, exhaled, and said nothing. She was obviously in over her head.

He looked her in the eye. "Okay. I've got a plan, but it may require that we do some things that are a bit outside the box. If you don't feel you can bring yourself to be involved, I understand completely. This is your livelihood, and I don't want to ruin it for you."

She looked down, then up. "Would any of these compromises happen in Manipi County? Where I live and work?"

He chuckled. "No, not initially."

"I'm in."

In his mind, Hatchett wanted this over and done. He didn't know who, or how, or what it would involve, but he wanted it over.

CHAPTER 34

In three days they were in Montgomery to deal with Cabot. Ward made the arrangements, took several days leave, and told Hatchett she had checked her badge in her overnight bag.

"What did the good lieutenant have to say when you asked for leave?" Hatchett asked.

"He said I'd been working much too hard, and that anyone who worked closely with you probably needed time off."

Hatchett looked at her and said nothing.

She didn't speak for several seconds. "Well, I will say this. The time I've spent with you hasn't been dull."

He nodded. "I'll take that as a compliment."

Hatchett really didn't have a plan for getting what they needed from Cabot. There were three possible scenarios: Cabot killed Lisa Lemon in which case there'd probably be evidence of it around his house - namely her tongue.

Or, two, Cabot had her killed by someone else, and he and his house would be clean of any sign that he was involved. Or three, he had no part in her death.

In his mind, the latter was the most likely occurrence. From their conversation with the professor, even knowing about his past and his violence towards women, he still didn't strike Hatchett as a man capable of decapitation and the accompanying tongue-ectomy.

They checked in at the Governor's House Motel on the south side on a Tuesday afternoon. Ward had gotten them two rooms on the front side, facing the highway. Hatchett wanted to take two or three days for surveillance, if necessary, before they made their move.

That night, at dinner, at the hotel, they both ordered fish. They were half way through the entrée when Ward stopped.

"Well, look who's here." she said.

Hatchett looked around. He saw no one except Glenn Cabot. He was sitting down at a table with a middle aged man in a five button suit. Both smiled at the waiter and then the suit got up and walked over to another table and shook hands with a man and woman already seated.

"Are you talking about Cabot?"

"Right. Do you know who he's with?"

"No."

"That's the Attorney General."

"No kiddin'? Wonder what they've got goin'?"

Ward forked up a small bite of fish and chewed quickly. "They're probably working on some crime study or something. One of those government grant things. Colleges do that; get government money to do studies about social problems."

Hatchett chuckled. "Like college rape?"

Five minutes later, a thin young woman wearing a blue dress and heels walked in and made her way to Cabot's table. She was a tall blonde with a patrician face who looked to be in her early twenties. Cabot rose, kissed her on the cheek, and helped her into her chair.

"Who do suppose that is?" Ward said.

"Well, if they're here discussing what you think they're discussing, my guess is a research assistant. I bet this project is just getting started and this is some kind of kickoff dinner."

Ward looked at the young woman. "I wonder if she knows what kind'a man she's with."

"Yeah. I wonder."

They finished their meals then adjourned to the bar until Cabot, the woman, and the Attorney General finished eating also. Ward watched the girl, while Hatchett got the car.

They followed her to a condominium off Carter Hill Road, and at eight thirty sharp watched her walk in the front door of what presumably was her residence. Hatchett parked down the street.

"What are we waiting for?" Ward said.

"Unless I miss my guess, she's going to have a visitor very shortly."

They waited forty-five minutes, Ward passing the time talking about her parent's upcoming visit to Mauvilla. The talk greatly bored Hatchett, who was used to solitary stakeouts.

"You've got a lot to learn about surveillance," he said interrupting her in the middle of a story about her mother's people in Shanghai.

Sure enough, at nine fifteen, Cabot parked his blue Chevrolet sedan on the street in front of the residence and walked, without knocking, through the front door.

"Told ya'," he said.

"How did you know?"

"She was sitting with two powerful men; it got her blood up."

Ward took out her binoculars and recorded the license numbers of both cars. She smirked.

"So, what good does this do us?"

"I'm willing to bet that this liberated young woman might not be so friendly with him if she knew he was such a heel."

"You think she'll cooperate?"

"There's only one way to find out."

The next morning, they took up a position in the University parking lot just as the students were assembling for class. At eight twenty, the young woman – who Ward had learned from license plate records was Jennifer Platt – parked her small white Datsun near the Liberal Arts building and walked inside. Cabot arrived shortly after nine.

Ward and Hatchett took turns getting out of the Merc and walking around so as not to attract attention. As the morning dragged on, students came and went. Two found time to make out in the car parked next to them, right around ten o'clock.

At noon, Cabot and Platt left the building, got in Cabot's Chevy and left campus. Hatchett and Ward followed them to a chain restaurant on the Atlanta Highway, about five miles away. After lunch, they spent another hour and a half back at school before leaving again.

"They certainly aren't concerned with office hours." Ward said.

"I'm surprised they were here at all."

"Where do you think they're headed now?"

"Where else? Her place."

In twenty minutes, through business traffic, they both drove up in front of her condo and parked. Hatchett and Ward took the opportunity to get food and water and then return, an hour and a half later. Cabot's car was gone.

"What do we do now?" Ward said.

"Now, we pay a visit to his little chippie."

They parked in front of her residence, and in a minute they were standing in front of Jennifer Platt's front door. Hatchett rang the bell. Ward looked at Hatchett.

"Let me," she said.

Platt answered wearing a light blue housecoat and slippers. It was three thirty in the afternoon.

"Yes?" Her voice was light and airy, with a southern accent.

"Ms Platt. My name is JoAnn Ward, and this is Mr. Hatchett. We're investigators from Mauvilla, down in the south part of the state."

Her eyes widened, and she grabbed the front of her robe near the neck. "Yes?"

"We wonder if we could talk to you for few minutes about a case we're working on." She saw her reluctance. "It'll only take a couple of minutes."

She looked them both over. Ward hadn't shown her badge, but slowly, Platt stood aside and invited them in.

"Thank you for seeing us," Ward said as they settled themselves in the living room.

"What's this all about?"

Ward took a deep breath and exhaled. "How well do you know Dr. Cabot?"

"We're colleagues, and friends, too."

"Do you know anything about his past?"

"What, his past? Well, I . . ."

She stopped. Ward said nothing, a fact that impressed Hatchett.

"Well, no, I mean, we're colleagues. We met here at the University, and we're working on a project together."

"How long have you known him?"

"About six months. What's this all about?"

"Dr. Cabot's name has come up in the investigation of a murder that occurred in Mauvilla."

"Murder?" Platt pulled her housecoat tighter around her neck. Her face was wide with surprise.

"Yes, ma'am," Hatchett said. "He's one of several suspects with a recognized motive to kill a young woman named Melinda Boatman. He has a history of predatorial conduct toward young women so, naturally, we are looking into his background. And, with your obvious relationship to him, well, we felt we had to talk to you. We were wondering if you could help us either confirm or eliminate him as a suspect."

"Murder? No, no, not Glenn."

"How can you be so sure?" Ward said.

"Well, I just know. Why, he couldn't hurt a fly. No, I think you're looking at the wrong person." She paused. "When did this murder take place?"

Ward supplied the date in the first week of April. "It would have been one or two days before then."

Platt looked up at the ceiling. "Wait a minute. She rose from the couch and walked out of the room."

"Was I diplomatic enough?" Hatchett said after she left.

"So much for letting me take the lead."

"You seemed to be moving too slow."

"I'd've gotten there."

Platt walked back into the room carrying what looked like an appointment book. She sat down and opened it to the date that Ward had mentioned. She ran her finger down the page.

"Glenn was out of town those days. I've got it right here in my book."

"How can you be sure?" Ward said.

"Well, I, I mark the days when we're, uh, together. I've got it down here that we, uh, he was out of town in California on the dates that you're talking about."

"Could I see that?" Ward said.

Platt nodded and handed the book over to her. Ward studied the pages. There, in a small and delicate hand, was the notation, *'With Glenn in LA. Grrrrrreat!'*

"I'd like to make a copy of these pages if I could," she said looking up.

Platt was hesitant. "Well, I guess, so. Who are you guys with?"

Ward took a business card out of her pocket and handed it to Platt. "I'm with the Sheriff's Office in Manipi County."

Platt nodded her head slowly. "I guess it'll be all right."

The three were silent as Hatchett looked at the notes. There was no way to tell when they were written, however, airline records and hotel reservations could be checked to confirm her entries. Platt provided the necessary information. Running this down'll be a good job for Ward, Hatchett thought.

"What was that you said about Glenn," Platt said looking at Hatchett, "that he was involved in, 'predatorial' conduct?"

Hatchett looked her in the eye. "We know of at least three cases, one of which may have involved our victim, where Cabot, as a college instructor, was cited for inappropriate sexual conduct with female students. Were you aware of this?"

Platt shook her head. She had a blank look on her face.

"No. I wasn't. It, it, sounds hard for me to believe."

"How so?"

She slowly shook her head. "His hands, they're so big."

Ward looked puzzled, and Hatchett chuckled. He knew exactly what she meant.

An hour later, they were back at the University and sitting in Cabot's office. He was nervous. Hatchett and Ward were stoic.

"We understand you were an instructor at Lower Mississippi Junior College, Dr. Cabot, back in the late sixties, early seventies," Hatchett said. "Is that correct?"

"Look, I know what you're going to say, but, but, it wasn't like that," Cabot said.

He fidgeted nervously and was breathing fast. Platt had undoubtedly called and confronted him.

"How so?"

"Back then, Mindy and I were in love. She was in my class yes, but, we cared for each other."

"Is that what you believed?"

"Of course."

"Is that what she believed?"

"Why, of course. I'm sure of it."

"So, what happened, did you rape her, or did she concede to you because you were her instructor and she was afraid of getting a bad grade?" Ward said.

"What? No, no. She wanted me." He spoke as if trying to convince himself as well as them. "I, I was her first."

Ward looked at Hatchett. Her jaw was tight and her eyes wide.

"So, what happened when you saw her in Birmingham?" Hatchett said.

"Well, she, we, she and I talked. We talked about how things were back then, and she said she regretted our time together. I told her she shouldn't feel like that, that our time was beautiful. I told her I could take care of her." He paused.

"Go on."

"She said she couldn't turn back the clock, and, and, she didn't want my money."

"Was she angry?"

He shook his head. "No. She just seemed sad." He paused. "That, that hurt me." He looked away. "Then she just laid down and said to get it over with." Cabot hung his head.

"So you had intercourse with her.?"

He spoke softly. "I made love to her, yes."

"So, did you kill her?" Hatchett said.

"No, I told you, no. I loved her."

"Did you pay to have anyone else kill her?"

"No."

Hatchett leaned back, and Ward leaned forward. When she spoke her voice was as soft as Cabot's.

"Dr. Cabot, you're a real piece of shit."

That night over dinner, they debriefed. Hatchett was resigned, Ward was frustrated.

"I was sure he was involved. It just all seemed to fit," she said.

"Well, don't clear him too early. You've still got those airline manifests and hotel reservations to check. He could just have had her set up his alibi."

"I don't think so. Platt looks like she's smitten, and his wife, even if she knew it all, would do anything to keep her family together. This is just a dead end."

"Love is blind."

She shrugged.

"Anyway, we need to move on," he said.

She said nothing. He continued.

"The next lead is the Birmingham thing. I like it. Even if it doesn't help us, no telling what we'll uncover if we bump that hornet's nest."

She shrugged. "I don't know. It all sounds kind of hard to believe to me - a murder for hire company? Now? Today?"

"It's the oldest crime in the world. People have been killing for five thousand years. Isn't it time they made some money off it?"

"So how do we go about it?" She paused. "I say we get the Bureau involved. This is a criminal enterprise and could fall under the Rico statute; there's sure to be some connection to the mob, and what'chu wanna bet they cross state lines to ply their trade?"

"The feds? Oh, no. They'll just take everything they learn and keep it to themselves, and probably never do anything about it. If there's anything there to connect them to our guy and our murder, we may never know it."

"What could there be?"

"Lots of things: an insider could turn; a witness could put our man in their building - which I haven't heard about by the way - there could be tapes or photos; anything. You know, I bet they even keep books, ledgers." He took a drink of coffee. "I'm against it."

She took a bite of a roll and washed it down with a swallow of water.

"I think we have to. They've got better resources - personnel and informational - and they've handled things, like taking this group down, before. Face it, we're not gonna be able to cowboy this one."

"I don't like it," he said matter of factly.

"And, the 'building,' as you call it," she continued, "is a private residence in Mountain Brook, just south of Birmingham. The property is owned by a woman. The Birmingham Police say it's a pretty ritzy neighborhood. They took a picture of the house and mailed it to me. It's a brick Federal on a large lot that backs up to some woods. It looks like a three or four bedroom, with a Florida room on the side. It also has a brick wall around it."

"Sounds like just the place."

"The place for what?"

"Cutting off a woman's head."

CHAPTER 35

The next Monday, Ward set up a meeting with a special agent at the FBI's Mauvilla Field Office on 1st Avenue, downtown. The office was in a modern glass and steel structure next to the Federal courthouse, a more traditional-looking gray, stone building.

They met Agent Adam Sheen on the fifth floor at one o'clock. He was a young man, very fit, with brush cut black hair and a tailored suit. He had a Roman nose, olive complexion, and dark eyes. In Hatchett's mind, Ward seemed to take a liking to him immediately.

"I'm JoAnn Ward, Sheriff's Office, and this is Mark Hatchett. He's a private investigator."

"Adam Sheen. Sit down," Sheen said, motioning to two gray, metal, government-issue chairs. He was smiling as he took a seat behind a desk made of the same material.

"We're here because we have some information that might be useful to the Bureau and could also be beneficial to us," Ward said.

"I'm all ears."

"We've developed some information that a sort of 'murder for hire' group is operating out of a house in Birmingham; Mountain Brook, to be exact. We think it might have some connection to a murder case that we're working on."

"And where did this information come from?"

"Mr. Hatchett was assaulted by two men in a vehicle that was traced back to Nashville, Tennessee. An informant up there supplied us with the phone number of a group that does that sort of thing for hire."

He smiled. "Would that informant be Mr. W.C. Cox?"

Ward's brows shot up. "You know him?"

"We've heard about this murder for hire club he's been pedaling for two or three years now."

"And?"

"Frankly, we've never been able to corroborate it."

Hatchett spoke up. "You think it's all a lot of bunk?"

"Unfortunately."

"Do you already have the information about the home in Mountain Brook?" Ward said.

"It's owned by a woman named Mary Etheridge. She's ninety one and in a nursing home."

"Who lives there?"

"Her son and daughter in law: Steve Etheridge, and his wife's name is, uh," he looked up, "Jane, I think."

"When's the last time you ran this thing down?" Hatchett said.

"The last time we, that is the Birmingham field office, looked into it was about eighteen months ago. It pops up every now and then. We get something on somebody, and they try to peddle this information in exchange for a deal. We've followed up on it on two or three occasions, and we've never found anything."

"So what do you think? Is there anything to it?" Ward's voice was pleading, in a way.

Sheen looked her in the eye.

"In my mind, no. I don't know how this got thing got started; whether it's some sort of urban legend or what, but I don't think there's anything to it."

Hatchett decided to bring the conversation back to earth. "Just exactly how deep did you go? How far did you check?"

Sheen took a deep breath and exhaled. He seemed anxious to get rid of Hatchett so he could spend his time getting to know Ward.

"We did background checks on the Etheridges. On one occasion, we got their consent to search the house. Needless to say there was nothing there. We even surveilled the place for a few days. There didn't seem to be any unusual comings and goings around the house, or in the neighborhood."

Hatchett was not impressed. He saw immediately several areas that the agent had missed: bank accounts, family members, utilities, and travel records, even a wiretap.

He looked at Ward. "Well, Detective Ward, it looks like we've reached a dead end. I guess we'll just have to look another direction." He tried hard, and in his mind succeeded, to hide the sarcasm in his voice.

Outside on the sidewalk, Ward was ambivalent. She knew Hatchett was not convinced, but she had no reason to doubt the competence of Sheen. She looked at Hatchett.

"You don't buy it."

"You bet I don't. Somebody took a shot at me, and I want to find out who it was; and I don't think the F-B-I," he said emphasizing the letters, "is capable of the job. 'Nothing there,' hunh. I've got a hole in my leg that says otherwise."

"He said they checked everything out."

"Shit. I wouldn't give you two cents for those ninety day wonders from Quantico. The government thinks you can train somebody to be an investigator in a four month course, most of which is spent learning how to drive and shoot." He looked at her with hard eyes. "It takes years to become an investigator. Most guys get that education out on the street in a patrol car." He shook his head. "You can't get it any other way."

There was silence between them as he realized what he had said. Though it was the truth, he wasn't trying to shame her.

She looked at him with hurt in her eyes. "I know I've got a long way to go. You don't have to remind me."

He paused to weigh his words. "But you've got a good teacher." He smiled.

She forced a smile also. "So, what now?"

"We'll have to smoke these people out. The one thing Sheen didn't do was call the phone number. My guess is they don't have it. We do."

"What do we say?"

"We say that I want to kill my wife."

Surprise painted her face.

"Don't look so shocked. I've been having marital difficulties for quite some time now." He smirked.

They walked toward Ward's car in silence.

"So, it looked like you and Sheen may have made a love connection," he said.

She smiled. "You're very perceptive."

"It's a curse," he said. He wasn't smiling. "He'd certainly be a good catch; big money, early retirement, your own foot in the door to a Bureau job."

"You think I'm mercenary?"

"Aren't all women?"

"There is such a thing as love, you know."

"No. You're much too pragmatic for that. You've got your checklist just like every other female. My guess is you knocked out about four or five of the top ten, right away."

She smiled and raised her eyebrows but didn't deny it.

He looked at her. "You two will make beautiful babies."

"Whoa. We're not there yet."

"That's step one."

"What?"

"'We're.'"

"I meant, 'I'm' not there yet."

"Hey, you can't fight it. Even Cupid has a bow and arrow."

Over the next two days, they made plans to spend time in Birmingham. Once again, Ward handled logistics, and Hatchett worked on strategy.

His script had to be just right. He would be from Mauvilla; he knew Peters from a convention that Peters had pimped for; Peters led him to Cox. Hatchett's guess was that Cox was probably wearing pretty thin as a procurer for this group. After all, if the police counted him as an informant, then this group was probably beginning to have their doubts about him.

Then Hatchett would simply tell them that he wanted his wife killed and was willing to pay to have it done. They would need flash money. Perhaps Ward could handle that.

The first step was to get the group's representative alone and have a heart to heart with him. After that, he'd know whether or not they knew anything about Lisa Lemon.

Of course, he'd have to figure out a way to ditch Ward. He couldn't let her see what was going to happen.

Marilyn from the answering service woke Hatchett up at two the next morning. He wiped his face hard and coughed.

"It's Larry. I think you need to call him," she said. There was tensity in her voice. "He sounded nervous."

"You got a number?"

She recited the exchange.

"Okay. Thanks."

He hung up and dialed Larry's line. It rang once.

"Larry? It's Hatchett. You need me?"

"Yeah, Hatchett. I gotta talk to you."

His voice was different. He sounded sober, and his tone was a little higher pitched than usual.

"What's the matter?"

"Just meet me at the usual place."

"What's the matter, Larry?"

"Just meet me."

"Okay. I'll be there in twenty minutes."

Hatchett dressed quickly. He made sure he had a couple of extra pistol magazines in the pocket of his vest, just in case.

Fifteen minutes later he was at the parking deck. All was quiet. The only sounds were from the tractor trailers on the nearby freeway.

Larry wasn't hard to find. His body was stretched out on the concrete near the southeast stairwell. Hatchett saw him, and then looked all directions before walking over to the fat man lying supine on the cold floor. There was a large puddle of spatter under his neck. Hatchett checked his carotid. He was dead.

Hatchett took a deep breath and exhaled. He shouldn't have, but he took a second to reflect on the end their relationship. Larry was by and large pretty worthless, but he wasn't a bad sort, and he shouldn't have died this way. At least, Hatchett thought, he can afford a nice funeral.

When the city police homicide detectives arrived, Hatchett was waiting next to one of the large pillars overlooking the deserted city streets.

"What's your name, pal?" a short, thin investigator who had identified himself as Connor asked.

"Mark Hatchett. I'm a private investigator. Larry, there, was an informant of mine."

"How'd you wind up here?"

"He called my answering service; said he needed to meet me. This is our usual spot."

"He working on something for you?"

"He was keeping his ears open for me. He hangs, or did hang out at a titty bar up on the north side called the Silver Platter, on the Merle Ray Highway. I'm working on the murder of a dancer. It's a county case."

"You know if he'd heard anything?"

"If he did, he didn't want to say over the phone."

Connor looked over toward the dead man. "Now, he'll never say."

Hatchett smirked. "No shit."

CHAPTER 36

That Friday morning, Hatchett and Ward checked into a chain motel in Homewood, off the interstate between Mountain Brook and Birmingham proper. Ward brought along recording and photographic equipment, and they both agreed that Hatchett would run the show.

Ward had never met Larry and was not affected by his death. She was unaware of the information that he had given to Hatchett regarding the bar patron who kept saying the Lisa Lemon's death was related to her drug activity. She knew only that he had been an informant of Hatchett's, and that was all he felt she needed to know.

That afternoon, they set up in Hatchett's room. Hatchett closed his eyes as if in silent prayer, and then picked up the receiver and dialed the seven digit number - omitting the local area code - which Cox had given him. He settled back in the cheap wooden chair, while putting his feet up on the cheap wooden table. Ward put on headphones and pushed the buttons.

"Yes?" A male voice answered. It was a baritone and devoid of accent.

"Yeah, look, I got your number from Cox. I gotta a job for you."

There was a pause on the other end. "Not interested." Click.

Hatchett looked at Ward. His face went from surprise to anger almost immediately.

"He's not gettin' off that easy." Hatchett dialed the number again.

"Yes?" It was the same male voice.

"Look, I need a job done. Is that your business or not?"

There was another pause. "Not interested." Click.

Hatchett dialed the numbers again.

"Yes?" This time the voice was female. It was an alto, with an airish quality.

"I'm not calling again. I can pay, and pay well."

"What is your name?"

"Call me, Andrew Jackson."

"Who sent you?"

"I told the guy, it was Cox. Peters in Nashville gave me his name."

She paused. Hatchett's guess was that she was running the names by the man she was with.

"Since we don't know you, we'll have to get a deposit."

"How much?"

"Five hundred; non-refundable."

Hatchett paused. "It'll take a few minutes."

"Are you in Birmingham?"

"Yes."

"Good. Take the money to the bank." She provided the bank, the branch, and the account number. "When the deposit has been verified, we'll call you back. What is your phone number?"

Hatchett recited the number and the room number.

"Stay by the phone." Click.

Hatchett hung up and looked at Ward. "Well, looks like we're in business." He stood up. "Have you got the money?"

Ward fished around in her bag. She handed him a manila envelope. "I guess it doesn't matter, but the bills are copied and the serial numbers recorded. It's all I could get. You want me to come?"

He shook his head. "No. They may be watching the bank, and if I'm supposed to be having my wife killed, you might look a little out of place." He checked his weapon and put the envelope in the pocket of his vest.

"I'll be back as quick as I can."

"Okay," she said. "I'll be in my room."

It took thirty minutes in afternoon traffic to get to the bank that the female voice had identified. It was located in the parking lot of a shopping center near the interstate, and Hatchett made it just before closing.

He made the deposit and picked up the receipt from the blonde teller. Hatchett's head was on a swivel as he stepped outside into the parking lot.

Back at the motel, he and Ward settled down to wait for the call. It came shortly after five. They must have a contact at the bank, probably one of the tellers, Hatchett thought. The phone rang twice, and Ward donned the headphones.

"Are you from Birmingham?" the male voice said.

"I'm familiar with the city," was Hatchett's non-committal reply.

"Go to the ball field on Ruffner Road, off Georgia Street, in Irondale. Just south of the lumber yard across from the ball fields, there's a dirt road that runs back into the woods. There's a trailer in a clearing about fifty yards off the pavement. Meet me there at eight tonight. If anybody asks, the land's for sale and you're checking it out." Click.

Ward took off the headphones. "Did you get all that?"

"Yeah."

Actually, he was familiar with Birmingham and knew right where the man had described. Now, he had to find a way to make the meeting without Ward following.

"All right, I'm gonna get a nap," he said. "I'll meet you here at seven. We can leave together. You can follow me."

"Right."

Ward left the room, and Hatchett immediately picked up the phone. He dialed the number again. The male voice answered.

"We have to change the meeting time."

There was silence on the other end. "Why?"

"She's coming back unexpectedly. I have to be home at eight. We gotta change the meet time."

"When?"

"Same place; two AM."

Silence again. "All right." Click.

At seven o'clock, Hatchett in the Merc and Ward in her county-issue Plymouth, left the motel enroute the meeting place off Ruffner Road. They communicated by walkie-talkie. Ward followed at a safe distance, and as they neared the site, Hatchett pointed at the ball field. She entered the dirt parking area, stopped in the far corner, and turned off her lights.

Hatchett turned down the dirt road and parked his car. He decided to give his ruse a good thirty minute wait before he exited the clearing. It was a clear evening and the crickets serenaded him.

At eight thirty, Hatchett started the car, drove to the ball field and parked next to Ward.

"He was a no show."

"What do you think happened?"

"I don't know." He shook his head. "Let's go back to the motel."

Thirty minutes later, they were back in Hatchett's room.

"Let's call them and see what happened," Ward said.

Hatchett shook his head. "No. They got spooked for some reason. I say we let the FBI hear the tapes, and you and Sheen take it from here."

Ward looked at him skeptically. She had never known him to give up so easily, however, his idea was a good one. She shrugged in acquiescence, though in her mind, it didn't add up.

"Be ready to check out at eight. I want to get back to Mauvilla before noon."

At one AM, Hatchett rose and dressed. He replaced the barrel of his pistol with the special one that he used for just such evenings as this. He listened through the wall for sounds from Ward's room, and hearing none, he opened his door and walked silently down the sidewalk to the Merc.

Hatchett arrived at the meeting place at five after two. A large black sedan was parked next to a dilapidated mobile home in the clearing at the end of the dirt trail.

He was not impressive, the man in the sedan. He looked to be in his late forties and was slightly over five and a half feet tall. He had a little bit of a spread and was noticeably short waisted. His black Hitler-type mustache matched his black horn rimmed glasses. His hairline was receding and his dark hair was combed straight back. He wore a black suit and black wingtips. He looked like a character in a nineteen forties film noir.

Hatchett walked over and stood in front of him. He eyed him up and down.

"Mr. Jackson?" the man said.

"That's right."

"What can I do for you?"

"I need you to kill my wife."

The man looked him straight in the eye and said nothing for thirty seconds.

"It will cost you ten thousand dollars."

"Minus five hundred."

He paused. "Minus five hundred."

Hatchett nodded. "All right. Ten thousand, hunh. I've got it right here. In my shoe."

He spun quickly and in one motion laid a heavy sidekick on the man's face sending him back against his car. He followed up the kick with two straight punches into his solar plexis, causing the man to bend forward.

Hatchett stepped back to see how much more the man could take. When he did, the man attempted to stand straight. Hatchett could see the small semi-automatic pistol in his right hand. Hatchett kicked him underneath his chin as hard as he could. The pistol went flying, and the man fell, out cold.

Bending over him, Hatchett pulled his wallet out of his suit pants pocket. His driver's license read: Michael Etheridge, Shiloh Road, Birmingham. Hatchett began slapping his face repeatedly until he started to come around. He grabbed him by his lapels.

"All right, Etheridge, I want answers, and I want'em quick. I know who you are and what you do for a living." He slapped his face again, hard. "Do you hear me?"

Etheridge nodded weakly.

"Lisa Lemon. Did you kill her?"

"Who?"

Hatchett slapped him again. "Lisa Lemon."

"Ohhhhhhhhh. I don't know who you're talking about."

Hatchett slapped him two more times. "Yes, you do. A stripper; from Mauvilla; worked for Peters; decapitated." Hatchett shook him.

"No, no. Stop, stop." Etheridge's face was a bloody mask. "No, wait, we didn't do that job," he said out of breath.

"Why not?"

"Because, Peters said, no," he gasped. "We turned it down."

"Who tried to buy it?"

"A guy from down south; he runs a junk business down there. I don't remember his name. He didn't have the money anyway." He paused. "Oh, please don't hit me anymore," he whimpered.

Hatchett stood up. He now knew who had killed Lisa Lemon. He pulled his forty five from the holster in the small of his back.

"You kill people for a living, Mr. Etheridge. But I'm afraid you'll have to crawl to your next job."

Hatchett took aim and discharged two rounds - one in each of Etheridge's knees. Then he reached down and calmly picked up the two spent cartridges, got in the Merc, and drove away.

CHAPTER 37

They arrived in Mauvilla at one the next afternoon, Saturday. Hatchett went to his office, and Ward made a stop at the Sheriff's Department before leaving quickly.

Hatchett checked in with his answering service. No one had called. He sat at his desk with his hands behind his head thinking; thinking about what he knew he had to do. But first, he called Mary Boatman.

"Hey, Ms Boatman. How are you and your husband doing?"

"We're holding our own. Ever day it gets a little easier. I go out to the plot, down near the lake. There's a large oak down there, and I sit and talk to her."

"Does she talk back?"

She paused. "Sometimes I hear her voice in my head. She tells me she's sorry for how she lived her life. She tells me she just had to get out and see the world."

"And, Mr. Boatman?"

"Oh, you know Arnold. He keeps everthang inside him. I can tell it hurts'im, but he tries not to let on."

"Does he go to the grave?"

"No. Well, no more than to cut the grass."

She paused. Her unspoken question was hanging in the air. Hatchett decided to answer it.

"We've run down a couple of leads that I think are pretty good. I hope we're getting close."

"Can you say anything?"

"I'd really rather not."

"Well, you sure have put a lot into finding out what happened. And, for that much, I thank ya; Arnold does too."

"It's worn me out, Ms Boatman. It really has."

He hung up and shut his eyes. He tried to imagine what was about to happen and, more importantly, the outcome. After a short twenty minute nap, he awoke, rubbed his face, and made his way down to the Merc.

It took only ten minutes in Saturday afternoon traffic to make it Louis Hart's junkyard and 'what not' shop. He parked right in front. It was two thirty.

Hatchett exited his car and walked up to the gate. A German Shepherd ran up to the fence and stood, barking loudly.

In two minutes, Louis Hart walked out front, smiling. He grabbed the dog by the collar and attached a leash.

"Hang on a minute, I'll put him up."

Hart towed the dog around to the back side of his house, and in another two minutes he returned, empty handed. He was still smiling.

"What can I do for you?" he said unlocking the gate and opening it wide. Hatchett took three steps in and turned around.

"Do you remember me? Mark Hatchett?"

He paused in apparent confusion. Then he smiled broadly and said:

"Sure, yeah. You came by lookin' for Lisa. I was sorry to hear about that, by the way. You had any luck on that thing?"

"No. Things kinda went stale." Hatchett was sizing up the man deciding how best to get what he needed.

"That's too bad. But, hey, you know, these cold case squads work miracles."

"They do."

"What can I do for you?" Hart said.

"I'm looking for a gift for one of the guys down at the PD. He did me a favor once, and he's always talkin' about African art. I did some research, and I want to get him one of those fertility statues. You got anything like that?"

"Oh, sure. I gotta guy that imports that stuff for me cheap. I can make you a real good deal."

"I wanted to get one that's made of monkey fruit wood. I've heard it's lucky. My friend and his old lady are tryin' to get pregnant."

Hart smiled broadly. "It's like you read my mind. I've got just what you want over here. Come this way."

Hatchett followed Hart across the yard to the north side of the outbuilding on the east side of the lot. Hatchett looked to his left and saw the dog chained to a pole ten steps from the back door of the brick house. He was glad the animal was out of the way. It really was a beautiful dog, and Hatchett was glad he'd not have to shoot it.

"Step into my showroom, Mr. Hatchett."

He was laughing as he used a key to open a padlock, after which he flipped the hasp and opened the wooden door. He stepped inside, flipped a light switch, and walked about four paces straight ahead.

The building was made of corrugated tin with a wood frame. It was about twenty five feet across and looked to be about fifty feet long. The floor was a dirty ply board sprinkled with wood shavings. The front, near the door was somewhat open space, but the rear was filled with every sort of furniture and junk, even a few bales of hay.

"They're over there, next to the window." He chuckled. "I've got about forty of'em. Take your pick."

Hatchett walked straight ahead then veered to his right toward the only window on the west side. He leaned down and made a pretense of looking at the fifteen inch high statues. They were pagan idols; female figurines with sagging breasts, bloated bellies, and bone piercings. Hatchett wouldn't spend a dime on one if his life depended on it.

But something else caught his attention. He let his eyes fall on a Mason jar sitting on the window ledge seven feet above the floor. He couldn't tell exactly what was in it, but somehow he knew. It was a human tongue immersed in liquid.

Hatchett stood up straight and turned slowly toward Hart. He was standing, no longer smiling, with a machete in his right hand. He was five feet from the door.

"Pretty stupid, leaving that jar out in the open like that," Hatchett said jerking his head toward the window.

"It's kind of a shrine." He looked up at the window. "It reminds me that I pay my debts." He paused. "When did you know?"

"For sure? Last night. But, I guess I knew from the first time that I talked to you. You had the best motive. Revenge is always a more compelling reason than any other."

He spat. "That bitch hung me out to dry; and robbing the place was her idea. Now, you don't rat on your friends like that."

"So how'd it go down?"

He shrugged. "It was easy. When I got out, I just went to see her and started spending time with her. She was a little hesitant at first, but I told her all was forgiven.

"The first of April, I invited her to a party - an April Fools party." He chuckled. "When she got enough coke in her, she passed out. After that, it was easy." He nodded toward the back of the building. "I drained her right back there, into the sink."

"You cut out her tongue?"

"She didn't know when to use it and when not to, so I took it from her."

Hatchett nodded. He had begun to perspire in the unventilated room. A bead of sweat was rolling down in between his shoulder blades. His pistol was secure in its place, and he began think about whether or not he could get to it before Hart made up the twelve feet of distance between them.

"What about Larry? What did he do?"

"The fat, white boy from the Platter? Well, he was good for spreading around that story about Lisa being dead because of her drug connections. Then one night, he said the wrong thing."

"What was that?"

"He said that maybe it was me that did the killing. He was smiling, and I guess he was makin' a joke, but I couldn't have him telling anybody that. Somebody might'a believed him. So, when I overheard him call you, I followed him to the garage and, well, I guess you know the rest. He squealed like a pig."

I'm going to enjoy this, Hatchett thought.

"And the girl in New Orleans, Darla Hedrick?"

"Was that her name?" He shook his head. "I never knew it." He paused. "She was just for practice."

Hatchett shook his head and began to reach for his pistol, when, without warning, the door opened, and Ward took two steps inside. Her badge was in her left hand. Her outstretched right hand held her revolver and her arm was extended to a locked position.

"Sheriff's Department. You're under arrest," she said. "Drop the machete." Her voice had an authoritative tone, but was not loud.

Hatchett saw what was going to happen even before it happened. He had his right hand on the butt of his forty-five and was pulling it from the holster just as Louis Hart swung the machete and struck Ward's arm at the elbow. She dropped her weapon immediately, and blood began to spurt from her radial artery. She bent over and then dropped to her knees while pulling her arm to her chest. The look on her face was panic, fear.

Hart followed through and was preparing to swing again when a shot reported. Hatchett's round struck him in the left hip. He spun away from Ward and onto the floor in the middle of the room.

Hatchett ran to Ward. He laid his pistol on the floor next to her.

"Where are your cuffs?"

"On my belt in the back."

"Put pressure on the wound with your hand," he said. She obeyed.

He reached around her to the small of her back and pulled out her handcuffs. Then he affixed them around her thin, feminine arm, just above the elbow, and tightened them as much as he could. The blood flow from the artery was stanched.

Hatchett raised her up, steadied her, and pushed open the door. "Go to the car and call yourself an ambulance." He looked over his shoulder at Hart. "I'll be along in a minute."

She looked him in the eye, knowing full well what he was about to do. She said nothing but turned and walked tentatively out the door cradling her right arm in her left.

Hatchett turned to pick up his pistol. In the meantime, Hart had lifted himself to his feet and was hobbling toward him.

Hart swung his machete downward. He didn't have a lot of force behind the blow, but the sharp blade was still capable of death. Hatchett threw up his left arm to block the strike that glanced off bone and sliced open his forearm. The blade put a six or eight inch laceration in the meat of his limb.

Hatchett felt the sting, but the pain wasn't immediate. He rushed Hart before he could draw the machete back again. Hart was stumbling badly from the leg wound. Hatchett closed in and kicked him in the groin with all the force he could muster. Hart doubled over and the blade went flying. Hatchett kicked him again, this time right under the chin. Hart fell back onto a bale of hay. Blood came out of his mouth.

What happened next took only about ten seconds. However, in Hatchett's mind the scene slowed to a crawl.

He walked over to Hart, who was hovering just outside of unconsciousness. Hatchett knelt down, putting his right knee on the man's chest. Then he reached inside his right pants pocket and took out his knife. The blade sprung open with a push of the button on the side. Hatchett grabbed Hart by his hair, held his head back, then cut deeply into the carotid arteries on first the left, then the right side of his neck. Blood spurted up into Hatchett's face and onto his white shirt.

Hatchett looked into the dying man's eyes. "Quick. Make your peace with Jesus."

Hart smiled and closed his eyes. In seconds he was dead and in hell.

Hatchett stood up slowly and looked down at him. He took two deep breaths to calm himself before he turned toward the door. On the way out he picked up his pistol and slid it into the holster. Then he walked out through the door and into the yard while holding his injured left arm.

When he turned the corner, he saw Ward leaned against her car. An ambulance drove up seconds later. Hatchett stopped and rested against the wall of the building. The pain from his arm was getting worse and his limb had begun to throb. Hart was gone. It was all over but the healing. Hatchett looked down and closed his eyes.

When he looked up, Ward was lying down on a gurney and attendants were strapping her in. McRae had arrived and was getting out of his car. As the ambulance left, two marked city police vehicles drove up. The lieutenant walked in the front gate and stopped.

"What's going on here, Hatchett?" McRae said.

He jerked his head over his shoulder. "Lisa Lemon's killer is inside."

"Dead?"

Hatchett nodded.

"How'd Ward get hurt?"

"The dead guy, Louis Hart, cut her with a machete."

"How bad are you hurt?"

"A few stitches; it'll heal."

McRae took a deep breath and exhaled. "Alright, we'll get to the bottom of this later." He looked around and motioned to the two city officers. "You guys secure that building."

McRae walked toward the outbuilding. Hatchett watched him then turned toward the front gate and the Merc. In seconds he was on his way, driving himself to the hospital.

CHAPTER 38

Hatchett reclined on the hospital bed in the first examination room closest to the swinging doors of the emergency room of Mercy Hospital. His left arm was outstretched, and it lay across a small metal table raised to the height of the bed. One nurse, a young, thin woman with brown hair, was gingerly cleaning his limb. Another nurse, an older one, was preparing to give him a tetanus shot in his right upper arm.

"Wait a minute," he said, "I just had one of those about a month ago. It was here, as a matter of fact."

The nurse stopped and laid down the hypodermic needle. "I'll check the records." She walked through the curtain and was gone.

Hatchett winced at the pain from his cut arm and then lay back with his eyes closed. As he rested quietly, in his mind, he could see the face of Louis Hart as he died. Hatchett had taken another life. It wasn't his first, and probably wouldn't be his last, but they all affected him, this one less than others.

Hart died with a filthy smirk on his face; a look that said that no matter what Hatchett had done to him, he had taken care of all his enemies. Perhaps he was prepared to die; that he innately knew that Hatchett would be coming for him. Hatchett wished he could have wiped that look off his face.

He was glad he had killed Louis Hart. Hatchett couldn't stand the thought of him languishing in a jail cell for the next forty years at taxpayer expense while serving a life sentence.

But not only for that reason. He was glad he could bring not justice, but some sense of closure to the Boatman family, a family that had seemingly done nothing to incur the pain of living through the death of their child. Now, they could know what happened to their daughter, and why.

He was glad he killed him for what he had done to JoAnn Ward. At that moment, he didn't know the extent of her injuries, but even if she didn't lose the use of her right arm, she would surely be incapacitated for a while.

Hatchett was also gratified that he had somehow avenged the death of Larry; Larry, who had lived his life imprudently, yes, but not imprudently enough to warrant his dying alone, in a parking garage. In his mind's eye he could see the fear in his eyes as he was being stabbed to death, as he was lapsing into unconsciousness, as his blood ran out of him.

Hatchett, in deed, felt no guilt or shame for what he had done. He felt only relief.

His cogitations were interrupted when Patrick McRae yanked back the curtain and stepped into the space. His visage was stern but there was no condemnation. The nurse looked up, surprised.

Hatchett spoke first. "How's Ward?"

"She'll be okay." He chuckled. "That was a pretty unique tourniquet. How'd you ever think of that?"

"Well, I wasn't about to take off my belt and put it around her arm. I read about it in a survival magazine once. If the victim's arm is small enough, like a female's, then a set of handcuffs works as well as anything else."

"Clever. She might have a little nerve damage, and her arm'll probably tingle a little when it rains, but they say she'll get full usage back. You got the blood flow arrested in time."

"Have you talked to her?"

"Yeah. She's shook up, but she'll recover. You know this is all new to her."

"I know."

"How are you doing?"

Hatchett lifted his arm and showed him the eight inch slice along the underside of his forearm. The doctor had not yet stitched it up and the skin was laid open, but there was no bleeding.

"I don't think there's much muscle damage. I can still move my fingers. It feels pretty superficial, really. Infection's gonna be the biggest problem."

McRae looked at the lacerated limb, grimaced, and blew out a large breath. He shook his head.

"That's gotta hurt."

"It would but for a wonderful thing called morphine." He smiled at the nurse who looked at him and smiled back.

McRae looked him in the eye. "Tell me what happened, Mark."

Hatchett chuckled. "Wow, that's the first time you've ever called me 'Mark.' Do I need a lawyer?"

"Do you?"

It was Hatchett's turn to chuckle. "No. But keep in mind I am under the influence of hard narcotics and my statement might be inadmissible." He grinned.

"I guess I knew pretty early on that Hart was involved. He just had the best motive. But I didn't have any physical evidence to link him to the crime and there were so many other people with motives. Then, when Larry started telling me about Hart, or a man that I thought was Hart, coming into the Platter and trying to mislead the investigation, I began to feel stronger about him." He paused and shook his head. "I hate that about Larry. He didn't deserve what he got.

"Then, I remembered about the piece of wood found between the victim's toes, and I figured that Hart might have something at that junk bin of his that was made of that monkey fruit wood. So, when we got back from Birmingham, I went over to see him.

"I guess Ward followed me. When we got in the warehouse, I saw Lisa Lemon's tongue. Hart picked up the machete, and we started talking. He intended to kill me, and because he thought he could, he confessed it all, including Larry and a prostitute over in New Orleans." He paused and readjusted his arm. "I guess Ward heard it, 'cause she came through the door with her weapon drawn and telling him he was under arrest. That's when he cut her.

"I shot him in the hip then went to see about her. I laid my gun down and helped her out the door. When I looked back, he'd gotten up and was swinging at me. That's when I got cut. I kicked him a couple of times then got out my knife, the only other weapon I had on me, and took a couple of swipes at him. Luckily, I hit him in the neck. He fell down and bled out." He stopped and looked at McRae. "That's it."

McRae nodded. "You're right. She did follow you. She told me that she's been suspicious of you and some of the things you've done for a while."

"I wish she didn't feel that way."

"Hatchett, you're a bang up detective. And the only reason I don't yank your ticket is because what you do really is a big help. You can get to the meat of things in ways a law enforcement agent can't. I need you. You get results." He paused and looked him in the eye. "Just be careful. You can't get by with it forever."

"Lieutenant, I always am."

CHAPTER 39

It was three days later when Hatchett and Ward met in his office. His arm was bandaged heavily and lying across his lap. He had his feet up on his desk when she knocked. He put his hand on his pistol and called out.

"Come in."

JoAnn Ward opened the door and entered. She had her right arm in a sling that was royal blue in color and matched perfectly the midi length dress and heels she was wearing. Her hair was down, and she was wearing makeup. Hatchett thought about how that she looked quite attractive.

"Well, look at us, a couple of birds with broken wings," he said. "Sit down."

She smiled and took a seat. "How are you feeling?"

"I've been better. And you?"

She held her arm away from her body. "They tell me it'll heal, but, confidentially, I don't trust doctors to tell me the truth."

"This coming from the daughter of a doctor."

"He's been lying to me all my life."

"So, how long you gonna be out of commission?"

"I'll be out for two weeks, and then on light duty for three months. But . . ."

"But?"

She paused. "But, I'm not coming back."

His eyes shot open wide. "Yeah?"

She shook her head. "It's not for me." She paused. "I think now I see how you feel and how you deal with it. But . . . I don't think I can deal with it the same way you do."

He looked her in the eye but said nothing.

"I know now how it affects you." She shook her head. "There's no prison sentence in the world that could ever make up for what I've been through."

They looked at each other in silence.

Hatchett spoke first. "How'd you happen to show up at the junkyard?"

"I followed you. When we got back from Birmingham, I knew you'd been up to something. The fact that you wanted to get back to town so quickly told me that you knew who'd killed Lisa Lemon, and you were on your way to do something about it. So, I called McRae, and then I followed you. After I watched you go into the building, I went through the gate and stood next to the back door and waited. I heard him confess, and when he finished, I went in." She chuckled. "It seems silly now, but I actually thought I could arrest him."

"You'd have done it, too. You just didn't know what you were walking in to."

"Anyway, when he swung that blade down, it scared me to death."

"Only a fool doesn't get scared."

"I thought I was going to die." She stared at the floor. "But then, when I looked down and saw my arm, a funny thing happened."

He looked at her with brows upraised.

"I got mad; so mad I could've bit nails. The very idea that he had the nerve to cut me; it incensed me. I wanted to stay there, get my gun, and put all six holes right in the middle of his face"

"Why didn't you?"

"I don't know if I could have. And, I knew I needed medical attention." She paused. "By the way, how did you know about that trick with the handcuffs?"

"The old 'nipper noose'? It's an old home remedy."

She nodded. Neither of them spoke for seconds.

Finally, she did. "Anyway, I just came by to say thank you."

"For what?"

"Well, for saving my life for one thing; and, for showing me the real world."

"Ahh, you'd have seen it eventually."

"Maybe."

She shrugged and looked at the floor. Then she looked up.

"Have you talked to the Boatmans?"

"I have. I told them everything, including about Cabot. I thought maybe it might take away some of their guilt." he said.

"Are they satisfied?"

"Oh, no, they'll never be satisfied. They'll always believe that they had some part in causing their daughter to step into the life she chose. They'll never get over that. But they're coping. That's really all they can be expected to do. It's done them good to know who killed Melinda and that the motive was because she did the right thing."

"I suppose."

"They did send me a hefty little bonus."

"Good."

"It'll just about cover the hospital bill."

"Don't forget the reward."

"I haven't. We've got a hearing on it coming up pretty soon."

"Sounds like you're landing on your feet."

"I try."

There was silence between them. Finally, he spoke.

"Look, don't do anything hasty, you know; about work, I mean. You might change your mind."

"Maybe."

"And as long as there are people like me, there can still be people like you. After all, you've got your way, and I've got mine. We actually made a pretty good team."

"We did? I thought I was fighting you the whole way."

He shook his head. "Nah. You just kept me on my toes. My kind of work has to be done in secret. You made sure I followed my own rules."

She smirked. "Well, I'm happy about that, I guess."

"What do your parents say?"

"My father said, 'I told you so.' My mother couldn't stop crying. She took it really hard."

He smiled. "Well, I guess there's always Agent Sheen."

"I don't think so. I think I want to get as far from this life as I can." She paused. "When my mother stopped crying, she did say one thing." Ward smiled.

"What was that?"

"She said, 'Chinese proverb say: Woman not made for heavy thinking, but should always decorate scene like blossom of plum.'"

Hatchett threw his head back and laughed heartily.

"What?"

"That's not an old Chinese proverb. That's Charlie Chan."*

The End

* from *The Chinese Ring*

CPSIA information can be obtained
at www.ICGtesting.com
Printed in the USA
LVHW031631051118
596009LV00001B/20/P

9 781496 947864